THESE SHALLOW WATERS

MADISON MOUSER

With Love Always ♡

Madison Mouser

Mimosa
Bookhouse

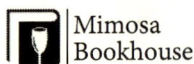

These Shallow Waters
Copyright © 2024 by Madison Mouser

Cover Design by Rotoscope Design
Edited by Between The Covers Editorial
Author photography by Laura Powers

First edition: May 2024

Library of Congress Cataloging-in-Publication Data
Names: Mouser, Madison, author.
Title: These shallow waters / Madison Mouser.
Description: First edition.
Fayetteville, Arkansas : Mimosa Bookhouse, 2024
Series: Deep Waters ; book 1

ISBN 9798989823628 (hardback)
ISBN 9798989823604 (paperback)
ISBN 9798989823611 (e-book)
Subjects: GSAFD : Fantasy fiction.

Printed in the United States of America
Printing 1, 2024

To all those brave enough to take on a new adventure,
even when all seems lost.

"*The selkie people are a peaceful clan, but there will come a time when they will have to choose between the peace they so desire or death at the hands of those unafraid to take the throne by force.*

All but one of the Royal clan shall be slain and, with the aid of a human woman, the remaining royal will reclaim the throne. In order to save the selkies, the human must become a royal to claim her coat and free her newfound family.

If she fails, the selkie people will exist no more."

—The Selkie Prophecy; prophesied by the Sea Witch, circa AD 1267

CHAPTER I

Lawson

THE FREEZING WIND WHIPS PAST MY FACE AS I RUN UP THE beach from the shoreline, my sea-soaked coat tucked under my arm. Dark curls slick to my forehead and create a perfect avenue for the rain and ocean water mixture to find its way into my eyes.

As the sand turns into grass, a large rock formation protrudes from the ground. I quickly shove my coat down in a crevice and look behind me to see if she is following. She's not here. Yet. I touch the golden ring on my finger, a nervous habit I picked up over the years. The glow from my coat dwindles the further away I move.

Lightning cracks across the black sky as I turn and spot a tiny church just inland. Free of the burden of my coat, I stretch my human legs and run toward the stone building. Rain pelts against my skin as I run, struggling to catch my breath. Chancing a look, I don't see anyone following me. When I make it to the church, I lean my back into the large door. It quickly gives way under my weight. Gasps come from behind me as I land on my backside, and my eyes work to adjust from the pitch-black outside to the warm glow inside.

"What is this?" I try moving my head to see who spoke, but I am already surrounded by people trying to get a glimpse of this stranger who has fallen into their laps. Feet clack along the floor, echoing in the sparsely furnished room.

"It's just a young man!"

"What on earth is he wearing?"

"He's getting blood everywhere!"

My breathing finally slows as the faces of the churchgoers start coming into view. A man in long black robes pushes through the crowd and takes my head in his hands. I'm reminded of Gabriel, as this man's robes flow gracefully, even with his smallest movements. It is suddenly too warm as a man drapes his dry coat across my body. Of course, he doesn't know that I don't need it.

"Son, are you alright? Where is your family?" the man in black asks.

Something wet covers my forehead. A damp cloth now soaked in my blood. I forgot about the gash from her claws.

"Son?"

"Hide ... She's coming ..."

CHAPTER 2

I STILL CAN'T BELIEVE WE ARE ACTUALLY HERE. ALL THOSE months I spent holed up in our ... my ... tiny apartment ended with the discovery of a single email. I had completely forgotten about Noah looking into his father's ancestry until someone asked if I had shut down his email yet. The answer was a resounding "no". I couldn't even bring myself to throw out his clothes, let alone see beautiful words he had written with his poetic brain.

By the time Caitlin arrived that night to drag me out to dinner, my plans to visit Bettyhill, Scotland were already formed. Caitlin, my saint of a best friend, dropped her plans to accompany me. When her boss told her she couldn't take that much time off on such short notice, she threatened to quit. Which, of course, scared them because she's a damn good accountant. So, safe to say, she got the time off. I wouldn't have made it through airport security with my sanity still intact if it hadn't been for her. And now, here we are. Caitlin, God bless her, is chatting up the cab driver so I can just sit here and take everything in.

Bettyhill is a tiny village on the northern coast of Scotland. With a population of about 500 people and beautiful rolling moors, there is no way I won't feel connected to my late husband's ancestors ... or something like that.

"I'm glad you like fish, El. Sounds like it's pretty common fare here." Caitlin sits back into her seat, checking for phone service while

3

her severe blonde bob sways with every movement. Her furrowed brow relays disappointment as she tucks the phone back into her oversized purse.

"Here we are, lassies." The middle-aged cab driver pulls up in front of the tiniest inn I have ever seen. I love it immediately. The exterior is a warm white, and mahogany shutters frame each crosshatched window. The deep red front door is adorned by a sweet welcome sign and wreath, clearly a gift handmade with care.

As we step out of the cab, the driver lifts out our bags and starts talking about all the wonders of the smallest village known to man. My long, chocolate-brown hair dances in the wind and I wish for the umpteenth time I had put it in a ballet bun before we left the airport. Pulling my coat closed, I look around at the small town surrounding us.

"Did you hear that?" Caitlin's voice pulls me back to the conversation.

"Sorry, what?"

"Bruce here said there's a fun little pub right next door we have to see. Let's go tonight!" She points to the building just to the right of the inn. It looks abandoned, but then, it's only four in the afternoon.

"Ehh, I dunno ..."

"El, come on, we're here. In Scotland. On a whim. Because of you. You are not getting out of this. No arguments!"

I can hear Bruce chuckling behind me as Caitlin shakes her finger at me like I'm two. I turn to glare at him, but he is already closing the car door and starting the engine. Picking up our bags and heading to the front door, Cait turns back to me with a softer expression.

"Ellie, don't worry. We won't stay long and, who knows, you may have fun. And you can even wear the muumuu I know you hid in your bag." She gives me a knowing smile, leading us out of the frigid breeze and into the warm inn to drop off our bags before getting ready for tonight's activities.

The music in this pub is louder than anything I've heard for the past year, aside from my own thoughts. Looking around, it is evident this is the place to be on any given night. The dark wooden walls paired with the dim lighting and an overwhelming smell of spicy whiskey notes make for the perfect place to get drunk while you try to forget the bitter cold just on the other side of the door. We snag a small wooden table near the back and start making our way through the menu. After we've gone through two rounds of beer and three appetizers of varying degrees of pub food, most of them including some kind of "tatties" and meat pie, Caitlin heads back up to the bar for her third round when a movement off to the side catches my eye.

"Aye, you lassies can eat!" A thinner, salt-and-pepper haired man in his late thirties takes a seat in one of our empty chairs.

"Umm ..."

"Name's Kenneth Gibson. I run the local bakery. I always need taste testers and you lassies look like prime candidates!"

I can't help but laugh. Loudly. My ponytail bounces, tickling the back of my neck with the sudden movement. It certainly is not the first time my eating skills have been noticed, but it was since Noah.

"That's the first time I've seen you laugh in a year." Caitlin returns with a third beer and a grin on her face. "Would that be your doing, sir?" She takes a drink and sticks out her hand for a handshake. I can't help the smile on my face, this scene reminds me of our college days when she would walk in a room ready to meet everyone and I hung back, praying no one noticed me.

"I was just noticing your mate's eating abilities. Yours too, of course!"

"Well, gee, thanks! We'd be willing to demonstrate them for you if you'd like to order another plate." Caitlin's saccharine smile only makes me smile wider while rolling my eyes. Kenneth drums his hands twice on the table and lets us know he'll return soon.

"Your confidence never ceases to amaze me." I pick at the remaining crumbs of appetizer number three while Caitlin shrugs at my statement.

"You should be confident, too, El. Trust me, it's not your looks that keep guys away." She eyes me over her beer. "See that guy at the bar there? Mr. Tall, dark, and handsome in the white sweater and dark vest? He's been staring at you since we got here. You should go talk to him."

"What? No. Absolutely not—"

"El, he's hot! And besides, it's not like it would *mean* anything. Just some shameless flirting with Hot Guy to help you loosen up a little." I put my chin in my hand, elbow propped on the table, and slide my eyes in the direction she pointed. There is no mistaking who she meant—he is clearly staring. The cold blue of his eyes stands out amidst the warm tones in the room, but he has the decency to look away when our gazes meet. He certainly is attractive. Actually, he may be about the most attractive man I've ever seen. *Dammit.*

"Cait, he looks kinda pissed ..." She laughs lightheartedly, clearly a little tipsy.

"Hm, did we kick any cats today? Could one have been his?" Her laughter is infectious, and I find myself giggling as well. "Y'know, I think it's time for your third drink, Ellie Hughes. Off you go."

I stand up, grasping my empty beer mug and press my lips firmly together, casting Caitlin one last joking glare as I head toward the bar.

There aren't many open seats, but the ones that are available happen to be right around him. Lovely. And easy. Normally, I would think a little more on that, but tonight I walk right up to the empty seat next to him. Though he'd been looking away as I approached, he is unabashedly watching me now.

"May I?" I nod to the chair. Honey brown waves tickle his forehead as he looks at the stool in question. It takes all my strength, plus that of every ancestor, to not reach out and brush the soft, unstyled hair back. Or rub my fingers along that second-day scruff shadowing his fair skin. Or maybe both. Either would suffice, really.

"You may, miss!" the man on the other side of the open chair answers for him. This portly man looks old enough to be my grandfather and reeks of whiskey. I sit down and channel Caitlin, giving the older man a smile so sweet I can feel the cavities setting in.

He turns back to his party, giving me the opening I need. I decide to just go for it as I climb into the seat.

"So, do you have a permanent scowl on your face, or did someone spit in your drink?" I mentally slap my palm to my forehead.

This clearly isn't what he is expecting to come out of my mouth, and his expression turns to bemusement as he looks back to his scotch.

My word vomit keeps coming.

"Because y'know, if you're gonna come to a place like this, you should probably look more approachable. Or at least not like you'll smite anyone that comes within five feet of you."

"You're really bad at this."

"Excuse me?" I don't think I could hide my annoyance if I tried.

"If you're trying to flirt, you're not doing it very well." He looks from me to his drink and smirks. The motion of his body causes the scent of sea salt and citrus to waft in my direction. And something else almost ... woodsy. It pisses me off how intoxicating he smells.

I realize I am just sitting there with my mouth hanging open, so I snap it shut and notice the bartender is close by. Asking for a refill, I take any excuse to look somewhere other than the annoying, gruff, clearly fit man beside me.

"Have nothing else rude or bothersome to say?"

I whip my head back to him.

"I could say the same of you."

"You forget, ma'am, that I live here. You are the annoying American who thinks she can say whatever she likes."

"You don't know anything about me."

"Just reading the signs," he says pointedly. The man turns away and rolls a now empty glass between his hands. *What the hell?*

"What does *that* mean?"

The older man to my right turns back to face us as a fresh drink is placed in front of me. "You'll have to excuse Mr. Lawson here, miss. Bit of a strange lad." He winks at me. "But if you're needin' some company, I can help ya out."

I blink rapidly a few times before finding my voice.

"Thank you," I whisper. It was what I said after my first kiss, anytime I am handed food from wait staff, or when I can think of literally nothing else to say. And at this moment, I am truly at a loss for words. I hear Lawson stifling a laugh beside me.

"Sorry, is something funny?" I turn back around to find Lawson grinning at his glass. Now I *am* pissed, and I don't give a shit if he knows.

Lawson shrugs and shakes his head, eyes never leaving his empty glass. Fine, if he is going to be a cryptic jerk, then he can do so all by himself. I grab my freshened drink and start to get up, muttering as I go.

"Stupid, arrogant, egotistical asshole ..."

My momentum forward is suddenly cut short as a large hand grabs my elbow, pulling me backward and whirling me around to face its owner.

"Let's get one thing straight. I'm a lot of things, but 'stupid', 'arrogant', and 'egotistical' are nowhere on that list."

Apparently I struck a nerve. Wow. I can almost see the smoke coming out of his nostrils. I smile sweetly at him.

"I notice 'asshole' is not a word you contradicted."

Well, I'm already in this deep. By now, most of the people around us have quit talking to watch what the stranger is going to say to someone deemed strange by the rest of this tiny village's standards. His cold, sky-blue eyes narrow as they bore into my own. I briefly wonder if my honey-brown eyes will warm him up since his are sending shivers through me.

"You don't know anything about me," he manages through gritted teeth. I can actually see each muscle in this man's strong jaw ticking.

"Just reading the signs, I guess." Recognizing his own words in my mouth, his eyebrows raise, a gesture I mimic back. I shake his hand from my arm with more strength than truly necessary.

Conversations begin again as I turn and head back to our table.

"What the hell was that about?"

Segues were never Caitlin's strong suit. I sit down between her and Kenneth in my original seat and look back to the place at the bar I had just occupied. Both my seat and the one next to it are now empty. I look at the door just in time to see Lawson's brown waves blowing in the sea breeze as he walks out and shuts the door behind him.

"Your friend here was chattin' up Lawson MacCallum. He's a strange one. Washed up on the shore 'bout fifteen years ago. Literally. No family or friends. They took him in at the local church and now he works at our sad excuse for a library. Not sure what he sticks 'round for, though. Best leave that one alone now, miss." Kenneth takes a swig from his mug.

I finally pull my eyes away from the door and back to our table. "Yeah, best."

"El, Kenneth was—"

"I told ya, call me Ken."

"Sorry, *Ken* was telling me about some new suppliers he was thinking of checking out down south and thought we may enjoy seeing the sights. May be something to think about," Caitlin says as she reaches across the table and touches his arm, their eyes holding each other's gaze longer than necessary.

Ah, it seems my friend may have found a friend. I smirk. Some things never change.

"Yep, definitely something to think about." I smile at her and take a drink.

Caitlin and Ken fall into easy conversation. At some point, another appetizer appears along with half the pub, thanks to Ken knowing everyone in town and Caitlin never having met a stranger. Just like in college, Caitlin is the sparkly new toy and I am the book-reading muumuu wearer. Between her golden hair, ample curves, and unapologetically effervescent personality, she is the sun and everyone else, Icarus.

At some point, Caitlin and Ken break away by themselves and stroll to the bar, heads huddled close together for what seems to be a pretty intimate conversation. All of my new friends now talk amongst themselves since the flames that had brought the moths here have moved. I have just pulled out my phone to read on any of my several book apps when one of the younger men turns to me.

"Bored of us already?" The tall blonde man is smiling as he takes a drink from his glass. Short curls move freely as he angles his head, looking at me curiously. Not mad. A good first step.

"Oh," I laugh awkwardly. "Not at all. I just never go anywhere without a book. Y'know, just in case." I sit my phone down on the table without locking it.

"May I?" He nods to the phone. Looking between him and the device, I nod back. He picks it up and starts to read. "*Pride & Prejudice?*" This handsome stranger locks the phone, setting it back on the table with his calloused hand and toned forearm on full display.

"You know Jane Austen?" I can't hide my surprise. He laughs with a smile that reaches his bright-green eyes and shows off the dimples in his sharp, clean-shaven face.

"We're not completely out of the loop here in Bettyhill, Miss...?"

"Ellie. Ellie Hughes." I quickly, and awkwardly, stick my hand out for a handshake. He continues to chuckle as he takes my hand in his, almost dwarfed by his size and strength.

"Miss Ellie Hughes. Hughes is Scottish. Are ya Scottish, Ms. Hughes?" He is still holding my hand as he smiles, encouraging me to answer.

"Uh, no. I'm actually a bit mixed." I smile sheepishly. "My late husband was half Scottish, though. So I thought, 'Why not go check it out?'" I wince a little as I wait for his inevitable reaction to my candor.

His eyes soften, but a gentle smile remains. And so does his hand on mine.

"I'm so sorry, Ellie. How long ago?"

"About a year. He, um, drowned." I sigh. "But this isn't to be a pity party. Only fun here!" I sit up a little straighter and square my shoulders, giving him my brightest smile. He finally lets go of my hand and smiles, readjusting in his seat.

"Well then, tell me about why ya chose the great Jane Austen tonight."

"Oh! Well, it's one of my favorite books. Has been since I was in high school, I guess. But I love how Lizzie and Mr. Darcy both act like idiots for a while and then both work to improve themselves for the other. Then they give the best versions of themselves to each other. I think it's beautiful. I think it shows that we, as humans, always have the opportunity for personal growth. Especially for the ones we love." I realize I am rambling and quickly stop talking.

I glance over and see he is simply looking at me. Simply listening.

"Wow, Ellie. If I didn't know any better, I'd say ya have a passion for books." I shrug.

"My degree is in english lit, so I guess you could say that." I smile at him and laugh. Suddenly, I realize something and grab his arm, which is now resting on the table. "Oh! I don't know your name?"

He covers my hand with his own and grins at me.

"It's Graham, love. Now then, if we're gonna talk about books for the next while, I think we need some fresh drinks. What'll ya have?"

"Just water, please."

"Two waters coming right up. Ya can, uh, resume your readin' for the moment." He nods to my phone as he stands up and heads to the bar.

I look around the pub and notice most of the people who had been here when we arrived are now gone. Caitlin and Ken are still huddled together at the bar, with Caitlin pulling out all of her signature moves. She is on the hunt and headed in for the kill. Good thing she changed from travel sweats to date clothes earlier.

"What's so funny?" I hadn't even realized I was laughing until Graham asked. He looks in the direction my gaze has been focused and chuckles to himself. "Ah, yes. Your friend is quite the life of the party." He sets a glass of water down in front of me and reclaims his chair.

"She's always been that way. And I have always definitely not been. But I love her dearly, even if she does dress for the party and not the weather."

"How did ya meet your friend?"

"I met Caitlin our freshman year of college. We lived in the same building and ran into each other in a mini kitchen on the floor in between us. It turned out we had both just been accepted by the same sorority. You could say we were fast friends. We both loved watching movies and reading books." I smile at the memories I haven't thought of in a long time. "She helped me be more social, and I think I helped her find some quiet time. We both had psychotic roommates, so we were able to find peace with each other."

"Sounds like ya were just what each other needed."

I take a drink of my water, a welcome contrast to all the food and alcohol I've had tonight.

"So, what about you? Is your official title Graham the Lion Tamer of Bettyhill?" Graham laughs right as the cup hits his mouth, causing the poor man to momentarily choke on his water.

"Sadly, no. More like Graham the Fishmonger. I have a booth down at the local fish market." He looks down to his drink, clearly embarrassed.

"Really? I'd love to see it!" Graham blushes and looks at me with surprise.

"Oh, Ms. Ellie, I doubt ya want to be somewhere as foul-smelling as the fish market. But there is a little coffee shop right by it."

"Well, it sounds like I need to come check out the fish market and then, since it's probably pretty chilly being by the shoreline, I guess I'll need a cup of coffee afterward. And based on Caitlin's moves tonight, I'll probably be alone. Know anyone willing to drink some coffee with me?" I grin at Graham, swirling what remains in my water glass.

"I'm sure I could b—"

"EL!" Graham and I whip our heads toward Caitlin, who makes a crash landing into our table and falls onto a chair. "Guess what! Ooh, who is this? El, he's really cute! You should go for him, especially if he likes you in that muumuu. He can't even see how awesome your boobs are!"

Graham is trying not to laugh, covering his mouth with his hand.

"How many drinks have ya had, there?" I grin at my friend. Resting my chin on my propped-up hand, I pass her my water glass with the other.

"Hmm." She starts counting on her fingers and holds up two,

"Maybe four? But the last couple were liquor, not beer." She shrugs, chugging the rest of my water and then taking Graham's half-empty glass and downing the remainder.

Graham and I share a "what can ya do?" look.

"Anyway, thinkin' I may go home with Ken? Is that okay? Will you hate me? Because I LOVE you, Eleanor Victoria Hughes!"

"Aye," Graham whispers. He raises his eyebrows in appreciation of Caitlin's current state.

Ken walks back to the table in time to see Caitlin's declaration of love for me and laughs. He is clearly not as drunk as she is. Almost.

"I promise to take good care of her and return her in one piece." Even drunk, he looks at her with a kindness I've rarely seen from men when it comes to Caitlin. I wave them off.

"Go, go. But if I don't hear from you by ten tomorrow morning, I'm sending the police after you," I call after them as they hurry out into the cold. When the door closes behind them, I turn back to Graham, who is already looking at me. "I shouldn't be worried about her, right? I mean, you know Ken?"

"Oh, Ken's harmless. Nice guy. No need to worry there, *El*." I smile at the familiar name on his lips, typically only used by Caitlin. I nod and glance around the pub again, noting the few employees are busy cleaning up for the evening. A quick look at my watch tells me it is a little past one in the morning.

Graham generously pays both our tabs, and we head out. As we step out the door, he turns and looks at me.

"My week has been shite, so I decided to come out for a beer. Now, I can't seem to remember why it was so bad."

I blush, looking down at my sneakers. We start walking toward the door to the inn.

"Well, maybe we make tomorrow a little better, too?" I dare to peek up at him, only to find him looking right back at me with a warm smile on his face. I find myself thinking about how my thin five-foot-five frame can easily wear heels with this man. He must be at least six-foot-two.

"I'd like that very much. I'll be at the market until eleven. Come by then and we can grab that coffee? We can even throw in some lunch, especially now that I've seen your eatin' habits!"

Smiling, I loop my arm through his and nod enthusiastically. We walk the rest of the way in silence. As we reach the front door, I turn to him and sigh. He reaches up and lightly touches my cheek. A light smile plays on his lips.

"See ya tomorrow, Ellie Hughes. I'll be countin' the hours." He drops his hand from my face. With one last smile, he turns and walks back into the night.

CHAPTER 3

Lawson

S *HIT, SHIT, SHIT. ODIN'S FUCKING FAT-ASS RAVENS.*

I throw a rock into the ocean as hard as I can and stand there breathing heavily, trying to decide if I want to hurl another into the black waves or if I am finally ready to go home.

It's almost one in the morning, so she will definitely be back in her room—or in someone else's bed. Not that I care. She's beautiful, almost exotic looking. So there's little doubt someone else threw themselves at her and charmed her into thinking they could provide quality company. Again, not that I care.

In the time since I've left the pub, I've run up and down the beach, stripped and swam a few hundred laps in the ocean, and thrown several dozen rocks of all sizes as hard as I could into the crashing waves. Getting out this anger seems impossible. Fifteen years of searching this tiny town and I'm not any closer to finding my coat. But now *she* has to show up.

All those years ago, I was finally well enough to leave the hospital, only to find my coat was gone. That could only mean one thing: the queen of those disgusting beasts had followed me to this tiny hamlet and stolen it. The one thing that would have allowed me to return to my people—or what was left of them, anyway. I had no way of knowing how many of them had escaped the Slaughter, other than the complete certainty I was the only one left of my family. I've spent years looking through every nook and cranny I could access for any place the queen could have hidden it. Now here I am, stuck working as a librarian in the saddest library known to man and creature.

I begin pacing again, picking up another stone to throw. I let out a growl when I release it, watching as it makes an audible smack on the ocean's chaotic surface.

Hopefully my people don't think I've abandoned them. They knew how this was hopefully supposed to go, we've all had the prophecy drilled into us since infancy. It was foretold that our people would be overtaken. It was foretold that my family would die. It was foretold that a human woman would save us. That woman. The one in the pub. *Her.*

My brother used to tease me, saying he would be the royal to survive because there was no way someone that beautiful would help us if someone like me asked her. But the faded, centuries-old drawings of her did not do justice to such divine beauty.

There is something different, though. Her brown hair is much darker and longer than in the picture. Her eyes are sadder, the amber not as warm and lively. It makes me wonder what kind of pain is hidden beneath her socially awkward surface.

I take off in a slow jog toward my apartment over the library in an attempt to distract myself from thoughts of the woman. I realize I didn't even learn her name in our conversation tonight.

Because of what I am, the cold has never bothered me. But tonight, there is something different in the air. The chill pierces through my jacket more than normal.

Coming to a halt, I look around. No one else is out, but it feels as if I am being watched. I realize I am nearly back to the pub when they come into view, and I peek around the closest building.

She and one of the local men are walking slowly arm in arm toward the inn. If words are being spoken, I can't hear them. When they reach their destination, I can't look away as the two stop and face each other. The guy ... *What's his name again? The guy with the fish stand ... Graham?* Graham touches her face as he says something.

I feel as though my nose is pressed up against some make-believe glass as I watch while he drops his hand and walks back toward the pub. I tuck a little further behind whatever building is keeping me concealed—my vest and jeans may be dark in color, but my off-white sweater doesn't really lend itself to stalking others in the wee hours of the morning.

My eyes flick back to the woman as she heads into the inn. The anger I thought I had quelched back on the beach threatens to rise back into my throat. Anger for her having to become involved in a world she has no idea even exists. Anger at the sea witch for prophesizing this fucked-up situation. Anger at the queen for putting all this shit in motion. Anger at the rest of my family for getting killed and leaving me alone to deal with this when I was only fifteen years old.

Geez, how fucked up is that? I'm pissed at my family for being slaughtered like animals and leaving me alone ...

Tears threaten my eyes as I lean against the cold bricks beside me. The only time I've ever cried throughout the past fourteen years was when I've thought of my family, and it never fails to piss me off. The last remaining royal shouldn't be a crier, especially over those who've passed.

But our people are social beings. We swim, hunt, live, and just generally exist together. No one of our kind has ever survived on their own for so long before now. I may be considered novel in how I've managed, but that doesn't mean it doesn't fucking suck, especially because my exile wasn't voluntary.

I need to start walking. Now.

Anger starts rolling off me in waves. I begin to stomp as quietly as I can toward my apartment when I hear the rumbling engine of a car coming up behind me. I know who it is before I even turn to face him.

"Aye, a bit late bein' out. Is it not, Mr. MacCallum?"

I turn to find Graham Brightley leaning out of the truck window, peering at me with the same judgmental eyes most people in this town cast in my direction. He is smiling, at least. That is pretty novel, in and of itself.

"Hello ..." I mutter.

I turn back to the road and continue walking, not so secretly hoping this is where our conversation will end. No such luck.

"Whatcha doin' out at this hour? Nothin' too scary, I hope."

Are the people here scared of me now? I sigh.

"Just couldn't sleep is all. But I'm almost back home now, so thanks for the stimulating company, but I have to go." I turn a corner, expecting him to drive away. Again, no such luck.

"I saw ya were talkin' to Ellie earlier tonight. She's somethin', isn't she?"

So that's the name of the poor, misfortunate woman. Ellie. A rather plain name for someone so important to my people. How annoying.

Graham takes my silence as an invitation to keep speaking as his truck matches my quickening pace.

"Not as obnoxious as her friend either, which is nice. We're actually havin' lunch tomorrow down at the coffee shop by the market. 'Haps I can convince her to stay awhile, even." He chuckles to himself.

I pull my hand out of my vest pocket and rub my face as I walk, willing him to shut up. A sigh escapes unwillingly. Well, maybe not totally unwillingly.

"Eh, Lawson?"

"YES, Graham?" I let out a big sigh and turn to look at him with exasperation written all over my face.

"We're at your place ..." He motions behind me, where I turn to see the door of the library.

"Right." I sigh again. "Well, this has been fun and thank you for the escort, but ..." I look around and shift uncomfortably from foot to foot.

"Well, I'll see ya 'round. Take a walk through the mysteries and thrillers section for me." He waves and drives off. *Thank Odin.*

I roll my eyes and unlock the door. Once on the other side, I lock it behind me and head straight for the back staircase that leads up to my small dwelling. Since I typically leave the apartment door unlocked, I walk right into my tiny kitchen and pour two fingers of scotch. The glass touches my lips and amber liquid hits the back of my throat as I head to the far wall where a map of Bettyhill is hung.

Red pins scatter across the terrain. Places I have already searched and come up empty. As the years have come and gone, the number of green pins have significantly decreased and been replaced by both a red pin and a few choice swear words sent directly from my heart to the queen.

There are only a few houses I haven't been able to gain access to and a few places that would be farther than I believe the queen would actually go to hide it. But then again, she is about the worst kind of creature to roam the land and sea.

After polishing off the scotch, I rub my eyes. Unsure of whether it's the late hour or the fact that *Ellie* has arrived to serve as a constant reminder of my failure, a heady mix of exhaustion and frustration sweep over me. Even though I know I should get some rest, past similar feelings have taught me I won't be getting sleep anytime soon.

A quick glance around the empty hunter-green walls of my flat would signal that I have always viewed this place as a temporary home. I've always been prepared to leave and meet my people at the Base. Nothing other than the map decorates my walls and a couple of dirty dishes clutter the counter. Even my bedding is a dull light gray. But fourteen years have come and gone, and I've been alone. Without so much as a picture to remember my family by.

I look down at the book laying open on my kitchen table—a mythology book I occasionally read for entertainment. Humans are so peculiar, thinking themselves safe from these creatures they deem make-believe. If they knew how real a threat many of these beasts pose, they'd never leave their homes again.

My kind has never been one to harm humans, exactly. Not that we've been particularly kind to them, either. But the people of Bettyhill have survived, blissfully unaware of what lurks in their waters.

What would she make of this situation if she knew?

With one hand still on my scotch glass, I turn to the sink to fill it with water. As the glass reaches maximum capacity, my mind wanders to the woman. Ellie.

Out there, she sleeps peacefully, not knowing her life will soon change. Strangely, our lore never spoke of what was to become of the woman once she had fulfilled her duties for us. Is she to go back to her life in the human world? Even if she does manage to fulfill the prophecy, it is possible she could perish in the aftermath.

I shake my head to try and clear my thoughts. Ultimately, it shouldn't matter to me what happens to her, so long as she does her part. But if I am being honest, how the hell am I supposed to get her to even become aware of her part in all of this? It wasn't like we got off to a stupendous start tonight. I think she got along better with the several plates of appetizers she put away than she did with me. So, first things first, I have to get her to not hate me. In truth, I actually need her to trust me. But trust is hard to come by in general, let alone with someone you just met. And I did plenty to keep her from trusting me tonight.

Then again, it appeared she did seem to find some kind of kinship with Graham Brightley rather quickly. And he did tell me where she would be tomorrow, late morning. Perhaps I could crash their little lunch date. If Mr. Brightley was so keen to share information about her with me tonight, maybe he would be amenable to me joining them for their meal together. Of course, he could have just been looking for someone to share the intimacies of his prowess with her and I was the first guy to cross his path.

A glance at the clock on my sad excuse of a nightstand tells me it is nearing two thirty in the morning. After rinsing out my glass one final time, I pull off my boots and clothes. I collapse on the full bed, willing sleep to come. If I am going to set this in motion, I am going to need some rest. With any luck, Ellie will have an open mind. Without luck, this is going to be even more painful than I originally thought.

CHAPTER 4

Ellie

M Y EYES FEEL LIKE SANDPAPER AS I PRY THEM OPEN. BUT NO headache, so the water at the end of the night did its job. The light streaming in the window of the inn pools on the bedspread. My joints pop, and to say I felt the stretch in my bones would be the understatement of the century. Clearly, I didn't move much in the night.

I look over to the rickety wooden nightstand's sleek and modern clock. It looks very out of place in this room filled with quilts, ornate antique furniture, and frilly throw pillows. The clock reads 9:58 a.m. Only two more minutes and I will be calling Caitlin.

Reaching up to rub my eyes, I think about last night and the bizarre turn of events. First, Caitlin convinced me to go out. No surprise there. It was college all over again. She was the life of the party, while I, the awkward one, found exactly one potential friend and spent the majority of the time eating and wishing it wasn't rude to read in front of everyone. Second, I met about the rudest man I had ever spoken to since my time spent at frat houses. Lawson something? How anyone can live in a town this small and be that rude is beyond me. Surely he's managed to ostracize everyone here? Third, Graham. Warmth creeps its way up my neck and into my cheeks. Yeah, that part was good. And I somehow ended up with a date? If Caitlin had been watching, she would have been so proud.

I grin to myself as I turn to look toward her empty bed when a small movement catches my eye near her pillow. Pulling the covers back, I get out of my bed and walk to hers. A piece of inn stationery with her chicken scratch handwriting lays on the pillow.

El,

Please don't be mad, but I've decided to go with Ken to check out those suppliers and do some exploring. I wanted to wake you and tell you, but you just looked so peaceful. And I know peace isn't something that's come to you easily this past year. Not since Noah.

I'm not sure how long we'll be gone, but I know this place is one of the best I could have left you. It's just a feeling I have (you know how I am haha). I love you so much, El, and I promise to call when I get somewhere with cell service. If that Graham guy tries to get in your pants, make sure you're ready and not just doing it because he wants to.

Please don't be mad. Please. I love you.

C

There are no words. Not in my mouth, not in my head. Nowhere. Nothing. She's pulled this kind of crap before, just not when we were in a foreign country. I take a look around and sure enough, her bags are gone. Her bags are gone? Oh shit!

I run to my bag and begin tearing through it. Nothing. Now is when the idea for her to keep my passport, ID, and wallet in her purse becomes the worst one we've had since I decided to take this trip. Especially because now, they are all with Caitlin, wherever the hell she is on this side of my nightmares.

We only prepaid for a few nights at the inn because we didn't know how long we'd be here, which now means I will have to find a new place to stay. No ID card, either. I can't even go get alcohol or rent a car if I want to. Or get on an airplane.

I sink down to the floor, hands covering my face. Maybe if I beg down at reception, they will let me stay until Caitlin comes back. It seems unlikely, though. This is a business, after all. Okay, that is enough. Time to get your life together. I lean back into the closest piece of furniture and sigh.

"Step one. Pack all your stuff in case they ask you to leave."

While I should feel silly talking to myself, it actually helps to hear something other than deafening silence. I look around at the cream carpet covering the floor, where most of my belongings now lay in a scattered pile that I am sure resembles my brain at this exact moment. Grabbing my clothes by the handful, I quickly shove them into my bags, the only interruption being an occasional sigh. Once everything is back in my luggage, I stand and look around the room.

"Okay, now. What's step two? Step two, step two ..." I mutter to myself. A shiver runs through my body as I am now away from the warmth of being huddled on the floor. Apparently, my ratty college T-shirt and PINK sweatpants don't hold a candle to Scottish autumn weather. Who knew?

Back by the bed, the clock tells me only a mere eight minutes have passed. How on earth have only eight minutes gone by? That is ludicrous. Between my peaceful waking, nocturnal reminiscence, crappy discovery, and minor panic attack, surely at least twenty minutes of my sad excuse of an existence have wasted away. I don't even realize I'm crying until the taste of salt invades my mouth.

My hands have just covered my face when a ding rings out from my phone on the nightstand. Sitting down on the bed, I lean over to grab my phone where a notification with a strange number waits.

> Chuffed I decided to go to 'round the pub last night. See you soon. 😊

Graham.

The same heat from earlier finds its way back into my cheeks. It may be too early to dump my entire life's crap into his lap, but maybe his knowledge of people in the town could come in handy. I'll admit it when I'm desperate.

While the market isn't far from the inn, I hurry to get ready. I pick out my nicest casual outfit which, other than a shimmery cocktail dress Cait made me pack, is the best outfit I have brought on the trip. A pair of dark skinny jeans and a fitted olive V-neck sweater paired with my one set of black heels will have to do. Caitlin would hardly approve, but then again, she isn't here.

After a quick shower, a little bit of makeup, and getting dressed, I start feeling a little better, until I look in the mirror at my typically cornsilk straight hair. The weather here does weird things to it, and the level of frizz is astronomical. Wielding my brush, I try my best to beat it into submission. I put it up in a ponytail, and then take it back down. I put it into a French-braid and leave it like that for all of thirty seconds before taking it back down again. By now, it has a semi-decent wave to it. It will have to do. I grab my purse for the sole purpose of carrying my phone and some lip balm, and head out the door.

The walk to the market is even shorter than I had anticipated, which is great considering my shoe choice for the day. But it is a pleasant surprise to find that the market is much bigger than I had expected. There are rows and rows of merchants set up for the day. Some booths hold beautiful fruits and vegetables that are far superior to any I have ever purchased from Whole Foods. The farmers stand proudly with their crops, speaking animatedly with anyone who will listen. Other stands showcase handmade goods. Dolls, purses, clothes, and soaps are only a few of the items available for purchase today. Walking through the different booths, I realize I recognize several of the merchants from the pub last night. How none of them look the least bit hungover is beyond me.

My phone dings with a text:

> Running a little behind. Meet you at the coffee shop!

> No problem. I'm enjoying checking out everything.

The salty air suddenly fills with a much more pungent smell: fish. It seems like whoever designed the market layout did so with peoples' noses in mind and put all the fish stalls together. This section of the market is much smaller, but it still offers a wide selection of choices. While Noah and I always enjoyed eating at Red Lobster and indulging in seafood when we went on vacation, I can't name any two of the kinds of fish that surround me.

Everyone seems friendly, even though it is obvious there is an outsider among them. Each person I make eye contact with stops for just a moment when they don't immediately recognize me, but jump right back into character as the happy and familiar salesman. True to who I am, I smile awkwardly at each one as I make my way through the maze of goods. A familiar scent fills the air as I get to the last of the fish stands in this row. Coffee and pastries are showcased on a poster in a windowpane. The coffee shop.

Stepping inside the warm shop, the smell of cinnamon and espresso invades my senses. Off to the side, a glass case catches my eye—ice cream. Homemade, by the looks of it. And they have mint chocolate chip. My favorite. I am once again silently cursing Caitlin for forgetting to leave my wallet behind. Even if they didn't have mint chocolate chip, I've never met an ice cream, or dessert in general, that I didn't love. I am still gazing longingly into the ice cream case when another reflection appears in the frosty glass behind me.

I whirl around, hand to my chest. But he finds his words before I can.

"Were you planning on leaving a nose print on the glass?" Lawson MacCallum gives me a lopsided grin, hands shoved in his vest pockets. Ah, yes. The dick from the pub. Lovely.

"Umm ..." I am finally beginning to regain some of my faculties, but apparently words aren't one of them. "I-I was just admiring the variety available. Lots of choices here." I motion behind me. Awkward, as always.

"Yes, they're known for their variety." He keeps his blue eyes on me like his life depends on it. "Miss?" The girl behind the counter is now behind us, waiting for our order. Trying to tone down the awkward as much as possible, I step to the side so he can order ... whatever he is going to order. "Can we get two single scoops of the mint chocolate chip, please? And two coffees." Lawson finally tears his gaze away from me and looks at the girl.

She seems genuinely shocked when Lawson offers her a sincere smile. But she recovers her professionalism and nods, getting to work on his order.

"Are you meeting someone?" The words are out of my mouth before I can stop them. There is no denying he's extremely attractive, so it's not outside of the realm of possibilities that he would be meeting a date. He gives me an odd look, which morphs into a smirk that I immediately want to smack off his smug face. I narrow my eyes at him. The girl returns with his order and he reaches out to take the first couple items from her.

"You mind?" he asks, holding out the two coffee cups. Politeness kicks in as I automatically reach out to take them. He gets the ice creams from the girl and turns back to me. "Shall we?"

It suddenly hits me what is happening, but I have to double-check. "I'm sorry, what?"

"Apology accepted. And we're having coffee and ice cream." He walks past me toward a cluster of empty bistro tables and sits down at one near the back of the room. "If you don't bring the coffees over, I may be tempted to think you're stealing them from me," he calls from across the room. The people in line begin giving me dirty looks.

I shake my head at them, shrugging my shoulders. They clearly think I'm an idiot. Frankly, so do I. Thankfully, I do a pretty good idiot run when needed, which I employ now as I make my way over to his table and set the coffees down.

"It'd be easier to eat sitting down." He motions to the chair opposite him. Unsure of what else to do, I slink down into the chair.

Lawson takes one of the coffees in front of me and exchanges it for a scoop of ice cream.

"What is this?" I ask, motioning to the items in front of me.

Lawson seems to down half of his coffee in one gulp. Not gonna lie, it's kind of impressive. "Coffee and ice cream. You like mint chocolate chip, right? It was the one you were staring at while you were practically drooling on the case."

"Yes, I understand the concept of food. I'm not an invalid, contrary to what you seem to think."

"Aye, that I know. I saw how much you ate last night."

"Wow, zero to creepy in five seconds." I nod my head and press my lips into a thin line as I think about him watching me eat the five hundred different types of pub food Caitlin and I tried last night.

Lawson laughs. "You should eat it before it melts." He takes a big bite of ice cream. "Easier to eat that way. Unless you prefer to drink it." A sip of coffee. He's not wrong. Approximately two bites in and this is without a doubt the best ice cream I've ever eaten. Did he lace it with something when I wasn't looking?

I chase the ice cream with a big swig of hot coffee. "Look, I'm not trying to be rude, but I was actually meeting someone here." As if on cue—

"Ellie! Hey, sorry I was—Lawson?" He looks between Lawson and me.

"Graham! I was—"

"Hey, sorry mate. I saw Ellie all alone by the ice cream and figured I should entertain her 'til you got here. And y'know, apologize for being a dick last night to her." Lawson shrugs nonchalantly and looks back at me, clearly waiting for a response. Meanwhile, I try to identify what I just felt when he said my name.

Graham glances awkwardly between us when I finally find my voice.

"Uh, well, that wasn't really an apology. But sure," I say, looking at Lawson and then Graham, not quite sure what is going on. Lawson gives me that half smile and holds my eyes. There is something mischievous behind them. Whatever it is makes me uncomfortable and I begin to squirm in my chair. Thankfully, Graham clears his throat and gives me the out I desperately need.

"Well, Ellie, if you're still hungry, I'd love to buy you lunch? Unless you already ... with Lawson ..." Graham looks a little lost.

"No! I'd love that." My cheeks hurt with how big I'm smiling. Or is it a mix of that and the cold ice cream with the lava-like coffee? I turn back to Lawson, who is already staring at me. "Mr. MacCallum, thank you for the appetizers and your ... apology ... but I'm gonna go. Eat. With Graham." I glance back to Graham to make sure he is still there. Thank God he is. And he is smiling at me. Both good signs.

"Of course." Lawson stands up from the table, gathering the trash. We had managed to finish off both ice creams and coffees. He locks his eyes on mine again. "It was nice to see you again, Ellie." What is it about how he says my name? He breaks our stare long enough to nod to Graham before looking back at me. "Hopefully I'll be seeing you again soon."

When he exits the coffee shop, I let out a breath I don't realize I'm even holding. I can feel Graham watching me as I turn back, smiling. It is an obvious assessment to make that Graham puts me at ease. Especially compared to Lawson.

"How's this table for today's festivities?" I motion to the table where I was just sitting like I'm Vanna White, wide smile and all.

Graham laughs and hangs his coat on the chair opposite mine, offering to go grab menus. As he walks away, defined back and arm muscles are evident, even through his flannel shirt and full-length sleeves. I cross my arms on the table to hide a quick drool check. The situation with Caitlin rears its ugly head again now that I have a moment to think.

After placing our order and chatting about hobbies and favorite foods, I begin the delicate process of eating the most delicious sandwich of my life.

"So, I need to tell you something." With my mouth stuffed so full, it's a wonder Graham catches anything I just said.

Graham stops with his sandwich in midair and looks me straight in the eye. "Please don't tell me you're a serial killer."

Now it's my turn to laugh and, given how stressed I've been since I found Caitlin's letter this morning and being accosted by Lawson in the coffee shop, it's a nice feeling. "No, no. Nothing like that." I sigh. "You remember my friend, Caitlin?" I shove in another mouthful of sandwich

"She's not easily forgettable. She's quite loud." Graham puts down his sandwich, wipes off his hands, and crosses his arms. He leans forward, resting his elbows on the table. His soft expression encourages me to continue.

"Well, she's ..." I swallow my mouthful, "Gone." His eyes go wide.

"What?!" His outburst quickly catches the attention of those around us. "Wait, like she died, or she ran off?" Thankfully, he lowers his volume when he asks if she's dead.

"Ran off. You think I'd be this calm if she died?" I exchange my sandwich for a handful of chips.

"Just had to check. I don't know you that well. Yet." Graham glances down at his mostly empty plate before reaching one of his hands across the table to cover my own. The one not currently covered in potato chip grease. "But I'd like to."

I look from my hand to his face, where kind eyes wait for me to find them. His beautifully chiseled features are soft, inviting.

"Now, tell me what happened and how I can help." His warm smile melts away any leftover worries in my mind.

I tell Graham all about how last night Caitlin put on her signature moves, so I had a pretty good idea where it was heading. About how this was pretty standard for her in general, but that she has never done this kind of thing on any of the trips we've taken over the years.

"And here comes the worst part." I sigh. "When I decided to take this trip, it was originally going to be just me. I had found Noah's ancestry tracing email and decided it was time to get out of my environment. During that time, Caitlin was coming by every few days to take me out to dinner to make sure I didn't become a wallowing hermit. When she got to the apartment that night and I told her my plans, she dropped everything to come with me. And while I've always been the more organized one, she suggested she carry all my documents, wallet, ID, everything, so that I didn't have a panic attack while standing in line for airport security. She wasn't wrong. That totally would've happened. I almost had a breakdown when they asked me to remove my shoes."

Graham's hand never leaves mine, occasionally nodding in encouragement so I will keep talking. But this time his nod is slower, like he finally realizes where this is going. "And when she took off, she didn't leave any of your documents or anything," he guesses.

"Yep. Which means I can't leave, even if I wanted to. And I couldn't even offer to pay for lunch." I pull my hands to my face, ensuring he won't see my eyes start to water. They aren't there but just a moment when Graham's hand pulls them down with his own.

"Hey, hey. Everything will be okay." He smiles softly, like he is trying not to scare a wounded animal. I sniffle while trying to keep my tears in check. How attractive. "Now, let's look at this one piece at a time. Ya need somewhere to stay or is the room paid for?"

I shake my head. "We didn't know how long we'd be here. Since I guess there isn't a big tourist crowd, the owners of the inn said we could pay for a few days at a time, but tonight's my last night that's paid for."

Graham nods, taking everything in. "And ya have basically no money except some spare change rollin' around in your bag, there?" I nod. Graham withdraws his hands and leans back in his chair. He crosses his arms, then pulls a hand out and rubs the nape of his neck. Looking down at the table and then back to me, he asks, "How are your housekeeping skills?"

To buy myself a moment, I slurp down some Irn-Bru and am once again shocked that the orange-colored soda isn't repulsive. I decide to tread lightly. "Pretty good ... Why?" Sensing my deep confusion, Graham chuckles to himself and leans forward again.

"I ask because my Aunt Isla lives on a large estate a wee bit up the road. Her live-in housekeepers are typically students home for the summer and hers just went back to school. I'm sure she'd love to have ya. You could stay as long as ya need. And she spends most of her time traveling, so you'd have the place to yourself quite a bit." He pauses, cheeks flushing. "And I know I'd love any extra time with ya, as well." I blink. It seems too easy. Or that potentially there will be strings attached. I swirl my cup to give myself a little extra time to think. Graham seems to know what I'm doing and offers, "I promise, no strings attached. I just wanna make sure you're safe and taken care of, Ellie."

A big sigh escapes from deep inside my chest, letting out all the pent-up anxiety I've held in since I decided to travel halfway across the world. Looking up at his striking green eyes, I feel a familiar warmth creep up my cheeks and gather in my core. "I guess if you promise she won't try to kill me, then I'd love to meet your aunt."

He grins like I just told him he won the lottery.

CHAPTER 5

Ellie

GRAHAM WASN'T JOKING WHEN HE TOLD ME HIS AUNT LIVES on an estate. He could have said she lives on her own private military base and it probably wouldn't be a false statement. I bet if I google "old Scottish castles", her home will even populate the search results. Once we turn down the long dirt drive, trees line our path and showcase the foggy moors surrounding us. When the trees finally break, a castle rivaling Edinburgh Castle itself looks down upon us. Vines scale the warm stone walls, weaving around the many windows looking over the front lawn. Turrets line the front wall and continue along the sides as far as I can see. The only things missing are a moat and drawbridge.

Surprisingly, the drive out wasn't too bad. I found myself thinking about how it would be nice to walk into town on decent days and how cozy it would be out in the country on rainy ones.

We didn't stop by the inn on our way out of town, just in case the guy at reception asked if I was checking out. I also told Graham I didn't want to show up at his aunt's house looking move-in ready. But when we arrive, she's waiting on the front porch with a warm smile on her face. She's much younger than I expected, no older than mid-forties. A jade green floor-length robe straight out of an old Hollywood glamour magazine covers white capris and a black blouse. Like Graham, her shoulder-length hair is ice blonde, making her bottle-green eyes and tall, willowy frame stand out, leaving little interpretation of their familial ties.

No sooner am I out of the car than I am being embraced by this strange woman.

"Oh, you poor dear! I can't begin to imagine what you've been through." She loosens her hug and holds me at arm's length. "One so young and beautiful should never have to go through such tragedy."

I look over to Graham with wide eyes, unsure of what to say next. But it's clear he's shared quite a bit with her.

"Don't mind Graham now," she continues, fixing him with a pointed look. "He was just trying to make sure you were so appealing that I couldn't possibly live without you. And that way he can spend as much time with you as possible." She winks at me. When I turn to look at him again, he just shrugs, and a sheepish smile crosses his face.

The woman drops her arms from mine and looks around, frowning. "Now Ellie, where are your bags? Are you not staying?"

"Oh. Well, I—"

"She didn't want to be rude and assume, Auntie Isla." Graham to the rescue. Again. I let out a sigh of relief. She waves a hand as if she was swatting at a fly. I have to lean back to get out of its path.

"Nonsense. Graham, you will go into town and gather her bags while I show her around."

"Yes Auntie." He kisses her on the cheek and grins at me as he heads back to the car. "I'll be back," he calls through the window, pulling away from the house.

Suddenly, I'm alone with this somewhat eccentric woman who's ushering me to the house and looping her arm through mine as we head toward the door.

"Graham tells me about your love of reading. Suffice it to say you will love the library. In fact, your room is quite close to it." There's something about her accent I'm trying to place when we cross the threshold and enter the most beautiful foyer I have ever seen.

The ceilings are at least twenty-five feet high and house an ornate crystal chandelier. *That'll be a bitch to clean.* Warm tones of burgundy, yellow, olive, and cream are spread throughout the room and across the plush, bold rug covering the majority of the floor. I can't help but think of Sleeping Beauty's castle if it were in modern times, save for a few decades. Time seems to have stopped in this place. Our arms remain looped as we move through the first couple of rooms like I've been here a hundred times before. Each room is covered in the same warm palette, filled with rich, plush furnishings, and lit by a warm glow from lanterns and bulbs alike.

Eventually, we reach the kitchen and it's the most beautiful kitchen I have ever seen. Much like the rest of the home, everything here feels rich and heavy. Large dark cabinets line the walls, almost reaching the ceiling. I notice there's a step stool tucked in the corner. The preparation table is made of the same dark wood as the cabinets. But where the rest of the walls in the home are dark yellow or olive, the kitchen walls are a light cream. In a similar fashion, the countertops are a stunning white granite without marbling. It makes the room truly striking.

As Graham's aunt continues telling me other general routines, I realize why her voice initially threw me off.

"But there's a pad and paper h—"

"Are you not Scottish?" I ask.

"Sorry, dear?" She was in the middle of explaining the menu preparation ritual. Oops.

"Sorry, it's just, your accent. You sound European, but you don't have the same inflections as Graham." She laughs.

"Oh, no dear. I didn't grow up here, unlike Graham." When she doesn't continue, I figure it's time to switch topics.

"This kitchen is stunning. I think I have one just like it on my Pinterest."

Her brow creases. "What's a Pinterest?"

"Oh, um. Basically an internet-based bulletin board of your favorite things all in one place," I explain. "On your phone." Why I feel the need to add that last part is beyond me, but I have the strange feeling Isla isn't living in the twenty-first century.

She perks up, seeming to remember something. "Ah, yes. Just so you know, I did get the internet installed yesterday. It may make your life a tad easier. Shall we?" She motions to another doorway on her right, opposite the way we came in.

I nod and follow her out of the kitchen, thinking there is no way I just understood her correctly. She just got the internet yesterday? As in, the day before today? What was she doing up until then?

We walk through a long corridor before stopping at a large oak door that's standing ajar. I can already see through the crack that I will spend most of my time in here. Isla throws the door open to reveal a library Belle would be jealous of. I can't help the gasp that slips out of me as I follow her into the room. The twenty-five-foot ceilings from the foyer reappear, but this time they're lined with floor-to-ceiling bookshelves that are crammed full. To my left, a fire roars in a fireplace that stands as tall as my five-foot-five frame, surrounded by an intricate mantelpiece, and a large dark wooden desk sits off to the side where a brass lamp was left on by its last occupant. As I turn back to my right, I notice the depth of the library. It must run the entire length of the corridor where we just were. An enormous oak table takes up the middle of the room, covered in books and what look to be giant maps. Isla works to roll them as I make my way toward her. "This place is absolutely incredible," I breathe.

"You're welcome to come here as much as you like, of course." She casts me a soft smile while putting away a couple of volumes. I pick up one of the remaining books on the table. It looks old. Ancient. I briefly wonder if Isla's some kind of antiquities dealer. Or a black market dealer.

"I don't mind doing that. It'll help me get more acquainted with the filing system anyway." This seems to satisfy her while she continues with a condensed general tour of the room before leading me next door to a small bedroom and en suite, where I will stay.

A full canopy bed takes up most of the floorspace, but the warm palette from the rest of the house finds its way in. It makes the room inviting in that "stay a few days, but then please leave" kind of way. I briefly wonder what the rest of the bedrooms look like if this is mine. It's not lost on me that I've been instructed not to bother with cleaning Isla's room and am only to worry about the main living areas. Like the bedroom, the bathroom is equal parts inviting and uninviting. Modern enough to be convenient, but out of date enough that it's evident visitors are not frequent here.

Graham returns with my luggage while we're roaming around on the second floor, so we stop for a quick dinner of some kind of local fish and chips. As we eat, Isla tells me not to worry about preparing dinners, and that she will take care of herself. When Graham hears this, he declares evenings can be when he will show me around town. This seems to satisfy Isla and she lets Graham take care of carrying the conversation with me. I glance at her throughout the meal, which she only picks at. While she continues to remain pleasant, it gnaws at me that something is upsetting her, like she's always a little bit sad. It begins to remind me of Noah toward the end, so I do my best to focus on the joyful man beside me. With plans to meet up the next evening, I go to bed that night wondering how on earth I ended up living in an old castle in Scotland.

The next morning, I wake up determined to build a solid routine. If Caitlin's gonna mess with my vacation plans, I'll create a new ones—though I'm not really sure I can call it a vacation anymore. After washing up and cooking some omelets for Isla and myself, I make quick work of tidying up most of the downstairs while I work on a routine in my head. By the time Isla and I sit down to lunch, my phone beeps. Seeing Graham's name appear across the screen sends a flush across my olive skin, not going unnoticed by his aunt.

"That Graham, dear?"

My blush only deepens as I smile in response. She nods approvingly, a satisfied smile settling on her face while she eats her salad.

"I didn't know this town had a theater?" I try not to sound like a complete moron.

"Oh, yes. We may be a small community, but we make sure to entertain ourselves, Ellie. Though it is mainly young ladies in the acting troupe, their talents are not to be discredited."

Something in her tone changed then, almost protective. "Are the actresses friends of yours?" I notice she's wearing another Hollywood robe, crimson today. Maybe she was an actress when she was younger.

"Everyone in this community is connected, my dear."

There was a sense of finality to her statement, so I let it drop. After a few minutes of only semi-comfortable silence, Isla nods and stands to leave. Being true to my people-pleasing self, I panic.

"Isla, I didn't mean to pry before. I'm terribly sorry."

Her gaze is cool and level. It's a practiced look. "No need for apologies, dearest Ellie. Your curiosity is not a bad quality. But you should be careful. One day, it could get you into trouble." She must notice the terrified look on my face because she lets out a musical laugh. "Have a good evening with Graham. And do try to relax—you look like you've seen a ghost."

With a small grin, she exits the kitchen and leaves me alone in deafening silence.

That night, Graham senses my uneasiness, the weight of the conversation with Isla still on my mind as I watch the beautiful, lithe creatures dance across the stage to an enchanting rhythm. He takes my hand and gives it a soft squeeze. When I turn to look at him, he's already watching me with a warm smile that fills my chest with a gooey feeling. There's something about this man. Between the ethereal music playing in the background and the way his eyes are practically glowing, something prickles at the back of my neck. He's able to put me at ease so effortlessly that it's almost scary. But I suppose I should just be thankful, given my current predicament.

We walk around town after the performance has ended and I tell Graham about the earlier conversation with Isla. He laughs, and it's such a beautiful sound, I stop in my tracks. He regards me curiously and I realize I'm staring. A blush creeps across my face as I turn to look away, but his fingers catch my chin and turn my face back to his. His eyes are kind as he drops his hand and takes mine, propelling me forward and into the night.

CHAPTER 6

Ellie

AFTER LUNCH COMES AND GOES, I REALIZE ALL THE BUSINESSES in town should be open since the weekend is over. There's still a couple hours before I'm supposed to meet Graham at the coffee shop, so I decide to check out the local library. Apparently, all the books on my e-reader and the massive library at Isla's estate are simply not enough.

I pull my coat tight around me as the wind bites at my face. For the eighth time since I left the States, I wish I had brought a scarf to cover my nose. It's a mercifully short walk from the estate, and I quickly find the library, located right in the middle of town. From the outside, the two-story building looks old and run-down compared to the pub close by. If this town's priorities were ever in question, they sure aren't anymore.

A tiny bell rings as I push open the front door and warmth cascades over my body. While I hate to admit I thought it would be all cobwebby in here, it's quite the opposite. Compared to the gloomy exterior, the main room is bright and well-lit with vibrant paintings and posters littering the walls. The bulletin board next to the exit holds colorful papers advertising livestock for sale, an upcoming bake sale, a community book club, and guitar lessons. I wander a little deeper into the first few shelves—autobiographies. Not really my thing after Noah, but I take a few minutes to peruse anyway.

After moving on to the fiction section, I find a book that catches my attention. When I get to the part about the love interest, a familiar smell fills the air. I turn around to see Lawson standing about a foot away, putting a book back on the shelf. Without meaning to, I take a deep breath and accidentally inhale his scent. Woodsy, sea salt, and citrusy. Homey. *Wait, what?*

Lawson clears his throat and my face flushes when I realize I'm staring. Willing myself to look anywhere else, I reach for a book still on the shelf and pretend to read the back.

"Finding everything okay?"

"Excuse me?" I pull my gaze up to meet his. Why does this man always seem to catch me off guard? It's terribly annoying. "O-oh. Yep. This is one of my favorites, so I just thought I'd check out the European version ..."

Lawson raises his eyebrows and looks at the book cover. Stretching the fabric of his green Henley, he crosses his arms and suppresses a laugh.

I look down at the book and just about die. *How To Speak Whale for Dummies* rests in my hands. Someone obviously put this in the wrong section as some kind of cosmic joke made just for me.

"Okay, then. An aspiring whale?"

"You mean whaler?"

"No, whale. Why else would you need to know how to speak whale?" He leans into the bookshelf and tries not to grin at my expense.

"Because I ... I ..." I sigh, "I grabbed the wrong book." He laughs softly and my heart stops. It's rough, like it's been a while since the man last laughed—which I fully believe. Not surprising, given his generally surly demeanor. I suddenly want to know what it would be like to hear him really let go. I try to gather my wits, which are now scattered all over the floor. "Why on earth does the library even have this book?" I ask, holding it up. The absurdity of the situation brings a laugh out of me. A sharp intake of air stops me in my tracks as Lawson looks at me like I've just said a long string of obscene curse words.

I let out an awkward laugh as I place the book back onto the shelf. "Well, anyway—"

"If you're interested in sea creatures, there are more interesting books to explore. I can show you, if you like." He shifts from foot to foot, like he's the one feeling awkward. Maybe people aren't typically this moronic here.

What am I supposed to say? I guess I could lie and say I prefer my feet solidly on land and would happily smack a dolphin into oblivion if it came near me? Who am I kidding, I would freaking love it if a dolphin came up to me.

"You know, you think quite loudly." Lawson's light blue eyes sparkle as he teases me. Jerk.

"Um, yeah, sure. Lead the way." I gesture toward the end of the aisle, giving him a sarcastic smile.

Lawson turns and begins walking away while I do my best not to notice how attractive he is. Nope, not even a little bit. *Maybe a little?* Once his amazing scent is no longer within my nose's reach, my feet finally decide to follow him.

I trail after him for a few aisles and then notice an unmarked door off to the side. It's away from all the shelves and a little off the beaten path. Curiosity gets the better of me and I take a couple steps toward the door when a hand wraps around my arm and turns me around. I look down at it and notice a small golden ring around the middle finger. I lift my head to see who it belongs to on the off chance it's not the stupidly handsome librarian.

"You're not very good at following directions, are you?" Lawson's much closer than I anticipated and the smell of him once again throws me for a second.

"Oh, I just saw the door and I—"

"Thought you'd go snooping?"

"What? No ..." Except that was exactly what I was doing. "Okay, maybe. But it wasn't intentional," I insist.

His straight-faced mask finally slips and gives way to a lopsided grin. It fans the annoyance flame, which only seems to please him more.

"If you must know, my apartment is up there. Which is why it's unmarked. For the nosy people. Such as yourself," he says, gesturing to me as he finally releases my arm. "Here." A heavy book is thrust into my hands.

"*Mythological Creatures of the Deep*," I read aloud. I cock an eyebrow at him and he shrugs nonchalantly.

"You look like the kind of girl who likes to live in worlds other than her own."

"I typically prefer regency or fantasy worlds."

"And what's more fantastic than a selkie? Or a siren?" He looks at me intently. But to my intense surprise, there isn't an ounce of mockery on his face.

"A siren? You mean, like a mermaid?"

Lawson shakes his head. "No, a siren. Very different."

"Sounds like I'm not the only one who lives outside their own world." I realize then he mentioned another creature, as well. I pull my brows together and frown. "What's a selkie? Do they wear a lot of silks?"

He gives me a small smile and shakes his head. There's about one too many seconds before he finally answers, and I wonder if he finally thinks I'm truly an idiot. Which is fine, I don't like him, anyway. *Liar.*

"Do you always spend so much time inside your own head?"

"What?" Is the helicopter spotlight finally on me with horns blaring? He sighs and runs a hand through wavy caramel hair before crossing his arms at me. Again. I certainly annoy him.

"Nothing. Is that all you're here for?"

"Oh, an absurdly attractive man giving me the world's weirdest book is definitely not what I came here for." As soon as the words are out of my mouth, I want to crawl under the front desk and wither away. Lawson doesn't seem to know what to do with my accidental confession and pulls in his lips to keep from laughing. He finds me much too amusing. I hate this man.

To avoid the risk of further embarrassing myself, I head toward the oversized checkout desk. It holds the most archaic computer I've ever seen. Lawson follows wordlessly behind me. Putting the book on the desk, a thought strikes me.

"I don't have a library card," I blurt out.

"Don't worry about it. You're with Graham's aunt, right?"

"How do you know that?" Did I send out a Change of Address card in my sleep?

"It's a small town, Ellie. People talk." He gives me a pointed look. "Most people here have never met her, but it's no secret where she lives." What?

"How does someone in this small of a place get away with not meeting everyone in a single day?" Lawson shrugs as he types something into the world's oldest system.

"Graham's always talking about her travels, so I'd guess that's how." His eyes slide over to mine and something about them pins me in place.

A bell singing in the background as another patron walks in brings a gust of the cold outdoor wind. I shiver in response, earning me a deep frown from Lawson.

"Do you not have a scarf or anything else to keep you warm?" He almost sounds offended.

"No." My voice comes out sharper than I mean it to. I clear my throat and try again. "I wasn't in a great mental state when I was packing. And then I just haven't bothered with buying one yet since I've been here." I do my best to appear indifferent. In reality, I am already dreading having to go back outside right now.

Lawson rolls his eyes and crouches down beneath the counter. After a moment, he stands back to his full height. Without taking his eyes off of me, he holds out a hand, in it, the fluffiest scarf I've ever seen. I briefly wonder if I'm drooling. When I don't automatically take the scarf, he lets out a big sigh and I figure I should say something.

"That's one fluffy scarf ya got there." I mentally slap myself on the forehead. Lawson just looks at me with bewilderment written all over his face. Yep, today would be a great day for lightning to strike me down. But with my luck, it would probably be in front of Lawson, and I wouldn't even be unconscious from the experience, if only to further my humiliation.

Before I am able to say anything else inept, Lawson rounds the counter and stops directly in front of me. I watch as he takes another step closer. His eyes never leave mine, asking permission. I nod and he wraps the scarf around my neck, finishing it off in a knot. My body temperature instantly rises about ten degrees and I'm not sure if it's the wool scarf I'm now sporting or the annoying but attractive man standing so close to me.

Lawson finally pulls his eyes away and I could swear there's now a slight pink tint to his cheeks. He straightens as he notices an older man standing in line at the desk with a couple of books tucked under his arm.

Realizing it's time for me to leave, I give him one last smile and a small nod. I turn to give the old man an awkward smile before I can help myself. Grabbing my book off the counter, I head out the door. Lawson's eyes burn a hole in my back the entire way.

By the time I arrive at the coffee shop, I'm still five minutes early. Walking into the warm building, even among the workday's end crowd, it's easy to spot the mess of curly blonde hair framing Graham's bright green eyes sitting at one of the black bistro tables. His red flannel shirt and jeans blend in with the local fashion, though flannels seem to be a favorite of his in general. Another local quickly surfaces in my mind and it dawns on me that I have never seen him in a flannel even once.

He spots me just as quickly and stands abruptly, almost knocking over his coffee in the process. I laugh and point to the counter to let him know I'm going to order before heading over, thankful that Isla paid me the first month's wages in advance. When I finally have a coffee and the pastry of the day in my hands, I head toward the table with a bright smile.

Removing my coat and newly acquired scarf, I am reminded again how easy being with Graham feels. I look at him over my steaming coffee to see he's already watching me. And smiling. A blush fills my cheeks as I smile back.

We fall into easy conversation and drink scalding coffee. He doesn't even seem to judge me as I stuff my face full of lemon pastry. When I see pastry flakes dropping onto the cover of my library book, I wipe my hands before cleaning it off.

"Whoops. I doubt the library would like their book returned complete with a new lemony filling," I say, hoping he doesn't think I'm a total klutz.

He laughs, reaching for the book. His eyebrows raise as he sees the title. "Doin' a little light research?"

"Oh, not really. Lawson, um, MacCallahan, or something—you know him, right? He was here the last time we were. Anyway, he recommended it. I accidentally picked up a book on learning to speak whale and I think he just suggested this one as a joke."

"MacCallum, yes. He's surely an odd one," he says, nodding.

I laugh. "That does seem to be the general consensus about him. Anyway, I only took it to be polite. I doubt I'll even crack it open."

Graham shrugs and laughs. "You never know what ya may find, Ellie. May be worth a read." He takes another sip of his coffee and looks at me over the cup.

Something like a shiver runs through me. I take a moment to look around the crowded shop. I've never considered myself prey, but right now, it feels like a predator is lurking. Graham's voice draws me back to our table.

"Ellie?"

"Sorry, what was that?"

"I asked if ya want to take a walk along the beach. It's a lovely evening and I think we should enjoy it a little."

Forcing a smile at Graham, I try to push the thought of being watched from my mind. "That sounds great. Besides, I imagine there are plenty of others who would like our table." I nod to the other patrons at the ordering counter.

He and I begin bundling back up just as the table vultures descend upon us. Laughing to himself, Graham puts his hand on my back and leads me out the door.

We reach the beach in record time since it is so close to the coffee shop. Graham's right, it's a beautiful evening. Vibrant pinks and oranges paint the sky as the sun begins making its descent into the horizon. The wind has finally calmed down and I can pull my face out of the scarf so I no longer look like a half-assed mummy.

As we walk, Graham takes my hand in his. I wait for the feeling of ease to wash over me like it normally does. But it never comes. The sound of the waves crashing pulls my eyes to the water while I recall my first date in high school. The poor guy tried to hold my hand and I yanked it away because I didn't like when people would touch me. Noah was the first person I didn't mind holding my hand. While it's not like this is the first time Graham has held my hand, it is the first time comfort doesn't automatically wash over me. But it didn't bother me this afternoon, at the library when—

"Hey, there's Lawson. That guy's crazy." Graham's voice snaps me back to the moment. He points out to the water where Lawson is doing laps. Literal laps in the ocean. Like a psycho. Graham laughs. "He's too far out there, otherwise I'd call him over and ask why he recommended such a weird book."

The air is suddenly filled with Graham's ringtone blaring from his pocket.

"Oh, sorry. I need to take this. Do ya mind?"

"Of course not." I smile at him.

He drops my hand and walks several paces away before answering. When I turn back to the water, I about drop the book from under my arm.

"Ellie." Lawson saying my name shouldn't feel this familiar. But it does. I silently curse the arrhythmia pounding behind my ribs as I actively work to not notice his very naked, chiseled chest.

"Lawson." *Eyes up top, Hughes.* "Weren't you just way out in the ocean? How'd you get up here so quickly?"

"I'm a fast swimmer." His smile is sincere, filling me with warmth. He pulls on a shirt and looks over to Graham. "On a date?"

"Erm, something like that. I guess. Maybe," I answer awkwardly.

"I think you'd know if you were on a date," he replies cooly. "At least, you would if it were with me." He laughs loudly at the surprise on my face. "Don't worry, you won't be subjected to such torture."

A pang of disappointment hits me in the chest. *What the hell am I supposed to say to that?* I pick a generally neutral answer. "Oh, well. Alright then."

Lawson watches me thoughtfully. "Alright then." A little dissatisfaction comes through in his remark. He looks over my shoulder and seems to immediately become bored.

"Lawson, bit cold out for laps. Don't ya think?" Graham's voice is so close it makes me jump.

"I don't mind the cold." Gone are the warm, familiar tones in Lawson's voice, replaced by weariness and the intense feeling of intrusion.

"Right, well. I best be gettin' this one home for the evenin'. Don't want her to freeze." Graham moves to put an arm around me and my body goes rigid at the contact. Lawson's eyes don't miss the reaction. Forcing a smile to cover up any awkwardness, my eyes seek out the darkening water. Really, anywhere but at the two stupidly attractive men standing with me.

"Of course. I'll see you around, Ellie. Graham." Lawson nods at me and looks at Graham, calm and cool. It would almost be frightening if I wasn't feeling so damn awkward.

I watch as Lawson walks toward a small pile of belongings a little ways away and Graham begins to lead me back toward town. As we make the trek back to the estate, I remember Graham's phone call.

"Was everything okay earlier? You were on the phone for a while."

"Oh, yeah. Just Auntie. She's interested in doing a bit of traveling to see some family and was curious if I wanted to go with her." Graham takes hold of my hand again.

"Oh, wow. Do you all have a lot of family in the area?"

"Loads. But we will have to travel a bit to get to them." I will myself to focus on the conversation and not how badly I would like my hand back.

"I didn't grow up with a big family, so I think it sounds like fun. When will you leave?"

"Day after tomorrow, actually. And we'll be gone for a few weeks," he says. "Will you miss me?"

His question catches me off guard. When I turn, his bottle-green eyes are nearly glowing in the sunset.

I answer honestly, "Yes, I will." His responding grin is heartwarming.

The next couple days pass uneventfully, with the exception of Isla also relaying the message of their impending trip during breakfast, and the two of them leaving the following morning. I spend the days cleaning, cooking, and studying the endless volumes in the library. A text from Graham lets me know things are going well, but that he may be out of range for a bit.

On Wednesday evening, I decide to wander into town for dinner. On a whim, I grab a bag and stuff a blanket and the book on mythological sea creatures in. Donning my warmest socks and favorite purple sweater, I lock up the estate and head down the road.

The walk isn't far, but I find myself pulling Lawson's scarf up around my nose not long after I'm out of the estate grounds. His signature aroma fills my senses and it's amazing. He may be a frustrating man, but I would pay a lot of money for his scent to be bottled up and spritzed on my pillow each night.

After enjoying a hearty dinner at the pub, the sound of the waves beckons me to the ocean. Taking the blanket and book out of my bag, I flip through the pages, reading various passages. Lawson wasn't kidding about this being interesting. I find the two creatures he mentioned and pay closer attention. Selkies seem intriguing, except for the women being trapped by humans thing. That's definitely horrible. Sirens just seem scary. Gorgeous, but frightening.

A large wave crashes not too far away, pulling me out of the book. It's gotten dark, so I make quick work of folding up the blanket and putting my things away. Before starting the walk back to the estate, a sound draws me closer to the water line. Due to the lateness of the hour, the water is nearly black, and I can't see anything past the surface.

My first unashamed thought is that it might be Lawson doing laps again. But then I hear the same sound further down the shoreline. The soft airiness pulls me toward it, even if I can't see its origin. I hug Lawson's scarf tighter to my front, protecting myself from the winds coming off the waves. The sound washes over me again, but there's more substance to it now, stronger and with more purpose.

"Ellie ..." I whip my head around so fast I'm pretty sure I pull something. I'd know that voice anywhere. It's the voice that lives in my nightmares, my daydreams, and hasn't left me since I first heard it when I was fifteen. *Noah.*

Frantically, I look up and down the shoreline, calling his name. But these shallow waters show me nothing beyond their frothy waves. With the sky now black, I give up and head home.

The next morning, I wake to the sound of rain pelting against the window—a direct parallel to my current emotional state. A quick breakfast and general cleanup later, I decide to spend some quality time in the library. Starting up the fire, I begin to peruse the shelves. After my first extended visit here, it was obvious there is nothing from the last eighty years on these shelves. Touching the spines as I walk the length of the room, my mind wanders back to the possibility of Isla being some kind of black market dealer. Some of these books are so old, they don't even look real. Most hold ancient or dead languages and are coated in dust.

I take the few volumes I've plucked from the stacks and head back to the desk near the fireplace. While setting the books down, a glimmer from the mantelpiece catches my eye. As I get closer, I see it's a small bronze hourglass. Like so many of the volumes, it also looks archaic. Leaning it forward to pick it up, a loud creak on the other side of the fireplace makes me nearly rip the antique timepiece from its secure spot on the mantel.

Torn between fear and curiosity, I slowly step toward the sound's origin. Where the fireplace typically meets the bookshelves, a doorway now stands wide open. Looking around, I grab a small wooden stool and place it in the opening. I've seen enough episodes of Scooby-Doo to know the secret passage door always closes on you. With the stool in place, a quick look back at the mantel lets me know the hourglass is still tilted forward. Reflections of the fire below it dance on the sparkling glass, daring me to enter the depths of hell. Even though my heart is about to pound its way out of my chest, I turn back to the hidden doorway and slowly step into the room.

The air is thick, like the ventilation must not be great. Midnight blue paint covers the walls from floor to ceiling and spotlights shine on various items in glass cases. The room isn't large, but the sheer number of items showcased are impressive. From old maps to expensive jewelry, it's evident this is some kind of vault. Without labels on anything, I have no real way of knowing what I'm looking at, but against the far wall of the room is what is clearly the centerpiece of the collection. I walk up right next to the case, and it takes me a minute to absorb what I'm seeing. The sheer size of the object is impressive to behold. Walking from end to end, I take it all in and realize the oversized, black-speckled, white canvas looks familiar, but I can't place from where.

Hanging on the wall above the behemoth trophy is a framed picture. The faces are beautiful, nearly inhuman. The one featured in the middle is absolutely striking. The way the others huddle around her shows she is clearly the leader of the group. They all show a great physical resemblance to the one in front and it's not a giant leap to guess this is some kind of a family portrait.

Deciding it's time to get some air, I turn to leave. Then it hits me where I've seen the thing in the glass before.

"Holy. Shit."

CHAPTER 7

Lawson

B Y THE TIME THURSDAY ROLLS AROUND, I NEED A DRINK. THE week has been spent running into Ellie time and time again, and usually with that cheery prick, Graham. Not that he knows what he's stepping into. But I will need to find a way to get her away from him so she can fulfill her duties. Then what? I bring her back and she returns home to wherever she came from? Or worse, she comes back to be with Graham.

Thinking about them together makes my hand begin to hurt and I look down to see my knuckles white from gripping my glass too tightly. I release the glass and a deep sigh simultaneously. Dragging a hand down my face, I'm finally honest with myself and admit that I don't find her annoying like I should. Chagrin washes over me. Twisting the gold ring on my middle finger, I fight the urge to throw my face down on the wooden pub table in frustration.

I never wanted more from another person. Never thought I would have the chance to even consider it. But if Ellie was not the single most important person in our culture's history and future, she would make me want more. Of course, she's also only a fragile little human. That's annoying, too.

But she's also beautiful, funny, quirky, and kind. Her laughter makes my heart stop, but in a way that makes me want to say anything that might allow me to hear it again. Her lack of consideration for herself is infuriating. She eats more than any woman I've ever seen. And she is simply amazing. But she's only a human.

The whiskey warms my throat as I take another swig. Then and there, a reluctant resolve moves through my chest, pushing down anything resembling a warm feeling toward Ellie. It's simply too dangerous. For me and for her. And I will not put any fuzzy feelings above the safety of my people.

Catching the bartender's eye, I raise my now empty glass. He only nods in response. In the background, the bell above the door chimes as someone enters the crowded pub. Something in my body lights up and I know who it is before I even lift my eyes.

When did my body get so attuned to hers? Fuck.

The chair on my right scrapes the floor and I look to see Ellie sitting there, coat unbuttoned and my scarf hanging loosely around her neck. She eyes the bucket of peanuts in the middle of the table. I haven't known her to be shy about food, but I scoot the bucket toward her anyway.

She flits her eyes up to meet mine before reaching for the peanuts. I watch in awe as she shells her handful faster than any grown man I have ever seen and shoves them all into her mouth.

The barkeeper sets my fresh drink down and looks to Ellie.

"Would ya like anything, miss?"

She looks up to him but doesn't immediately respond.

"She'll take a light draft beer. Whatever you have on tap is fine," I order for her. It's what she was drinking that first night in the bar nearly a week ago. The barkeeper nods, letting me know he'll be right back.

By the time he returns with her drink, Ellie still hasn't said anything. Nor does she ever look directly at me. Deciding I'm done with the silence because it's making me nervous, I take a stab at making conversation.

"It's a little cooler this evening." Crossing my arms, I lean further into the table. I bet she didn't know she would get such stimulating conversation.

She finally looks at me, nodding slowly. I take a chance even if I really don't want to know.

"Where's Graham tonight?" I make a show of looking toward the door in an effort to find him. Clenching my fists, I pray to Odin she can't see how nervous I feel.

"Out of town," she finally says, lifting her eyes to meet mine. The amount of relief I feel at her response is truly annoying. But this does give me a little more time to prepare her for what's coming. Hopefully she looked at the book I gave her.

"Oh. Well, in that case, you're more than welcome to—" I'm cut off by a ringtone coming from her bag.

Ellie looks down at her bag with confusion covering her face. Digging through the contents, she pulls out her smartphone. A frown settles as she reads the caller ID and she answers with what looks like reluctance. Even I know it's crossing a line if I hope it's Graham that she doesn't want to speak with.

"Ana?" *Nope, not Graham.*

I can't quite make out what the woman on the other end of the line is saying, but it's clear she's highly intoxicated. And not speaking English. Ellie uses her free hand to shield her eyes from me. Her long, chocolate-brown hair helps by falling around her face in a makeshift curtain against the world.

"Ana, please ... I ... I didn't know ..." Ellie sniffs and quickly wipes her eyes.

Rage begins to course through me. *Who has the fucking audacity to make her cry?* I clench my jaw and begin shoving peanuts in my mouth so I don't rip the phone out of her hand and verbally assault whoever's on the other end.

"I-I'm sorry, I ... Paul, please," her voice quivers. She listens for another few seconds before moving the phone away from her face. The dark screen showing that whoever it was hung up on her. *Assholes.*

Ellie takes one of the paper napkins on the table and violently wipes at her eyes. When one of her hands finally rests on the table, I indulge in a human moment and cover it with my own.

"Ellie? El?" The amber eyes that meet mine aren't hers. Rather, they're the eyes of the person she's been hiding since she arrived that first night. Someone broken.

She gives me a wavering smile and sniffs again. "I'm fine," she says, and gestures to the beer sitting in front of her. "Thank you for ordering this. How did you know that's what I wanted?"

Pulling my hand away, I lean back in my chair. I shrug and do my best to appear nonchalant. I decide to go with honesty. "You were drinking it the last time I saw you here. The night we met."

From her silence, she's not quite sure what to say. Can't say I really blame her. Ellie finally nods. The swig she takes next could put any man to shame, me included. "What's the bartender's name?" she asks.

"Uh, Thom. Why—"

"Thom!" Her volume that close to my ear nearly causes me to jump out of my chair. "Another round? Something stronger? Thanks." She gives him a wave.

"Er, Ellie. Is everything okay?" I eye her curiously.

"Weird day followed by a shitty phone call. In my world, that means it's time to drink. Cool?"

The woman was just crying on the phone and now she's sassing me like it's her job.

"No objections here," I say, holding my glass up to her. "So ... what made today so weird?"

Ellie wags her pointer finger at me like I'm two. "Uh-uh. The first rule when drinking to a weird or bad day is not talking about said day." She takes another swig, and the rest of her beer is now gone. The woman just drank a whole pint of beer in two swigs.

I down the last of my second whiskey as Thom appears with our next round. Whatever he brought Ellie isn't beer this time, but I can smell its potency from here. She doesn't waste any time taking a long sip.

"Uh, Ellie. I can't say I know you all that well, but I'd really love it if you didn't die from alcohol poisoning tonight."

She proceeds to flip me off. A man at the next table laughs loudly at her boldness. I pin him with a glare, making him shrink into his chair.

"I'm not gonna die. I was in a sorority. Got lots of practice." Sip.

"What in Niflheim is a sorority?"

Ellie's drink pauses halfway to her full lips. "You're serious?" My blank expression must be all the answer she needs. She continues, "It's a group of women at universities who focus on philanthropy. But they really like to have fun, too."

I'm guessing she means by drinking when she polishes off her liquor. She points to my still full glass of whiskey.

"You gonna drink that?"

Knowing the right answer, I slide the drink across the table. This one she at least sniffs before taking a drink.

Thom, the astute man that he is, shows up with another round. I quietly let him know to close out the tab before turning back to Ellie. Having licked my glass clean, she goes to pick up the fresh drink in front of her.

"Ellie, talk to me."

"Why?"

I rest my elbows on the table and lean toward her. "Well, for starters, you are the one who sat down at my table. I didn't interrupt your drinking." I smile at her as sweetly as I can manage, though I imagine I look more like a cat with a canary in its mouth.

Ellie considers this while working on some more peanuts. She finally looks down at the table.

"The phone call. It was someone who blames me for their son's death," she says quietly. I'm not sure what I was expecting. But it wasn't that. She continues before I can say anything, "He drowned in the ocean back home. Just walked right in and never came out. They blame me, saying I should've seen the signs."

At first, I'm surprised she's not tearing up at having to share something that horrific. But then I figure she must be pretty numb thanks to the alcohol. Thank Odin for small favors, I guess.

"El, that's horrible. But it's not your fault. You know that, right?" My hand takes on a life of its own as it finds hers again. To my intense surprise, she grips mine back. Hard.

"Honestly, I go back and forth sometimes," she sighs. Her words are starting to slur. Time to go home. I run my thumb across the back of her hand.

"Hey, El? I think it may be time to head on out. Do I need to call Graham's aunt to come get you?"

She looks up at me with hazy eyes. "She's gone. With Graham."

So, she's all alone. *Odin's bony ass, I'm gonna regret this.*

"Okay. Well, you probably shouldn't be alone since you probably can't even walk that well at the moment." Watching as she tries to stand, I will myself to not look at how well her red sweater and jeans fit. She stumbles and I jump up to catch her. "Yeah, that's what I thought."

Her eyes close as I wrap her arms around my neck for stability. She begins to hum softly while I button up her coat and tie my scarf securely around her neck. Knowing she won't catch it, I grin at the thought of her wearing something of mine. Alright, time for the beginning, or the end.

"Okay, El, let's go." Turning back to wave goodbye to Thom, I loop my arm around Ellie's waist and help her out the door. To my surprise, she's compliant. A bit of a fight would not have surprised me.

Walking with Ellie through the dark street earns us a few dumbfounded expressions. Mainly because I'm walking while she is mostly being dragged and humming some inane pop song. About halfway between the bar and the library, I give up and scoop her into my arms, bridal style. She nuzzles against my chest, and I force myself to focus straight ahead. By the time we reach the library, she starts mumbling about random things—her favorite cookies, the time a big dog farted in her face, and the time her professor made a pass at her.

When I'm fumbling for my key while trying not to drop her, I chance a quick look. And then I almost drop her anyway because she's already staring at me with the warmest cinnamon eyes and a lazy smile that stirs something deep inside.

"Y'know," she slurs, "just thought you were ... bein' weird when you gave me that creaturey book ..." *That's fair.* She laughs a drunken, carefree laugh. *Odin's fat-ass ravens, that sound.*

Shaking my head, I try to remember the promise to myself. Our empire's survival is not worth a few moments of my selfish happiness. Ellie continues muttering something about the book while I think about where in Niflheim my coat is, the pile of dirty socks by my bed, not accidentally making us fall down these stairs. Anything but Ellie.

"But then ... I actually saw one ... couldn't freaking ... bleeve it," she practically shouts.

Laughing as I throw the door open to my apartment, I indulge her. "What couldn't you believe, El?"

She lets out an exasperated sigh. "That I saw one!"

I sit her down on my bed and take off her shoes, scarf, and coat. Helping her under the blankets, I wrap her up in a cocoon as she moves to lie down. A piece of hair covers her eyes, and my hand takes on a life of its own as I wipe the strand away. Sighing softly, I can't help but smile at her.

Her heavy eyes start opening less between blinks as sleep threatens her. But I humor her one more time.

"Saw one what, sweet Ellie?" I whisper. Here, where no one will ever know and she will never remember, I can revel in my feelings for her that I will always deny.

She roots around in my sheets and nuzzles into my pillow. A gratified hum escapes her throat. Certain she's not going to answer, I move to grab another pillow and blanket from the closet.

I'm halfway to the living area when she whispers, "S ... selkie coat."

I'm pretty sure my heart falls out of my ass.

Panic attacks were pretty common for me when I first washed up in Bettyhill, and it may have been a while since my last one, but there is no fucking doubt that is what's happening now. Ellie may be drunk and mostly incoherent, but what just came out of her mouth was clear as fucking day.

I turn around so fast I almost fall over in the process. But by the time I reach her, she's fast asleep. My eyes roam over her face as I contemplate shaking her awake so she'll say more words. But the longer I look at her, I know there's no way I would get anything useful at the moment. Raking my free hand over my face and through my hair, I reluctantly leave her to snore peacefully in my bed.

Lying on the couch, my mind races with all the fragments of information floating around in there. Even with her inebriated confessions, there are still so many pieces missing. Knowing Ellie will be asleep for quite a while and that sleep won't be coming for me anytime soon, I get up and start making preparations.

CHAPTER 8

Lawson

B Y THE TIME ELLIE COMES TRUDGING INTO THE KITCHEN area, everything is in place. Sitting on the couch pretending to read, I look up to see her hair standing up in every direction and eyes heavy from drink-induced sleep. Her coat and shoes are still off, so she's clearly not awake enough to fully process things quite yet. She sees me and gives a look just short of disdain. *I guess she's not much of a morning person.*

"Morning, sunshine," I say cheerfully. My grin is so big it's openly defying the human laws of physics.

Ellie scowls at me before realizing she has no idea where she is. Before she can ask, I offer, "You're in my apartment. It was much closer than trying to get you back to Graham's aunt's estate. And you were absolutely no help when it came to walking." She raises a critical eyebrow at me. "I carried you most of the way here," I say. Shrugging, I turn back to my book so she can have the moment of embarrassment I know is coming. "Oh," I add, "coffee's on the counter."

Shuffling on the floor lets me know she takes me up on the human offering. A moment later, the droopy couch sinks on the opposite end. I look up, expecting to see annoyance, frustration, outrage. Instead, Ellie looks contrite.

"I'm ... sorry," she whispers.

"Why?" I keep my tone light. If last night made me feel anything, it certainly wasn't regret.

"Being forced to take care of someone you despise while they're drunk after they interrupt your lonely drinking time isn't very nice. And on top of that, you were so nice that you let me kick you out of bed because you were being a gentleman and obviously slept on the couch, and now you have coffee for me and—"

"Ellie, breathe," I say. "And I don't despise you. At all. Not even a little bit." Giving her a small smile seems to make her believe me.

She finally allows a deep breath to come out and sinks a little further into the couch.

"Thank you for the coffee, Lawson." She takes another sip from the steaming mug while my heart catches inside my chest. She's never said my name before. But the way she says it is familiar, like she's done it a thousand times and will say it every day for the rest of her life.

A quick glance at the other end of the couch tells me she's already looking at me, waiting for an answer. I have to clear my throat before I figure out that I can't yet form a coherent sentence. I settle for a nod.

Step one: she wakes up. Time for step two.

"I didn't know if you had time to join me for a quick breakfast down at the coffee shop?" I aim for nonchalance but land more in the panicked curiosity realm.

She seems to consider the offer. I had no idea it would be such a weighty decision on her part. Maybe she really does hate me.

"Okay, breakfast would be nice." I don't miss the hesitation in her voice, but I'll take what I can get. I watch as she looks quizzically around my apartment. "You don't have a lot of personal items. Any, really."

I frown. "Never been one for personal effects. This place isn't really my home."

Ellie gives me a questioning look, but I distract her by asking about her favorite breakfast pastries – all of them, of course.

Once we're both dressed and fully awake, we make our way down to the coffee shop. It's a crisp Friday morning, so we have the place mostly to ourselves. Ellie had asked on our way out if the library being closed would be a problem. When I told her I run the place and therefore I can set the hours, she seemed amused, but at what I'm not sure.

While our order is being prepared, I lead her to a small table in the far corner of the open room. Our items are delivered right to us due to the lack of customers. Even though my nerves are threatening to take over, I ask the question I've been wanting to ask since she fell asleep.

"Ellie, do you remember telling me something about seeing a selkie coat?" Her cup freezes halfway to her mouth. "I promise I won't judge anything you say about it," I quickly assure her, hoping she'll feel more confident that way.

Setting her cup down, she looks at some crumbs on the table. "You're gonna think it's dumb. Monumentally dumb. Absolutely ridiculous."

"Try me." I level a look at her. Not a hint of amusement shows.

She sighs.

"Remember that book you let me take from the library?"

"Vividly."

"Okay, well," she pauses for a bite of blueberry muffin, "a couple nights ago I was bored so I went down to the beach." Her cheeks flush at the memory and I assume she's leaving something out. "Anyway, I took the book and a blanket—"

"Are you trying to tell me you lost the book to the ocean?"

"No!" She laughs. "I'm trying to say I actually read that crazy book. First, let me say, there are a lot of terrifying creatures in there. But I remembered you mentioning a couple and, me being me, I just had to check those out too." Her face falls.

I watch her closely, anxiously awaiting the next words. When she doesn't continue, I prompt her. "And what did you think?"

Ellie looks at me. Surprise crosses her face when she sees I'm genuinely curious. "Well, I honestly thought the sirens seem pretty terrifying. I'd hate to meet one of those." She laughs, clearly uncomfortable with sharing her honest opinions.

"That's fair." I nod. "What about the other?"

"Oh, the selkies? They were pretty weird. I mean, I've never heard of anything like them before. But the concept was cool. Except for the part where the women are taken captive as humans and have their coats hidden from them. That really sucks."

I realize I've been holding my breath and I try to let it go a little at a time so as not to scare her.

"So, is that what upset you yesterday? Reading about things like that?" I ask.

"What? No, no." She shakes her head. "That's not it." She swirls the coffee in her cup.

"El? What is it?"

She takes a deep breath.

"Yesterday, I was in the library at Isla's—er, Graham's aunt—and I was gathering some books to look through. When I took them back to the desk where I was working, I noticed this really neat hourglass on the giant ass mantel, so naturally I had to go check it out."

"Naturally." I smile. Ellie smiles back and shoves another handful of muffin into her mouth.

"So, anyway, when I went to pick up the hourglass, this, I dunno, secret door next to the fireplace opened up." She winces, waiting for a negative reaction. When she doesn't get one, she continues. "I found a stool to block the opening in case something happened, but the next thing I know, I'm in this crazy vault of some kind."

I don't think I've ever been this still in my entire life. My breathing becomes shallow as I wait to hear what I now know is coming.

"There were all kinds of things in glass cases in there. Jewelry, old maps. But at the far end of the room was this giant seal skin. Easily over six feet long. I swear it could've been worn by a grown ass man, even you." She gestures at me like my six-foot-two height is offensive to her. "I just thought it was really weird. But when I went to leave ... I remembered a picture I'd seen in that creature book." Ellie looks down at the table again, focusing on the uneaten remains of her muffin. "It looked just like a selkie coat," she whispers.

I must be staring pretty intensely, because she immediately starts to backtrack.

"But y'know, it also could've just been a hunting souvenir or something? Do people even hunt seals or is that just polar bears?" She waves her hands around like they're on fire.

I capture them in mine and pull them to the table. I don't want the restaurant staff thinking we're arguing. In the calmest voice I can manage, I say, "El, calm down. First, a question."

She looks down at our hands but doesn't attempt to move them. "Okay ..."

"How long has Graham's aunt lived in that house?"

"I don't know." She shakes her head. "But she said something about recently getting the internet installed, so I'd guess not long? So it's very likely she has no idea that room or, um, *thing* is even in there."

"That makes sense," I say, nodding. "What did you do next?"

"Um, well, I was pretty freaked out. Especially if that thing really is what it looks like, which, even if it's not, it's fucking weird it's just sitting in some secret room in that house. So I put on my coat and scarf—"

"*My* scarf" I smirk at her. A warm blush spreads over her olive cheeks and I fight the urge to reach out and touch her face.

"Uh, right." She pulls her hands out of mine as she leans back in her chair. "So, then I decided I needed some air and ended up at the bar, where I saw you. Since you're the only one here I really know," I raise my eyebrow at her, "I-I just mean, I've talked to you several times and—"

I laugh. "I can honestly say you know me better than anyone else here, Ellie."

That seems to please her. She smiles warmly at me. "Anyway, I was needing familiarity, so I sat down at your table. Then Noah's parents called and, well, you know the rest."

I nod and lean back into my chair to give her some space. *Okay, now or never, MacCallum.*

"Did you read the part about the selkie prophecy?"

Ellie frowns and shakes her head. She looks at me intently and it encourages me to continue.

"So, a long time ago, supposedly, the Selkie Empire was vast and spanned through all waters and lands across the Earth. But the great

Sea Witch foretold the fall of their people. Apparently, someone would try to take over the selkie throne and slay all they captured. Whoever it was that conquered the selkies could only be killed by a human, who would come to their aid. But once that was done, the only remaining selkie royal would reclaim the throne and free their people." When I finish, Ellie's frown seems to have only gotten deeper.

"This was in that book?" she asks. She downs the last of her coffee and looks at mine longingly. *Right, hangover.* I push my cup toward her.

"Uh, yep. Crazy, right?"

She shakes her head. "Wow, I can't believe I missed that. I read it pretty thoroughly." She lifts my coffee cup to her full lips, and I want to expire on the spot.

Instead, I shrug against my chair.

"There's not much print devoted to it. Practically there and gone. I'm not surprised you didn't see it."

Ellie blinks rapidly a few times before scratching her nose. "Hm. Yeah, I'll have to double-check that when I get home." Pushing up the sweater's sleeve, she takes a quick glance at a small silver watch. "Which I guess should be sooner rather than later. Just so it's not sitting there empty."

And she gives me the opening I need.

"Why don't you let me walk you home?" I offer.

"Oh, no, that's okay." Ellie shakes her head and I sense my window of opportunity rapidly closing. "You've seriously done too much already." She turns to pull on my scarf and her coat.

"Honestly, I'd feel better knowing you made it home safely. Please, Ellie. Let me finish what I started." I hit her with big puppy dog eyes, hoping to make her laugh so she doesn't think I'm creepy. Thankfully, it works.

"Okay then, Lawson. Finish what you started." She grins at me.

CHAPTER 9

Ellie

W HEN WE ARRIVE BACK ON THE ESTATE PROPERTY, WE'VE
found a comfortable rhythm for conversation. Lawson asks
a question about my interests, current favorites, or time at college.
I answer. I ask him anything about his childhood or where he grew
up. He deflects by asking me another question. It's a wonderfully
honed system.

"So, you're really not going to answer any of my questions, but
expect me to answer every single weird thing you ask?" He raises a
thick eyebrow at me.

"What did I ask you that was weird?" he asks innocently.

"Like when you asked if I have a favorite color of grass? That was
weird. Especially since there's only green and brown." My hands fly
around in front of my face as I gesticulate to all the grass around us. I
stop in my tracks. "Hey, not fair. That was another distraction," I say,
frowning up at him.

He chuckles. Rolling my eyes only makes him laugh harder.
Turning my face away, I try to hide my smile.

"Woah," I hear him say.

I turn to see he has stopped a few paces behind me and is staring
straight ahead. Right at Isla's home. Pausing for a moment, I let him
catch up.

"Oh, yeah. That was my first response, too. Huge, right?"

Lawson finally catches up to me and we head to the front door, where I pull the largest skeleton key known to man out of my bag. Lawson whistles as I work it into the keyhole. When the door swings open, the awkwardness of our situation hits me. Am I supposed to send him on his way with a holiday ham? Do I chase him back down to the road with a croquet mallet? Can I invite him in? And just like that, I know that I want him to stay.

I walk through the door and turn back around.

"Um, would you like to come in?" He looks genuinely surprised. *Shit, wrong call?*

I breathe an internal sigh of relief when he smiles and heads in past me.

"This is quite the place," he says, looking around.

"And to think, you've only seen the foyer." He watches me as I take off my coat and scarf and lay them on the massive entry table. "Uh, can I take your coat?"

A look of discomfort comes over his face, but he recovers quickly. Taking off his coat, he lays it with mine on the table. I give him a quick tour of the general living spaces downstairs, the kitchen, and my room. I can't help but be baffled that my own introductory tour was barely a week ago.

He walks around my small room, cataloging every tiny detail. When he comes to my closed suitcase, he looks back up to me.

"You haven't unpacked?"

"Erm, no. I guess I'm a little, uh, nervous." My answer confuses him. I give my fingers their very own Chinese finger trap.

"Why are you nervous?" he asks genuinely. I take a couple of deep breaths before answering.

"Well, on the one hand, if I live out of my suitcase until Caitilin decides to show back up, I'll be ready to go back to real life at the drop of a hat." I release my fingers and sigh as I sit down on the bed. Lawson watches me carefully. "On the other hand, if I unpack and Caitlin decides to show back up, I'll *have* to go back to real life. A life where I no longer fit in anywhere." I twist the silver and blue ring on my middle finger, an old travel souvenir.

The bed dips as Lawson positions himself, facing me off to the side. After a moment, he covers both of my hands with one of his own.

"Ellie, what do you mean you no longer fit in your life?" he asks softly.

Turning to look at him, he's a lot closer than I expect. To my intense surprise, I find I'm not uncomfortable around him anymore. Not even a little. I dare say this surly man may even be my friend. I give a small smile and shift to face him.

"Before I came here, I quit my job. Moved my things into storage. Didn't really make a plan for when we got back. After Noah died, I just didn't really care about things anymore. Caitlin was really the only one who made sure I didn't fall off the face of the Earth."

"Noah was your best friend, wasn't he?" If I pay too much attention to Lawson's face, I'll see the small amount of jealousy I hear in his voice. And as much as I want to, I just can't do that right now. So, I nod.

"Yeah, he was. That's why his parents blame me so much for his death. They say if we were so close and honest with each other, how could I not have seen him deteriorate?" I trace the patterns on the blanket beside me. When I look back at Lawson, he's watching me like I'll explode into tears at any moment. My brows pull together and a frown takes over my face as I turn to look at the window. "But y'know what? I don't remember anything until that day. We had gone to the beach with Caitlin and her roommate. We were sitting down to eat our lunch while Caitlin and Morgan, I think, went to the bathroom. I remember he turned toward the ocean with this wistful look on his face. I thought it was weird because he was always so happy. We'd known each other since we were fifteen, just over a decade, so it's a safe bet to say I knew his general attitude."

My voice gets thicker and I feel the tears begin to slip down my face. I slap the burgundy bedspread in frustration, shaking my head. Lawson flinches in the corner of my periphery. Releasing a sigh, I lean back a little and prop myself up with a hand. My eyes settle on the opposite corner of the bed.

"And then he put down his sandwich. And just walked into the fucking ocean." The laugh that slips out of my lips holds no humor.

"Without even saying goodbye. Without even looking back," I whisper.

A movement catches my eye in time to see Lawson's hands just as they reach my face. He wipes my tears with his thumbs while I look at him through wet eyelashes. The tender look on his face would wash away any embarrassment if I had any, but I realize I don't. Probably because, unlike with Graham, I've never worried about whether Lawson finds me attractive. We've just existed around each other. And now, we can be friends who don't hide stupid crap like emotions from one another.

Lawson finally removes his hands and I sigh, immediately missing the contact. *Move on, Ellie.*

"Well, the last really cool place downstairs is the library." I try to change the topic as smoothly as possible. Honestly, I have no freaking idea if I succeed because Lawson stiffens in front of me. But I decide to take another chance, anyway. "Want to see the weird thing? And, y'know, the vault room?"

Lawson swallows. He almost looks guilty. But he puts me out of my misery when he finally nods and gets up from the bed. He holds out a hand to help me up, which I awkwardly let go of once I'm off the bed. *Do guy and girl friends hold hands? Did I just hurt his feelings?*

I don't give myself long to dwell on my new internal quandary as we enter the library and the old scary thing re-enters my brain. Looking up, I watch as Lawson looks around the room.

"This way."

I lead him to the cold fireplace. Sitting in the same spot is the hourglass. If I believed inanimate objects had feelings, I'm pretty sure this one would flip me off. Feeling Lawson standing directly behind gives me courage. God knows I need all of it I can get.

Reaching for the hourglass, I tilt it forward. The same creaking sound explodes through the silent room as the hidden door opens. Leaving the antique timepiece pulled forward, I grab the stool again as I look to Lawson. He's already watching me. Nodding to him, we both head into the room.

If the library is cloaked in silence, this place is a vacuum. But my ears don't miss Lawson's sharp intake of breath. I watch as he bypasses all the other objects and heads straight for the featured piece. Quickly putting the stool in place, I follow.

Just as I reach him, something shifts in the air. A low hum fills the space around us, and a soft light begins to emanate from the seal skin. Using Lawson's arm to balance myself, I lean down to look closer at it. But he shakes off my hand, causing me to nearly tumble into the glass.

Somewhere between incredulous and annoyed, I turn my now wide eyes to Lawson. Determination paints his features, and his face is fixed in a deep scowl. With his eyes focused on the seal skin, he lifts his right hand and presses it to the glass. I track his motion and then I notice it.

Holy shit, his ring is literally glowing.

The plain gold band begins to glow the same soft hue as the encased skin.

"Lawson?" I ask nervously. When he doesn't respond, I try again. "Uh, Lawson? I'm kinda freaking out over here ☒" A nervous laugh accidentally comes out.

Again, he says nothing. Nothing to even acknowledge my presence. Looking back to his arm, I can see the muscles working beneath his fitted cream Henley sleeves as he seems to push harder on the glass. Suddenly, the case shatters beneath his hand. Lawson hisses as the glass slices into his skin while I let out a scream as it pebbles all around us.

Lawson turns around and walks out of the room. I'm left standing there feeling dumbstruck as I stare after him with my jaw hanging open. Behind me, I can *feel* the glow receding from the skin. Like something flipped a switch and turned it off.

The only thing my mind can focus on is all the glass. I begin using my shoes to scoot it around to create a path on the floor. Because safety is clearly the most important thing here right now.

Lawson returns a few moments later. With his face still set in a frown, he holds up a giant, ancient-looking duffel bag. He walks straight up to the skin, and it begins to glow once more. Closing his eyes for just a moment, he lets out a deep sigh, like this is a moment he's been waiting on for a long time. When he opens his eyes, he begins unceremoniously shoving the skin into the bag.

I hear the zipper being pulled when I'm finally done being ignored.

"Excuse me!" I yell, waving my arms around like a lunatic. "Would you mind sharing what in the ever-loving hell you think you're doing?"

Lawson seems to remember my presence and turns to face me from his now crouched position. Shock covers his face and I can only assume it's at my volume. Or the withering stare I'm currently giving him. Without answering, he turns back to his bag to finish sealing the skin inside.

Standing up to his full height, he turns to leave. Unsure of what else to do, I trail behind like a lost puppy. Once we're out of the library, he turns to head toward the front door. Reaching the foyer, he finally stops at the entry table. Moving the bag from one hand to the other, he awkwardly puts on his coat.

Deciding I've had enough, I run up and body block the doors. Because obviously, there's no way this muscular six-foot-two brute of a man could take all five and a half feet, one hundred and forty pounds of frowning me. When his outer layer is back in place, Lawson looks at me with amusement. He puts all his weight onto his left foot as he crosses his arms. It's not very smooth since he now has a huge bag to contend with.

"Ellie ..." He smirks at me. This man has the audacity to *smirk* at me. "What are you doing?"

"Would ya look at that? He talks." I throw my hands up, talking to no one in particular. I pin my balled fists to my hips and glare at him.

His brows shoot up.

"Have you been talking to me?" Lawson tries for innocence, but I just continue to glare at him. He sighs. Using his non-bag hand, he rubs his forehead.

"Fine, what would you like to talk about?"

"Oh, well, please excuse me." I move my hand to cover my heart. "I don't mean to interrupt your active larceny with my desire to know what the actual fuck you're doing."

Lawson looks at his empty wrist before looking back to me.

"First, it's not larceny if you take what's yours. Second, I'm late, so if you don't mind—"

"You're not even wearing a watch! You just looked at your bare wrist!"

He shrugs and smiles.

"Saw some guy do it in a film once. Looked like fun. Now, seriously, if you don't mind." He motions for me to move.

I do my best to stand up straight, though heaven knows Lawson could probably move me with only one of his fingers.

"No," I say with the most confidence I can muster. "You're stealing something that is potentially Isla's. I was left in charge of her home while she's gone. Where that thing goes, I go."

Lawson frowns, but nods while considering something.

"Okay," he says.

He turns back to the entry table and grabs my coat and scarf. He proceeds to throw them to me and, like the athletic marvel I am, I drop them both. I can hear him choking back a laugh as I gather the items from the floor.

He takes that opportunity to rush past me and out the door.

"Wha—Lawson!" I yell after him. I fumble in my pocket for the key and manage to drop it twice. I finally succeed in getting the front door locked and have to sprint to catch up with him, thanks to his stupidly long legs. All while pulling on my coat and scarf.

I pepper him with questions of the "what the hell" variety, all of which go unanswered in his Lawson-like fashion, until we end up on a secluded beach north of town.

"Lawson, whose boat is that?" I ask, not even expecting an answer anymore.

He walks right up to it and tosses the bag inside. When he turns around to face me, he looks nervous. But he finally answers.

"It's mine," he pauses. "And if you're following what's in the bag—"

"You mean the thing that *glowed*? Yeah, I'm following it. Mainly because you stole it from my current employer."

As I speak, he watches me with something akin to fear etched into his features. Maybe it's his first robbery. After a moment of silence, he finally continues.

"If you're following what's in there," he points to the bag, "Then you'll have to follow me into the boat, too. And wherever it may take us." He looks at me, clearly waiting for an answer. When I don't give him one, he tries again. "What do you say, Ellie? Are you in? Or are you out?"

I swallow as I continue to stare at him.

"I'm in."

CHAPTER 10

THERE IS NO PART OF ME THAT CAN BELIEVE I GOT ELLIE TO climb in the boat uncoerced. I was nervous I would have to throw her in there kicking and screaming. Or unconscious.

As we cast off, Ellie tries to settle and finds most of the supplies I packed for her. Snacks, blankets, a hat, warmer shoes, and her e-reader. The contents of her suitcase have also been transferred into a bag of mine. She still doesn't know her suitcase at Isla's sat there empty when we were in her room earlier. Frankly, I think it would just piss her off if I revealed I went through her underwear trying to pick the right stuff before just dumping it all into my bag.

From the corner of my eye, I watch as she wiggles in the seat before moving to get a blanket. And a Slim Jim. I shake my head and try to hide my smile but catch her eyeing me warily. Hell, she probably thinks I've kidnapped her.

We begin to pick up speed as the shoreline slowly disappears into the background. The water around us turns deep oceanic blue the further away we travel. Salt slaps me in the face as we speed through the frothy waves. Too bad I didn't think to shave off my scruff before all this.

Ellie's been quiet since we cast off and I've had enough. Since we're in open water now, I slow the speed of the boat and turn around to face her. Ellie's eyes are focused on the duffel bag that holds my coat, like she expects it to reach out and bite her.

Suddenly, my nerves are wringing themselves together in my body. *What if she rejects everything I tell her? What if she rejects me?*

Her eyes wander warily out to the water and I know it's finally time to fill her in.

"Ellie?" I say softly. It wouldn't do well to scare her right off the bat. She looks up to meet my eyes, but doesn't say a word.

"Ellie," I try again, "I need to be honest with you about a couple of things." I wait to see if she will acknowledge what I'm saying. No such luck. Releasing a sigh, I run my hand through my hair, not quite sure where to start. "Do you remember the story I told you? About the selkies and their royal family? And how they would be overthrown? Imagine if all of it wasn't just some story ... and was actually ... true ..."

The only sign Ellie is listening is when she furrows her brow at me. She hasn't started laughing yet, so I take it as a sign to keep going.

"A long time ago, the Sea Witch ... I ... can't seem to remember her name," I shake my head in annoyance, "anyway, she's considered the oracle of the ocean. She told my people about the Slaughter that would one day come." Turning the boat off, I let us idle with the waves. When I take a seat in the captain's chair and fully face her, Ellie is staring hard at a spot on the floor. The frown seems to be frozen on her face. I clear my throat before continuing. "And about how only one member of the royal family ... *my* family ... would survive." I lower my eyes as I feel Ellie's finally find my face. A blush creeps up my neck as I continue. "My mother, the queen, had already put my older brother and me to bed ... It was dark when the sirens came for us. I had just fallen asleep when I heard the first ones—the screams. Our people knew the prophecy and had been taught and conditioned to get the royal family to the Base, a place our people had prepared for when the day would finally come." My fists ball in my lap and I try not to let my frustrations show. Our people had to put themselves second so my family could live. I work my jaw before finding Ellie continuing to stare at me. With no objections from her still, I finally share what happened after fourteen long years of solitude. "Our guards were caught by surprise when the Siren Queen herself found her way through the castle's secret tunnels in the Black Waters. My parents were first." I squeeze my eyes shut as the memories invade the present. "More sirens came for us, my brother and me. We ran through the carnage of their bodies, which had been torn to shreds. Because when a siren kills, they eviscerate you, leaving only your face intact so they can look at the fear they wrought for all eternity."

Ellie gasps, her first sign of life in a while. But I can't bring myself to look at her. Not yet. Not until this is all out.

"We'd almost made it to the Coat Room," I can't help but smirk at our kind's joke at the human world. I gesture to the duffel bag beneath Ellie's feet. "I was halfway into my coat when I heard Lorcan—er, my brother—call my name. By the time I turned to find him, *she* was running her pointed nails across his throat, surrounded by more of her kind. His eyes were on me the whole time." I take a deep breath as the rage starts to come over me and I do my best not to shudder. "He managed to tell me to run before he ..." I swallow the lump in my throat before I'm able to clear it. "After that, I pulled the last bit of my coat on and was in the ocean. But I got lost. It was storming that night, and I couldn't find the rest of our citizens. I ended up on the shore, the one by the church. I stashed my coat in some rocks, thinking I could come back and get it, but by the time I returned, it was gone. It had been taken." I chance a look at Ellie.

Her frown is still in place, but she's looking at the duffel bag instead of me or the floor. I know that look. She's overthinking about something. Pulling in her lips, she brings her eyes to meet mine.

"Have you ever gotten ... I dunno ... treatment? For, uh, this delusion of yours?"

"I'm sorry?"

A short laugh of disbelief escapes her lips. Shaking her head, she finds a whole cookie to shove in her mouth. "You've got to be kidding. This," she points to the duffel bag, "this is just some hunting trophy or something."

"You were singing a different tune last night—"

"I was drunk—"

"And then this morning?"

"I just ..." She runs a hand through her loose hair. "I thought you were just telling me some story or something. I sure as shit didn't think you, y'know, actually believed it!" Another cookie is violently popped into her mouth.

I pinch the bridge of my nose but keep my eyes locked on her. Mostly to make sure she doesn't try to jump overboard or anything.

"Ellie, I've spent the past fourteen years searching all over the area for it. There have only been a few places I haven't been able to look, one being the estate where you've been staying." She opens her mouth to protest again, but I hold up a hand asking her to wait. To my intense surprise, she begrudgingly obliges. "I don't know who owned it before Isla, but it's always been so out of the way, I've never really considered it. Until you came into the bar last night and got drunk. Then you started saying all these things ..." My eyes plead at her to believe me. If this woman wants me to get down on my knees and beg, I will.

"So ... either way ... you used me," Ellie whispers. Her gaze from me never wavers.

"What? No, I—"

"That's why you were being so nice to me when I got drunk. And before that too, because you knew where I was staying and you already wanted to check it out."

"Ellie, no, wait. It's you! You're the one who is to kill the Siren Queen. It's been—"

She jumps up, fists clenched and glaring at me. The rocking of the boat makes her unsteady and I can tell she's having to work to not fall on her ass.

"No, *you* wait. Even if you are absolutely insane—which you are, by the way—you needed me to get back into the estate so you pretended to be my friend in order to get what you needed." Her voice drips with venom as she looks at me. Her usually warm eyes are now glowing embers, threatening to burn me.

The swaying of the boat finally proves too much, and she starts to fall toward me. Without thinking, I throw my arms up and around her. Pulling her into my chest, I try to tell myself it's so she will be safe. But denying my attraction is proving to be more difficult than I originally thought. Too bad she's royally pissed at me.

She sinks into me only for a moment before seeming to remember herself and pushes me away with more force than I would have thought possible from someone so tiny. I don't want to admit it hurts more than just my chest.

"I can't fucking believe this," she mutters to herself.

"El, come on," I beg.

Ellie makes her way back to her spot and only glares back in response. Leaning forward to dig through the snacks again, it's clear when she decides she's done listening to me.

As desperately as I want and need her to believe me, I can't help but feel the irritation begin to bubble up within. If that's what she truly wants to think of me, I won't try to change her mind. It's better this way. My jaw sets with a frown as I watch her munching on a bag of crisps.

Storm clouds to the east catch my eye. I decide to give Ellie some space. If she thinks listening to me talk about all of this is ... anything short of real, wait until she meets Gabriel.

I turn the boat back on and steer us north toward the Base. There's no fucking way I could have found this on my own at fourteen. Having spent half of my life away from my kind, nerves crawl beneath my skin at the thought of seeing them again. To make matters worse, I will have to rejoin my colony as their leader. Some will surely think me unworthy. The shitty part is that I don't entirely disagree with them. What qualifies me to lead them other than the blood that runs through my veins?

Nothing.

My conscience rears its ugly head. But I know it's right. In the background of the rolling waves, I can hear Ellie asking me something now that I'm lost inside my own head. She has no idea how hard I'm working to not drive the boat straight down into the water to avoid all of this.

Ellie huffs from behind me, but I don't acknowledge her. She can sit and stew for a while. It won't kill her. She continues grumbling to herself and it takes everything in me to not bang my head against the boat's steering wheel. At least she still hasn't figured out I went through her suitcase and saw her underwear yet. She might have my balls for that one. With any luck, I will be nowhere near her when she sees her things.

Finally I see it in the distance. Its stone castle's Keep protrudes above the mist giving cover to the shoreline. I can't help but stare as I feel my jaw drop. After all these years, I finally made it. Sadness overwhelms me as I realize I'm not even sure who made it out alive. Swallowing the lump in my throat, I push the boat faster toward the island.

In the rearview mirror, I allow myself only a moment to watch Ellie's face as she takes in the sight before us. Incredulity covers her features, and she says my name again.

"Lawson, where are we?" Her voice is coated in nerves, though I can tell she's trying not to let them show. I can't bring myself to answer her, because I still don't fully believe we made it just yet.

"Lawson?" Somewhere between annoyed and nervous, she tries again.

Knowing we have already been seen by the guard, I begin slowing the boat's approach. The water beneath us begins to become shallow. Deep ocean blue begins taking on a slight green hue the closer we draw to shore.

"Lawson!" Ellie's booming voice cuts through my concentration this time.

"Ellie," I state, pinning her with a stare. Something she sees surprises her because she quiets and sits down. Ellie turns her gaze back to the shore, which becomes clearer by the second. As more of the militant castle comes into view, so does the thick tree line, concealing the village from any outside eyes.

Finally, I see them waiting for us on the shore and my chest swells. Pulling the boat up to the sand as carefully as I can manage, I cut the engine.

Bryant, my oldest friend and now apparently a high-ranking officer, and five other soldiers I only vaguely recognize, help pull our boat further onto the beach. Gabriel barely stands out among the sea of charcoal gray military uniforms, dressed in his standard black High Counselor robes. Turning back to Ellie, I give her a curt nod and help her out of the boat.

She doesn't seem to know where to look. She's obviously still irritated as hell at me, but she doesn't know the others. I can see her weighing which evil to choose.

I take a moment to grab the bags and toss them onto the beach, where the soldiers take care of grabbing them for me. When I finally hop out of the boat, Ellie is watching me with wide eyes as she practically rips the blanket around her in half from how tight she grips it. I hold her gaze for only a moment before turning to Gabriel and then landing on Bryant. A grin spreads over my face as I head to embrace my childhood friend for the first time in over a decade.

CHAPTER II

Ellie

T HE MAN IN FRONT OF ME LOOKS LIKE HE COULD BE MY grandfather, if I had ever known either of them and they dressed like the pope. Or Dumbledore. His tanned skin and kind, crinkly eyes radiate the warmth sorely missing from this frozen place. I love him immediately. It takes everything in me to not run straight into his arms and have him tell me that I'm only dreaming. But his dark flowing papal robes surrounded by six men in deep gray military uniforms are the wake-up call that whatever is happening is very real.

I'm not sure if it's being surrounded by a bunch of strangers (never my favorite) or that it's twenty degrees outside, but I pull the thick blanket tighter around my shoulders as the wind whips my hair across my face. Not for the first time since climbing into the boat after Lawson, I'm thankful for something to hold on to as I look around at the face of each man standing in front of us. Surprise hits when it finally registers they are looking at Lawson with joy. Reverence, even. I will admit, it's the first time I've ever seen anyone truly happy to see Lawson since I met him.

A movement to my left has me turning to see Lawson grinning and going to hug one of the obnoxiously tall men with short dark hair and sharp features in one of those weird man handshake-slash-hugs where they clap each other on the back. The man whispers in Lawson's ear as he locks eyes with me over the shoulder of the only non-stranger in our little group.

Heat rushes to my cheeks as I snap my head forward and catch the eyes of the old man. The kind smile is still on his face, but it no longer reaches his eyes. He steps forward and I instinctively take a step toward him, my eyes searching his face for some indicator of home I desperately need.

He brings his hands to rest on my shoulders and lets out a small sigh. "I am Gabriel, and it is my pleasure to welcome you, my dear. I do hope Lawson has been accommodating ..." His eyes slide over to the man who has been nothing but a weird nuisance the past week before looking back at me. I glance over at Lawson, who is still talking to the same uniformed man. Unsure of what to say, I simply give the man a slight smile so he might continue. Thankfully, he does. "I am quite sure you need something to warm you up. Come, let us go inside. No doubt you have many questions."

I realize I'm shivering like I'm going through crack withdrawals. Gabriel guides me forward like a child being led by a concerned parent.

A sound draws my attention to the right of us and I turn in time to watch a beautiful gray and black seal swim onto the beach from the water. An involuntary gasp escapes and I can feel the shock showing on my face as an honest to God *human* seems to be birthed from the middle of the seal's stomach. He stretches, fully clothed in a uniform that matches the others around me. Seeing our group, the man salutes before picking up the lifeless, deflated seal skin on the ground beside him and starts off in the opposite direction. The seal skin that looks just like the one in Lawson's duffel bag.

"My dear?" Gabriel's voice pulls me back to the moment. I'm certain my jaw must now be covered in sand and, any moment now, some proper lady of society will try to use my eyes as teacup saucers.

Maybe my eight new best friends managed to somehow miss what just happened. Or I accidentally drank some peyote this morning. What was in that coffee earlier?

Looking back to a very calm Gabriel, I do my best to rearrange my features to a more neutral setting. But I don't even dare chance a look at Lawson. Not yet.

With his guidance, Gabriel and I get back to heading somewhere out of these freezing winds. I'm immediately aware that the rest of the uniformed men flank us. It reminds me of those regency movies Caitlin used to make me watch, where the royalty could never even take a walk through the garden without a handful of guards there to protect them. Apparently, you never know when you'll need a hanky, or a stray bullet may try to take you down.

"What is this place?" I barely even whisper, not wanting to draw attention from anyone other than Gabriel. But I know he can hear me.

"A safe haven, my dear. For our people." His voice is guarded, while his eyes never leave the path ahead of us.

My breathing quickens as I think back to the conversation with Lawson that was only this morning. And then, of course, the more recent discussion on the boat. *The seal creatures. The sirens. The Slaughter. There's no possible way. Is there?* I'm telling myself not to hyperventilate when I feel a warm breath near my ear.

"I can hear your overthinking from here, El." Lawson's voice is so low I almost didn't hear him. That smug little fucker. *Are we speaking again?*

But I also didn't hear him come up behind me. Noah would have been disappointed in my lack of situational awareness. A pang of sadness fills my chest at his memory. Knowing I can't make whatever this is any harder than it is already, I make the decision to actively keep Noah out of my thoughts while I deal with whatever the hell is going on here. My face drains of emotion and is replaced by a mask I learned to perfect over the past year. Part of me wants to smack Lawson for the memories he's managed to stir, but the number of uniformed men in our immediate vicinity stops me.

Gabriel must feel the change in me because he doesn't try to engage in any more conversation as we walk along the wide dirt path winding through the forest. Laughter catches my attention and I look around to find the path leading to a small village, where several children and adults gather in the streets to play and gossip. I feel my mask drop a little at the sight of the children, the need to protect them from whatever is going on here is very strong. All around them, the buildings look ... old. Really old. They remind me of what I've seen in history books of early settlements. The people match the setting, with out-of-date clothes, dresses and trousers from centuries past. Time seems to stand still here.

More people come out of the surrounding buildings to see who Gabriel has brought to them. From their unabashed stares, they aren't expecting whatever I am. As we get closer, I see the women and little girls all have on some kind of necklace. Light reflects off the small pendant that hangs from each of them. Only when Gabriel clears his throat beside me do I realize he is trying to guide me away from the townspeople. I've been looking at them as much as they were studying me.

Instead of continuing into the town, Gabriel turns us toward a split in the path and I finally bother to look up. I'm met with a large gray stone castle that looks more like an army base than a home, with guards stationed at each entrance. The same castle I saw from the boat.

Beside me, Gabriel nods to them as we approach and they open a side door so short, I briefly wonder if the other guards with us will have to duck to fit through it.

Winding through sparce, lantern-lit stone hallways, we finally come upon a pair of large wooden doors with ornate metalwork covering at least 60 percent of the surface. Two of the militant men come to the front of our group and I watch as they easily open the heavy doors, knowing full-well I would have to be bitten by a hundred radioactive spiders just to confidently approach said doors. Warm light spills from the next room as the doors swing open. A gasp escapes me as we head through the doors. A library. With a fireplace.

All the men file in behind as I look around, taking in the sheer number of volumes in this room. I wouldn't be able to read all of these in three lifetimes.

"Are you okay, miss?" I turn to see one of the soldiers eyeing me with concern. I open my mouth to answer when—

"She loves books," Lawson says as he walks by. As if it were a simple fact he had known his entire life. Like he knows me. That man makes my blood boil. Balling my hands, recently clipped fingernails bite into my palms while I work to contain my annoyance. A large, circular oak table takes up most of the floor space in the immediate area. Lawson takes a seat, lounging in a large wingback chair with the nonchalance of a spoiled rich kid and drops *the* duffel bag unceremoniously on the floor.

Deciding to ignore him, I look around to see the rest of the men taking their own seats around the table. Gabriel seats himself on Lawson's left, while the soldier Lawson greeted upon our arrival sits on his right. I notice an empty chair on the other side of Gabriel, in front of the fireplace. I take the chair without needing an invitation. The warmth from the fireplace consumes me instantly.

A tall, blonde woman, maybe in her early twenties, enters the room carrying a tray with a single teacup. She makes her way directly to me with the grace of a ballerina and pours a steaming cup. I watch with wide eyes as she gives me a bright smile before hurrying out of the room. A quick look around the table lets me know no one else received such a kind service. I reach out to take a sip. The hot liquid is bitter, but it warms my insides and I hum in appreciation, earning myself a quiet laugh from the rest of the room. Well, from everyone except Lawson.

"She seems easy to please." I look up from my tea to see Lawson's right-hand man smiling at him. Unable to help myself, I shoot a glare from across the table. That doesn't do much but get me another laugh from the others.

"Enough, Bryant." Gabriel speaks up. Like me, he also sends a chastising look at the man. I knew I liked him.

I continue to sip my tea, waiting for someone to say something. Because there is no way they're waiting on me. Once my cup is about half empty, Gabriel puts me out of my misery.

"What is your name, dear?"

My eyes flick over to Lawson before landing back on Gabriel. I clear my throat before I murmur, "Ellie."

Gabriel gives me an encouraging smile. "Well, Ellie, where shall we begin? Has Lawson filled you in?"

I break my eyes away to stare at the table like it's a complex math problem—with a deer in the headlights look like I've just been called on in class for the answer.

"I gave her the basic rundown. Our history, the predicament, that kind of thing. Twice, actually. But I don't know that it all stuck, given the face she's making right now." Lawson takes the liberty of answering for me. Again. I can hear the smirk in his voice.

"Lawson." We can all hear the warning in Gabriel's statement. If I were five, I might have snickered into my hand.

Channel Caitlin, 'cause she's a freakin' badass.

With a deep breath, I square my shoulders and put down my teacup. Turning to Lawson, I give the sweetest smile I can muster and start, "Thank you, Lawson." Then I turn back to Gabriel and continue, "Unfortunately, the story was a little incredulous. So some of the details are a little fuzzy. From what I remember, the gist was: a sea witch lady foretold a prophecy, a bunch of mermaids came through and killed a bunch of seal creatures, and then Lawson escaped. But somehow I'm the one who is supposed to kill the mermaid queen." All around me, the soldiers shift uncomfortably in their chairs. Even Gabriel looks uncomfortable. He finally clears his throat.

"That's the general gist, yes." He looks between Lawson and me, like I managed to leave out some key piece of information.

"Is there a magical sandwich I forgot about, or something?" Bryant and Gabriel both chuckle softly, breaking the tension.

"No, no, dear." Gabriel sobers quickly. "I assume you know Lawson is the prince of our people, yes?"

"He mentioned something to that effect. But he also seems like a pompous, embellishing ass, so I figured he was just making that up." I don't have to look at Lawson to know he's fuming while his men are all laughing at his expense. Then, something dawns on me and I look back to Lawson, who refuses to meet my gaze. "Why doesn't he need anything to get warm?"

Gabriel continues, "Lawson is used to the cold and is built to withstand it. We all are." He nods to the other men as I take in the fact that none of them are dressed for the weather. "Now, while I can't be sure of what he told you, I can assure you the part about him being royalty is true." I nod, more than a little annoyed that part is factual. Does that mean he will expect me to obey him like the rest of his people? Because, no thank you. "The other piece I'd like to focus on for now is your part in all of this." I nod again.

"My part ..." A wisp of a memory from the boat comes back. "So, I ... well, a human ... has to kill this mermaid queen ... And you all think it's me? Is now a bad time to mention I'm a vegetarian? Well, I mean, not really. But I'm still not super excited about killing anything."

"Siren, Ellie. That's an important distinction you need to keep in mind. Mermaids are peaceful creatures ... to other creatures of the sea. Sirens ... sirens have no conscience. They do whatever will benefit them. They don't care who they hurt." I would have laughed, but Gabriel's eyes hold no trace of humor.

The joking is over.

I swallow, unsure of what to say. "Okay ..."

"But, yes, Ellie. You, and only you, can kill the Queen of the Sirens. Hundreds of years ago, the Sea Witch told the prophecy of the fall of our people. Many would be killed, including the royal family. All but one. When the Slaughter was upon us, Lawson was just a young boy. The queen intended to end the royal line, so that she may take over and rule the selkies." He paused and looked at each man at the table before continuing. "Knowing what was to come, we prepared an army. But it wasn't enough. So many lives were lost. Those of us who remained fled here, a place we had prepared for when the time came for those who survived the massacre. Of the royal family, the MacCallum line, only one made it out alive, just as the prophecy said. But instead of making it here, he became lost and washed up onto the shore of the human world. He was only fourteen."

I look at Lawson, who seems to have found something quite intriguing in his lap, while red creeps up his neck and into his cheeks.

"Those remaining in the Selkie Empire sought refuge here, awaiting the day their lost prince would return to the Base as their king. But the prophecy mentioned another. Another from the human world who would bring an end to the Siren Queen. A woman."

Aside from Lawson's, all eyes in the room are now on me, tracking my response. I look at each man, but I don't find mockery, hilarity, or contempt on any face. Only hope and fear. Fear of my rejection. I end with Gabriel's face, where he waits patiently for me. "And you think that's me ... What makes you think I'm this woman?"

He nods, clearly expecting this question. "When the prophecy came to light, a description of the woman was also given. Like other ancient civilizations, the selkies used drawings to tell their stories. The woman was also captured in many drawings by past generations." From beneath the layers of his robes, Gabriel pulls out a small scroll and hands it to me. "There are many renditions scattered all over the Earth where our people have roamed. But I figured you would like to see one upon your arrival." Feeling the age of the artifact in my hands, I carefully unroll the paper. And then, all the air in my lungs vanishes.

It may as well be a photograph of me. Nausea rolls through my stomach.

"It's not a perfect likeness." Finally, Lawson speaks up quietly, reminding us of his presence. I snap my gaze to meet his, as does everyone else in the room. "That first night, in the pub. I knew it was you. But in the drawings, you always appear happy. That night, you were anything but. You looked sorrowful, lost. Anxious. And your hair is much longer." Lawson looks at me with curiosity, now that my part of the story is the one on display instead of his.

"Ellie, dear, what did bring you to this side of the world?" Gabriel asks gently. I pull my eyes away from Lawson and look to my lap, willing myself to maintain control. My teeth bring blood from my bottom lip.

"My husband," I start. I clear my throat before continuing. "His genealogy report said his father's family is from this area."

"You're married?" Gabriel's shocked voice startles me, and his eyes search for a wedding band that I no longer wear on my finger.

I pull the matching ring set hanging on a chain out from inside my shirt. "No. My husband ... he ... passed away. Last year. Drowning." I let the necklace go so that the rings fall to lay flat on my chest.

"Noah," Lawson says quietly as he pieces things together. "Noah was your husband."

I swallow as I meet his gaze.

"Yes, he was."

Lawson nods, looking away.

Gabriel lays his hand on top of mine. "My dear, I am truly sorry for your loss." He shifts uncomfortably in his seat, like whatever he has to say next brings him physical pain. "However, that does bring me to the next item of note. In order for you to take on the Siren Queen, you must first accept your selkie coat." Unsure of what he means, my brows pull together while my eyes float to Lawson, who seems equally perplexed.

"But she's a human. How is she supposed to do that? There is no history of a successful coat acceptance." Lawson's frustration rolls off him in waves.

Does he know nothing about his own culture?

"The coat acceptance is said to only be successful once the Willing already has familial ties to the Selkie Empire. And the prophecy does tell of the woman becoming a royal before she can claim her coat." Gabriel levels his gaze to meet Lawson's. An entire conversation happening between the two of them no one else is privy to.

Looking around the room, I see varying levels of understanding and surprise. Everyone but Gabriel looks between Lawson and me. Some kind of realization slowly begins to dawn on Lawson as his face and jaw drop. He leans forward, hiding his face in his hands. If one couldn't feel the agitation emanating from his body, they'd think he was crying into his palms. But then he stands abruptly, body rigid. His knuckles white from how tightly his fists are balled.

"Are you out of your mind?" he hisses. It's less of a question and more a curse. If I ever believed love was a burning flame, it wouldn't even come close to the fire behind Lawson's eyes, which are now locked on Gabriel. Nobody else in the room utters a single breath. Gabriel stands to meet his height. I briefly wonder if Lawson's going to hit him.

"It is the only way." There's a reverence to Gabriel's voice not even the pope could contend with. "I am not surprised you didn't remember the royalty clause. So much time away from your people and your coat would diminish your memory of some details." Gabriel nods with understanding as he speaks, though it does little to quelch Lawson's anger.

My fingers find the rings around my neck while I watch the two of them. Bringing my eyes back to the teacup in front of me, I whisper, "Can someone please tell me what's going on?" A sharp intake of breath invites my gaze up, where it meets Lawson's scowl. His knuckles turn white as he continues to stare. Suddenly, the six feet between us doesn't seem like enough.

"Apparently," he grits out at me, "you have to become a selkie royal in order to hold up your end of this. And—"

"My '*end?*'" Something in me snaps. I stand to face him, crossing my arms and dropping my blanket in the process. "Excuse me, *Prince Lawson,* but I have no *end* here. I was on vacation and wound up in the middle of nowhere being told I have to kill some mermaid—siren, whatever—queen and you have the fucking *gall* to tell me I have an '*end*' to uphold? Absolutely. Fucking. Not." I'm pretty sure none of the other men in the room have released a single breath in about two whole minutes. My chest rises and falls more quickly now, red beginning to blur my vision. Seething, I turn to find the exit when a frail hand grasps my arm and makes me pause.

"Ellie, please. This is just as much a surprise to him as it is to you."

Turning back toward my new surrogate grandfather, I take several deep breaths and close my eyes. Without opening them, I bring my hand to massage the bridge of my nose. Another couple of breaths and I mutter, "You were saying, Lawson?"

"I was *saying* that there's only one way for you to become a royal." He pauses and I briefly wonder if he's done before he continues with, "Through marriage ... to the only surviving member of the royal family ... me."

My eyes pop open to find him now fully facing me, and Gabriel no longer standing in between us. I recross my arms while I try to come to terms with what he just said. I blink my eyes at him before saying, "I'm sorry, I think I need to look up the symptoms of a stroke to see if I just had one." To his credit, he looks calmer. Like having to explain it to me makes it less real for him. He tries again.

"In order for this to work, you and I will have to get married."

"Hmm. It seems you left out that tiny detail earlier today," I say sweetly, still trying to figure out if he's kidding or not.

"It's not like I did it on purpose." Lawson crosses his arms, clearly annoyed I would think he is trying to trick me into marriage.

A giggle bursts through my lips as I plop back into my chair before I'm overtaken by a full-on fit of laughter at the sheer absurdity of what we are discussing. By the time I come back to Earth, I look around the room to see six soldiers, a now-sitting Lawson, and a returned Gabriel all staring at me. *I wonder how badly it would hurt to jump into the fireplace and die?* Running a hand through my hair, I look back to Lawson.

"So, let's say, for just a sec, that I'm really buying everything you're laying out here." Lawson lets out an annoyed grunt, but I continue, "You're telling me that, in order for me to do the dirty deed of murder, I have to marry you because I have to accept a coat of some kind before I'm able to murder the queen."

"More or less, yes."

"I'd like more rather than less, please."

Lawson lets out a sigh as he drags a hand over his face. "In order for you to kill the queen, you have to accept your selkie coat. Before you can accept your coat, you have to be selkie royalty through a marriage to me, since I'm the only one left. Once we're married, you become my ... wife, giving you familial ties to our empire. But during the wedding ceremony, you will also be crowned Queen of the Selkies, giving you the status of royalty." We continue staring at each other while all of that information processes in my brain.

Finally, my brain regains function. I pull in my lips and slowly nod. "Is that all?" I ask.

Lawson shrugs. "After you kill the queen and we reclaim our castle, you'd live there and help me rule the empire. Given that you survive the battle, of course."

"Lawson." Gabriel's voice startles me, harsher than I've heard come from him. He continues chastising Lawson, but I don't hear him as everything that is my new reality takes hold in my mind.

This won't be a one-and-done thing. If, because it's now an "if" I survive this, I'll live in a castle. With Lawson. As the queen of a group of mythical creatures. What about Caitlin, my career, my apartment? All of my pictures of Noah and me, as we grew up and started our lives together. Am I just supposed to accept that it's all gone and I'll never have anything else to remember him by again? Holy crap. Am I expected to have children with Lawson? That's what kings and queens do, right? They produce heirs. If these people are some kind of seal creatures, I guess that means they eat a bunch of fish. Can I really adjust my diet drastically if I have to? Why are my hands hurting?

"El?" Lawson's use of my over-familiarized nickname stops my spiraling and I see the death grip I'm giving the table in front of me. "Did you hear me?"

I look up at him and shake my head. He sighs.

"I said I'll do it if you will. Since it seems to be the only way. The marriage. All of it." For the first time since he realized what was happening, Lawson sounds ... sad. I take a moment to look at him as he truly lets his guard down for the first time since I've met him. The sight makes my heart constrict and it strikes me that I don't like seeing Lawson upset this way. So, I say the only thing that pops into my mind.

"Okay."

Lawson nods once and moves to stand in front of the fireplace, my eyes following him the entire way.

Gabriel releases the other men, telling them to spread the word and for all citizens to be in the chapel at dusk.

"At dusk?" I ask him.

He nods, but my face must not convey a look of confidence because he continues, "For the wedding."

"It's tonight?!" I shriek. I look to Lawson for help, whose back is now ramrod straight and eyes are wide. Gabriel takes my hand as the other men file out of the library, whispering amongst themselves while the one called Bryant tries to talk to Lawson.

"My dear, we must move quickly. I know this is a lot to sacrifice and absorb, but yes, I am afraid we must wed the two of you tonight. For after the wedding, you will face the arduous task of accepting your selkie coat." He continues to hold my hand in his when he turns to Lawson, who's watching me carefully. "Bryant, take Lawson to his chamber to relax before he has to get ready. Ellie and I have much to discuss about what she will face."

That catches Lawson's attention. "I want to stay and listen. To know what will happen to her."

Gabriel shakes his head. "I'm afraid you cannot. Only the Willing can know what to expect."

"But—"

"C'mon, mate," Bryant whispers to Lawson as he grasps him by the shoulders and guides him out of the library. Lawson keeps his eyes locked on mine until they're around the corner.

Once the doors are shut behind them, I turn back to Gabriel with determination written all over my face. "Okay. What do I need to know?"

Gabriel smiles.

CHAPTER 12

Ellie

THE ROOM WHERE I'M TAKEN IS MUCH WARMER THAN I HAVE ever thought a stone castle would be. And the size makes my room at Isla's look like a broom closet by comparison. Fragrant flowers fill the room, as if they're trying to cover the smell of mothballs and disuse. Overwhelming, but not unpleasant. Even my favorite peonies sit in a vase by the obnoxiously tall window. I walk in to find the young blonde woman from before over in the bath area, filling the tub with steaming water and some kind of floral-scented bath oil. She looks up and a wide grin spreads on her face.

"Hello, miss. It's wonderful to meet you," she says eagerly.

"Uh, hi." I offer her a shy smile. While it's not like I've never met people before, I will be the first to admit I've never really made a great first impression.

Setting down the bucket of steaming water, she walks quickly over to me and offers her hand. I look at it for a moment, eyes wide. Thankfully, my manners are restored, and I go to return the gesture. She beams down at me before continuing.

"I'm Mary Emma. What's your name?"

Wow, this woman is not shy. A grin spreads across my face as I'm reminded of Caitlin. I like this girl immediately.

"Ellie. It's nice to meet you, Mary Emma. Uh, do you work here?" I gesture to the room.

"Yes," she gushes, "I'm to be your personal chambermaid. I can't wait to get to know you better, Miss Ellie." She tenses and the smile fades from her face. "Wait, you're to be royalty. I'm told I'll need to be more professional once the royals arrive, and that's you, so ..." she says more to herself more than me.

"No, no, no," I say quickly as I wave my hands in front of me, proving I'm too spastic for a career in air traffic control. "Please don't treat me like some kind of royalty." I pause at her confused stare. "I'd really rather you just be my ... friend, if that's okay?" I know I'm looking at her like a puppy at a liver treat, but I am so out of my depths I don't even care.

The tension melts from her body and her radiant smile returns while she nods in agreement.

Crisis averted, hallelujah.

I have to stop myself from doing a victory dance. As I look around the room, I notice one of the bags from the boat ride sitting in the corner. Seeing the confusion on my face, Mary Emma giggles.

"Those are your belongings. Prince Lawson said they were to be brought to you straight away." She continues to giggle as she goes to open the bag. Sure as shit, there are all my things ... including my underwear. A deep blush spreads over my cheeks at the thought of Lawson seeing my granny panties. "He's so dreamy. I can't believe you get to marry him."

I snap my eyes to her. "You already know about that?" Shock colors my voice, eliciting a knowing look.

"Ellie, the maids know everything," she says mischievously, grinning at me.

I'll definitely have to keep that *in mind.*

"Ready for a hot bath? I thought you could use one after being in the cold for so long." Mary Emma looks at me thoughtfully and I have to resist throwing my arms around her. I settle for enthusiastically nodding. She offers me a musical laugh before finishing the water and getting the bath products ready. After a moment of watching her work, she gives me a curious look before releasing a small laugh. "No need to be shy, Miss Ellie."

When I realize she means it's time for me to get naked, my already present blush deepens. "Uh, right ... will this be, uh ... normal? You helping me bathe?"

She seems caught off guard by the question. "Oh. I suppose so." She considers something for a moment. "Though I imagine once you and Lawson are married, you will bathe together instead. If you wish, that is," she says matter-of-factly.

I nearly expire on the spot. Even when I considered that we would have to have children, I hadn't even thought about the fact he would have to see me naked. While I keep my body healthy and relatively trimmed, I imagine my workout routine is nothing like Lawson's. Especially since I don't really have one, namely just an incredible metabolism. The spiraling is beginning to threaten when Mary Emma's voice catches my attention.

"I can't believe how Lawson grew up. He looks just like a grown version of himself as a boy."

"You knew Lawson when you were younger?"

"A little." She nods. "He was always rather surly, unlike his older brother. Lorcan was like the sun. Everyone wanted to know him, and he loved everyone in return. Lawson wanted nothing more than to stay out of the spotlight and was happy to let Lorcan have it."

Somehow, I'm not surprised to learn Lawson was a sullen boy.

"But Lawson was always so smart. Always reading. The king and queen would have to drag him out of the library to attend functions, or even meals. He always had a book in his hand, even when I would see him with Lorcan practicing with their swords." Mary Emma laughs at the memory.

"Were he and Lorcan close?" I finally gather the courage to start removing my clothes and fold them neatly by the tub.

"Oh yes, miss."

"Please don't call me 'miss'. It's too formal and it sounds weird," I plead as I step into the tub.

"Very well," Mary Emma smiles as she begins washing my hair. The smell of roses fills the air as the oil lathers in my tangled strands. "Lawson was only a few years younger, but Lorcan always made sure he was his equal. Lawson loved his brother more than anyone." She gets quiet for a moment. Finally, she says, "I was only seven during the Slaughter. My parents didn't make it, but they had worked for the royals just as their parents before them. Gabriel allowed me to take my place in the Royal Service when we made it here."

I reach my hand out to grasp hers that isn't still in my hair.

"Mary Emma, I am so sorry ..."

She squeezes my hand and gives me a small smile. "It was a long time ago. And they are always within my heart."

"That doesn't mean it's any easier." I release her hand.

We fall into easy conversation as she asks about where I'm from and other trivial things. The conversation stays light and I am beyond thankful. My eyes finally land on the large bed and the garment bag lying on top of it. Mary Emma follows my gaze and answers my unspoken question.

"Your wedding dress."

"My what?" I whirl around to face her. My shock is met with her confusion.

"What did you think you were going to wear tonight?" she asks, frowning.

"I honestly hadn't thought that far ..." Mary Emma helps me out of the tub and into a fluffy black towel.

"Ellie, I'm not going to tell you this is a lot to take in. You already know that. But I will tell you that I'm here for you, both as your maid and as your friend. If you need to talk to anyone, just know that you can always talk to me."

I throw my arms around her, barely aware of the fact that I am dripping wet. She returns my hug and a calm feeling comes over me. A feeling that maybe I can do this after all. Leaning back and bringing my hands to her shoulders, I look her in the eyes.

"Mary Emma, can I ask you something?"

"Of course." A look of confusion marring her dainty face.

"Will you be my maid of honor?"

Her answering grin is infectious.

Mary Emma fixes my hair and helps me into the most beautiful bridal gown I've ever seen. The simple cream silk hugs my body perfectly, with the boatneck giving it a regal quality. The veil is cathedral length, so we decide not to put it on until it's time to leave. I keep my makeup very simple, mainly because I've never been very good at applying it. But also, there's less to ruin if I cry. I'm slipping into a pair of nude pumps when Mary Emma brings me a small open box. A pair of ornate gold and pearl drop earrings stare back at me.

"They were the queen's," she whispers.

I'm not sure if my heart swells or clenches. All I know is the significance of my wearing these in my wedding to Lawson.

Turning back to the mirror, I put them on and take in the full view. I don't recognize the person looking back at me. I am Ellie Hughes. A bookish, muumuu-wearing, introvert. The woman in the mirror is breathtaking, regal, unapologetic.

The sight makes my heart ache. By agreeing to this, I will never have the possibility for a normal future. Noah was my first love, and I will never forget him. But any possibility for a next chapter is gone. And as Lawson pointed out, I may not make it out of this alive. While I don't second guess my decision, I am suddenly grateful there will be no one to mourn my death. Even Caitlin will think I am simply ... gone.

Mary Emma is pinning the veil snuggly into my chignon when there's a knock on the door.

"Come in," she calls. Her eyes never leave my hair as she pushes in the pins with precision.

The door creaks open and Gabriel walks in wearing robes the color of expensive champagne. A warmth reaches his eyes when he sees me, and I once again resist the urge to embrace him.

"Ellie, my dear," he says, "you look beautiful. Like the queen you were born to be." He walks forward and places his hands on my shoulders. I'm beginning to think this is a very normal gesture for him. Very papal, to say the least. "I see you've met your chambermaid, Mary Emma." He waves to her as she gathers my makeup from in front of the mirror.

"Yes," I breathe, grinning at my new friend. "She's actually going to be my maid of honor."

Surprise flashes across his face, but it disappears as quickly as it arrives and is replaced with an approving smile.

"I thought you two would get along nicely. I am glad to hear she has made you comfortable." He turns and asks her something I hadn't thought of. "Mary Emma, do you have a dress to wear for the ceremony?"

Looking down at her black servant's frock, she frowns in response. She hadn't thought of it either. I suddenly remember the tea-length golden shimmer dress Caitlin had made me pack.

"Actually, I might have something you could wear if you'd like?" I offer. "It may be a bit shorter on you than it is on me since you're taller, but it would look beautiful with your hair color."

Mary Emma's blush stains her fair cheeks and she looks to Gabriel for approval. I guess accepting clothes from the future queen isn't normal. He nods and I move to pull the dress and matching shoes out of my bag.

Gabriel leaves us to finish getting ready, stating that someone would be by shortly to lead us to the ceremony. As the door closes behind him, Mary Emma lets out a squeal and gushes about the dress. I don't think I've ever seen anyone remove their clothes so quickly to try something on.

As predicted, the dress looks absolutely stunning on her. We pin back some of her natural curls, add a little makeup, and we're both ready to go. Right on time, a knock on the door tells us to make our way to the chapel.

"Wait," Mary Emma runs over to the windowsill on the far side of the room. When she returns, she holds a large bouquet of the most beautiful white hydrangeas, light pink peonies, and peach garden roses I have ever seen. My jaw hurts from how far it's dropped and I'm pretty sure it's touching the floor. "Lawson said these were your favorites and wanted to make sure you had them."

She hands over the bouquet and the tears start to pool in my eyes.

"No crying yet!" she insists. Grabbing a tissue, she dabs at my eyes. "Good thing you didn't go heavy on the makeup." She grins at me.

I chuckle, thankful to have found such a sweet friend in her so quickly. Looking at how the flowers are bound together, I'm able to wiggle a few out of the bindings and hold them out to her.

"So you'll have something to carry, as well." I grin at her.

Using the same tissue, I dab at her eyes in return.

Once we deem each other ceremony ready, I cast one more look into the floor-length mirror and I feel the doubts start to creep back in.

Another knock comes through the door, this time a little more insistent. On the other side, a young soldier looks at us, clearly feeling awkward and apologetic.

Mary Emma gathers up my veil and train before looking at me, calmer and more poised than I have ever felt in my life. Seeing her holding the excessive fabric does nothing to help my panicking. But maybe, if she remains calm, so can I. Mary Emma gives me a soft smile.

"Are you ready, Your Majesty?"

CHAPTER 13

O F ALL THE SCENARIOS THAT HAVE GONE THROUGH MY HEAD when I imagined killing the queen, a wife being by my side was never one of them. How the hell did we get here? It was only a little over a week ago when she and her obnoxious friend walked into the pub. I knew who she was immediately. There was no doubting it. Aside from the ancient drawings, there was some kind of magnetic pull to her. Not just because she is so beautiful, but she radiates a warmth that will soon come in handy during her battle on our frozen lands.

But it was her friend who kept looking at me. She even tried starting conversations when she would come back to the bar for refills, leaving her friend alone to fend for herself. Odin's bony ass, she was annoying. The girl finally got the hint when she bothered to follow where I was looking. I would imagine that's when she sent Ellie my way. The woman who would become our queen, thanks to the royalty clause.

That fucking royalty clause ... And there is no other way to make her a royal. She has to become my wife. My *wife*. Even with my feelings for her, I don't want her to marry me out of obligation. It will taint everything we've built, and everything that could be.

I release a sigh as I turn toward the full-length mirror, Gabriel standing over my shoulder. My black attire and light brown hair stand out in contrast against the backdrop of his light robes.

He reaches around me from behind and straightens my bowtie, bringing his hands to rest on my shoulders once he finishes. Regal champagne robes flow with the soft breeze of his movements. My eyes anxiously meet his in the mirror.

"You look like the king you were born to be, Lawson." His words sound sincere, but they hold no sense of pride. "Your mother and father would have been proud." I look away before I'm able to glare at him. *How dare he bring them up right now?* I shift from foot to foot, needing something to do other than punch him. That wouldn't be productive. "Don't worry. I'm sure your bride is just as nervous as you are."

"I'm not nervous," I mutter. "I'm just—"

"I know what you are, Lawson. You were a surly little boy who grew up into a surly teenager." He turns me around to face him while he brushes off the lapels of my black wedding tuxedo. "You were forced into a terrible situation that caused you to be alone for so many years. Now, in order to do what is best for your people, you are forced to marry someone you do not love. And after all those years alone, you were hoping to maybe have that one piece of freedom, of choice. Choosing who you get to spend the rest of your life with. But now that's been taken away from you as well."

My mouth opens to argue that he doesn't know the whole story, but he looks at me just as a father would have. Just as my father would have. That look silences me instantly. His dark eyes take on a weary quality, like he's suddenly reminded of his age.

"So now, Lawson, you are a surly man who is thinking only of himself, while a frightened and confused young woman is on the other side of the castle. Right now, she's getting dressed in a bridal gown to marry a man she doesn't know and be crowned Queen, to join a fight that isn't hers, for a civilization she never knew existed until a few hours ago." He sighs. "I've served your family for many years. I watched you grow, learn, and train for your future. You never wanted to be king, making it no secret you hoped that duty fell only to your brother. Always resentful of doing anything that was not your idea. And it seems all those years in exile didn't change your way of thinking. So yes, Lawson, I know exactly how you're feeling." Gabriel's eyes never leave mine. I feel like a young boy caught swimming in the Black Waters again. I didn't wear my coat for weeks as punishment.

My eyes fall to the floor in shame as Gabriel turns to leave me alone in the suite. I don't turn to watch him go. Slippers shuffling across the stone floor echo throughout the room and the heavy wooden door creaks with protest as he opens it to leave. When I don't hear the door click shut, I dare to peek up at him. Well, glare at him. He stands in the doorway with his back to me. He knows I'm seething, even though I do my best not to show it.

"I know you're angry about all of this, Lawson. But everything will be okay. Your mother and father believed in you. I believe in you." With that, he pulls the door to the small bedroom closed behind him and leaves me alone.

When High General Bryant comes to retrieve me, I have my anger under control. It won't look good to my people for me to be clenching my fists as I say my wedding and coronation oaths.

"Your Highness? Lawson?"

I turn from the window overlooking the ocean to see Bryant in his deep hunter-green dress uniform. With a curt nod, we exit the suite and head through the corridors. As we enter the Main Hall, I see Gabriel waiting at the end of the aisle. The last remaining slivers of daylight stream through the stained-glass windows and reflect off two crowns sitting beside him on a large violet pillow. My mother and fathers' crowns. I do my best to not blanche at the sight. Bryant escorts me down the aisle as I look around at those in attendance.

Built large enough for nearly 2,000 humans, seeing the number of my people here brings conflicting emotions. We were once a great people, numbers in the tens of thousands. After the Slaughter, we are barely over a thousand souls. A fire builds within me, seeing my people here. A fire that will carry me to avenge my family's death and that will help me rebuild us to what we once were. But pride slips in, too. These people are survivors. They escaped a gruesome death and have charged on here on this island for the last fourteen years, waiting for me to return with the one who will slay the queen.

We reach the end of the aisle and Bryant squeezes my shoulder as I stand, looking coolly at Gabriel. I look over as Bryant steps off to the side, my only groomsman. My only real friend left after all this time. Simple orchestral music starts somewhere behind me, and I realize Bryant and I walked in to pure silence. I would feel awkward if I thought about it too long, so I turn over my shoulder to see where Gabriel and Bryant are looking in order to distract myself.

My eyes find the spectacle and my breathing stops. Ellie walks down the aisle toward us, her head bowed and eyes downcast. A young woman I recognize as Mary Emma walks behind her, carrying her dress's train. Once Ellie reaches us and turns to face me, Mary Emma lays out her cathedral train perfectly behind her and takes her place as Ellie's only bridesmaid. I realize I'm still holding my breath and it comes out in a big sigh, making me accidentally sound impatient. Ellie slowly pulls her eyes up to meet mine. A thin and simple floor-length veil covers her face, but it doesn't hide the look of resignation in her eyes.

Her dress fits her perfectly, another by-product of the Sea Witch's prophesying ability. Strangely, it also seems to fit *her* perfectly. The floor-length dress is fitted and sleek with long sleeves and a boatneck. With no beads or crystals, it is perfect and elegant in its unadulterated simplicity. She turns her head to look at Gabriel and I see her hair has been swept up into some kind of chignon, just like my mother used to wear. Her pearl drop earrings look familiar as they dance when she returns her glance back to me, then down to the bouquet I requested, resting in her hands.

With a clearing of his throat, Gabriel begins, "Dearly beloved, we are gathered here today to witness the union of this man and this woman in holy matrimony." Gabriel looks between us. "It is not to be entered into unadvisedly or lightly, but reverently and soberly. Into this estate, these two before us come now to be joined. If anyone can show just cause why they may not be joined together, let them speak now or forever hold their peace."

I look at Ellie as he pauses, waiting to see if she's going to back out or soldier on. Her eyes remain glued to the flowers between her hands. I watch like an absolute ass as a single tear slips down her cheek. But she remains silent. The anger I've felt today begins to dissipate as realization strikes me. I am getting the future I desire either way. But Ellie … Ellie is the one sacrificing any kind of a normal life. The weight of this thought hits me harder than I would like to admit, mixing with guilt in my mind. I look back to Gabriel to distract myself and find him watching me, waiting. With a nod from me, he continues.

"Lawson and Ellie, you have come together this day so that Odin may seal and strengthen your love and our kingdom. In the presence of this gathering, I ask you to state your intentions. Have you both come here freely and without reservation to give yourselves to each other in marriage? If so, answer by saying 'I have.'" He looks at me.

I look to Ellie. As much as I hate to admit it, this is her show. One word from her and this whole thing goes to shit. She finally raises her eyes to fully meet mine. I no longer see resignation. While fear lives there, so does a deep strength. Rightfully so, she's frightened. But she's strong, and now she's asking me to be the same. Any anger left in my body melts in her liquid amber eyes.

"I have," I say, with enough volume to be heard several rows back in the crowd.

"I have." A small but strong whisper rings out beside me.

Gabriel gives Ellie an encouraging smile and is handed a thin golden ring from Bryant before turning to me. "Place this ring on her finger and repeat after me: 'I, Lawson Alexander MacCallum, take you—'" He pauses. "Um, what's your full name, dear?" he whispers to her.

"Eleanor. Eleanor Victoria Hughes." From beside me, Ellie shifts uncomfortably as she shares her full name. Gabriel smiles softly and nods.

He looks at me and begins again. "'I, Lawson Alexander MacCallum, take you, Eleanor Victoria Hughes, to be my lawfully wedded wife. To have and to hold, in sickness and in health, for richer or poorer. In good times and in bad, so long as we both shall live.'"

He passes me the ring and I reach for Ellie's hand, feeling its small but sturdy frame. She holds her hand's weight as I slip the ring on her slender third finger. My fingers linger on the band as I repeat the vows to her. The intimacy of the moment surprises me and I will her to look at me, but her eyes stay on her bouquet. When my vows are done, I drop her hand awkwardly and return my gaze to Gabriel.

Mary Emma hands him my matching wedding band and takes the bouquet from Ellie. Gabriel then hands the ring to Ellie, giving her the same instructions he gave to me. Ellie turns to face me fully and slips the wedding band onto my finger. She finally brings her eyes to meet mine for the first extended amount of time during our wedding ceremony.

"'I, Eleanor Victoria Hughes, take you, Lawson Alexander MacCallum, to be my lawfully wedded husband. To have and to hold, in sickness and in health, for richer or poorer. In good times and in bad, so long as we both shall live.'"

Her voice is soft but confident. While she is sure of her decision, her voice gives away no emotion. It sounds like she's reading from an industrial manual. I try not to wince in front of everyone. She looks back to Gabriel, who appears satisfied. One oath down, one to go.

Gabriel reaches behind the crowns and retrieves a large golden sceptre and a jewel-encrusted orb, both bearing a valknut at their heads. Placing the sceptre in my right hand and the orb in Ellie's left, he motions to our open hands.

"Please join hands."

A look of surprise crosses Ellie's face as I reach out and grasp her hand. It's cold as ice. My thoughts surprise me as they turn to all the ways I could help her warm up, and I feel the heat rise into my cheeks, my fair skin hiding nothing. Thankfully, Gabriel starts talking again.

"Lawson and Eleanor, will you solemnly promise and swear to govern the people of our kingdom, its realms, and the territories to any of them belonging or pertaining, according to their respective laws and customs?"

I give her hand a reassuring squeeze. "We will," we say in unison. I see her glance at me in my periphery.

"Will you both, to your power, cause law and justice, in mercy, to be executed in all your judgements?"

"We will." Two voices. I feel her fingers close tighter around mine, but I can't tell if it's because she's nervous or if she's reassuring me.

"Will you, to the utmost of your power, maintain the laws of Odin and the true profession of the Light? Will you, to the utmost of your power, maintain and preserve inviolably the settlement of our kingdom, the doctrine, discipline, and government thereof, as by law established in our histories?"

I chance a peek at Ellie. She's already looking at me. She appears ... calm. Assured. Regal. She exudes more confidence now than when she was saying her wedding vows.

She was born to be royalty.

Together we say one final time, "We will."

Gabriel takes the sceptre and orb from us, but our hands remain linked. Not that I actually mind. Before he proceeds, he lifts Ellie's veil and leaves it so I can see her face clearly. My wife's face.

One at a time, Gabriel places our crowns on our heads. Each time he whispers, *"Sará geh parishi."*

Long live the monarchy.

He steps back and raises both hands like he's having a religious experience. "By the power vested in me, I now pronounce you husband and wife. Sovereign Rulers, King Lawson Alexander MacCallum and Queen Eleanor Victoria MacCallum. All hail the King and Queen!"

"ALL HAIL!" From behind us, the hall echoes with the voices of our people.

Gabriel smiles. "Your Highness, you may kiss your Queen."

Ellie pulls her hand away as I turn to look at her. She wrings her hands together, apparently more nervous for this than any other part of the ceremony. Suddenly, I'm nervous, too. I hesitate a moment too long.

"Your Majesty?" Gabriel whispers to me, more a command than a question.

Looking back to Ellie, I slowly close the distance between us. Her breathing has quickened, unsure of my next moves. I glance down at her hands and take them in mine. It's meant to be reassuring. Instead, I feel her breathing stop altogether. As I look back up to her eyes, one of my hands follows and rests gently on her face. Giving her a small smile, I remind her, "Breathe."

She lets out a small breath of air as I close the final space still between us. Our lips meet and I feel her fully relax into me.

Interesting. I file that away for later, unable to stop the smile that plays on my lips. When I pull away, I can see her cheeks are a beautiful pink. From the corner of my eye, Gabriel smiles approvingly while the rest of the room cheers for their new leaders. For us.

Unsure what to do next, I pull my hands back to my sides and step back from her, trying my best to give her some space.

"Brethren!" Gabriel's hands are lifted, asking for silence and rapt attention. He's given it. "You may now see yourselves out as our new queen still has one more task this night. I promise you will have plenty of opportunities to greet her in the coming days."

Beside me, Ellie's eyes go wide. *Her coat.*

Whispers begin as those in attendance begin filing out the door. Word had spread quickly about what was to follow the wedding tonight. Ellie will have to receive her coat before being fully accepted into our kingdom, and everyone knows it is not something that's been done before. Successfully, anyway.

As everyone else exits the Main Hall, Gabriel looks to Bryant and Mary Emma.

"Unfortunately, I must ask you both to leave, as well."

Mary Emma's face gives away her surprise and she opens her mouth to protest when Gabriel holds up a hand to silence her.

"I assure you, Mary Emma, Ellie will return in one piece to her chambers this evening. Go and wait for her there."

I watch as Mary Emma gives Ellie's hand a squeeze and a reassuring look. They have apparently become close rather quickly. Surprising, given Ellie's penchant for solitude in social situations. But

I find myself smiling, glad she was able to find someone else in my kingdom she could feel safe with.

Bryant gives my shoulder a squeeze and I move to shake his hand before he leaves. He nods before offering Mary Emma his arm and escorting her out the side door. Ellie looks lost as she watches her lady-in-waiting leave the room.

Fully aware of our remaining audience, I walk over to my wife and take her hand. She turns to me with wide eyes, apparently surprised by my gesture.

"She'll be there when we return. Don't worry," I whisper to her. This moment feels too intimate even to let Gabriel hear us.

Ellie nods but doesn't look less anxious. I know Gabriel gave her a rundown on how this next part would go, but I wasn't allowed to stay and hear, much to my annoyance. From what little I managed to catch from gossiping staff, it will be painful and arduous. Now, I especially wish I knew details to help curb her stress. It's the least I could have done. But the selkie partner cannot know about the ritual beforehand, only the Willing is allowed to know what they're up against.

Ellie brings her worry-filled eyes up to meet mine when Gabriel shifts behind us. I pull my eyes away from my wife and look at him, his hand resting on my shoulder.

"Your Highnesses, it's time."

CHAPTER 14

T HE GOLDEN CIRCLET WEIGHS HEAVY ON MY HEAD AS LAWSON
and I follow Gabriel through the winding corridors. Mary
Emma was kind enough to take my bouquet back to the suite, leaving
only Lawson's hand available for me to squeeze the life from. If the
length of time he's let me hold onto him while my hand is drenched
in sweat is any indication, we should be good to go for any future
childbirths. To my intense surprise, he is also helping carry my
obnoxiously long train and veil in the hand not currently glued to
mine. He may make a good husband, yet.

Passing several security checkpoints, we weave further underneath
the castle grounds. And the deeper we go, the fewer guards are present
at various stations. Beside me, Lawson looks around furtively. Trying
to not make me any more nervous, I assume. Even though I am the
one who actually has an idea of what's about to happen, he looks
like he's about to be sick. And if he knew what was coming, he might
have already puked a time or two. Lord knows I would like to. When
Gabriel was describing the Ritual of Acceptance to me this afternoon,
even he seemed to be apologizing as he depicted *her* and the hoops
I will have to jump through. Maybe I should have asked to bring my
purple sweater. It's gotten me through plenty of shit before.

Around us, the walls become narrower and the lanterns more
infrequent, making my eyes adjust to the increasing darkness. The
floor turned from bricks to dirt a while ago and is now clearly on a

downward trajectory. I briefly wonder if we are going to walk straight into the ocean at any moment and consider ditching my shoes here.

"El?" From beside me, Lawson quietly whispers my familiar nickname. My skin warms in response, and I am instantly thankful for the darkness surrounding us.

Not wanting to lose sight of Gabriel, who is now several paces ahead, I only squeeze his hand in response. Just like during our wedding, I want him to know that I'm here with him. No matter what. Thankfully, it seems to satisfy him for the moment, and he doesn't push for any other acknowledgement from me.

Several more minutes pass before we finally catch up with Gabriel, who is waiting before a small, plain wooden door. Compared to the doors throughout the castle, this one is almost a letdown, considering what should be behind it. Slowing as we reach him, Gabriel turns to face us. His eyes flit to Lawson briefly, before looking at me. Sorrow fills his eyes and something deep within me begins to sink as I understand what he's trying to say.

This will be so much harder than I could have imagined. And now there's no going back.

"Ellie," Gabriel sighs, "I am truly sorry, my dear." Lawson's hand tightens around mine as he pulls me closer.

"What ... what do you mean?" Lawson's mouth opens, closes and opens again as he tries to grasp what's going on, but how would we even begin to explain it to him? "Why are you sorry?" I turn to face my new husband, offering whatever reassurance I can.

"Lawson," I whisper to him, pulling his attention from Gabriel. There's no need for Lawson to be angry with him, after all. This is just what has to happen. No matter how terrified I am. "I know you don't really know—"

"El, why is he telling you he's sorry? What's about to happen to you?"

"Look, this is going to be very ... not fun for me ..." My eyes find his as I place both of my hands on his broad chest. He takes my hands in his own, keeping them tucked tight. "But you won't be able to help me ... so ... so, you'll just have to trust that I ..." I quickly swallow the lump forming in my throat. "That I can do this. Okay?"

His wide, anxious eyes take in my serious expression. Even through his tux, I can feel his heart beating rapidly with the hand covering his heart. But he nods reluctantly.

Dropping my hands, I turn back to Gabriel. A small tear slips down his cheek, nearly invisible in the dark passageway. Nodding to him, he takes a deep breath and opens the door behind him.

A bright, cold, green glow spills into the hallway, making all three of us shield our eyes as we step through the doorway and into a cavernous, dark room. Looking around the chamber, my eyes land on the only source of light, a large green orb floating about eight feet off the floor in the middle of the sparsely furnished room. The glow emanating from the globe is blinding, sending light to most parts of the room. But it's where the illumination doesn't reach that worries me. Like the passageway, the floor is packed mud near the door, but it turns back into the stones used throughout the rest of the castle a few feet into the room. The earthy smell from the passageway continues on into the room, mixing with something else. Something rank.

Whatever was holding the heat in the hallway is obviously outmatched here. Goosebumps begin to rise up and down my arms, and I'm not sure if it's from the lingering chill in the air, or what I know is lurking somewhere in the shadows of this room. Gabriel stands off to the side looking faint as my eyes sweep around the chamber, finally adjusting to the strange lighting. The walls follow the style of the rest of the castle, as stones flow upward as far as the mint green light can reach. But beyond that, darkness hides any remaining architectural secrets. No windows break the monotony of the stones. Wherever we are, we are deep into the dark. A shiver runs through me at the thought of what may lie outside these rounded walls. A small vanity and bed shoved up against the far side of the room catch my attention, and the idea of this place being nothing more than a bedroom brings me a little comfort, even if I am lying to myself. Because this place is not a room for comfort. It's a prison.

Lawson's warmth seeps through the thin silk covering my back as he steps up close behind me, keeping a solid grip on my hand.

"Come now, Your Highness," a smooth, sultry voice from behind us causes both Lawson and me to jump as I whirl around to find its owner. "You don't really think I would harm your blushing bride, do you?" Wet slithering sounds echo throughout the room.

As my eyes frantically search the darkness behind us with no success, Lawson drops the dress's train and throws both arms around my shoulders, crushing me to his broad, firm chest. I immediately grab hold of his arms.

"Show yourself." His growl rumbles through his chest and my own. I instinctively sink backward into him, causing him to tighten his grip.

"Tsk, tsk, Lawson. Is this how you greet an old friend?"

"I don't know you—"

"Yes, but I know you."

The voice turns harsh, now coming from in front of us. I squint my eyes as what looks like hundreds of black tentacles slowly begin to take shape behind the floating green ball. I angle my head back toward my husband.

"Lawson."

"Yeah, I see it too," he whispers back to me.

My heart picks up speed as the tentacles begin to pile onto one another, mimicking the silhouette of a towering woman in a black tentacle-created halter dress. Above the ball of light, glowing yellow eyes with obsidian centers focus on us. Dull black hair flows like seaweed down to the floor in braids, adorned with starfish skeletons and pearls. Taking a step from around the green orb, her thin black lips stretch into a mischievous grin over ashen skin.

"I've known of you long before you were born, young King. I've known the fate your loved ones would suffer, and of the rage that would flow through your veins. I've known of the blood sacrifice your new bride will have to make to finally become one with your kingdom." Lawson's grip on me tightens. I stretch my shoulders to bring his attention back to me. This woman intentionally antagonizing him is seriously starting to piss me off.

"Leave him out of this. Whatever tonight is, it's about me, not him."

Her booming laugh causes vibrations to run through the floor and her tentacles begin to glow a soft yellow, matching her eyes. Faster than I can even see, dozens of smaller tentacles shoot out from underneath her and latch onto Lawson's legs, pulling him to the floor. A cry escapes from me as he yanks out my veil for something to hold onto as he is drug across the floor to the far side of the room. Newly escaping tendrils fall heavy down the back of my dress as hairpins begin to lose hold of the thick mane.

"Lawson!"

Chest heaving, I look to my left for Gabriel, who is kneeling toward the center of the room with his head bowed. From here, I can hear him muttering some kind of prayer for deliverance from this. From her.

"My dear, he is just as much a part of this as you."

Her voice is much closer than I expect, and my hair whips my face as I turn back toward the center of the room. My heart beats rapidly within its ribbed cage when I see the Sea Witch's face is mere inches from my own. This close, her onyx irises are much more defined into a nonagon with severe edges, and her breath reeks of rotten fish. As strong as the desire to vomit is right now, it wouldn't help anything. Taking a deep breath through my mouth, I square my shoulders and channel Caitlin. Leveling my gaze with hers, I narrow my eyes and try not to think about Lawson lying on the floor in pain where I can't see him.

"Fine, Witch. Let's get this over with."

A burst of light at her side draws my attention. Opening her palm, she reveals a choker necklace with a single, small golden pendant. Surrounding it are some kind of sage and ocher gemstones. But what catches my attention isn't what's there, rather, what is missing.

"Where is the clasp?"

"Oh, Your Highness, this is not the kind of piece you remove each night." The witch closes her palm back around the necklace once more. She smirks, exposing barnacles that cover her nasty teeth. "Now, Eleanor, are you ready?"

"Yes." I don't dare even blink.

"Good answer."

Tentacles slither up my legs, underneath my dress, and grip my thighs, jerking me to the ground. The breath is knocked out of my lungs as my torso hits the solid floor, causing my crown to fly from my head and land on the floor with a clang. Using all my strength, I do my best to keep my head from bouncing off the stones. Lawson calls my name from somewhere in the distance, panic coloring his voice, but I can't focus on where. Above me, the light from the orb glows brighter as something dark comes into focus within it.

"Queen Eleanor," the Sea Witch's voice fills the cavernous room, "Tonight, you took vows to this man and to his people." Tentacles hoist me up in the air, high above anything I could have seen from the ground. Now standing by Gabriel, Lawson watches while a mix of horror and desperation paints his face.

"Ellie ..."

I manage to hear his whisper above all the noise in my head. My wide eyes stay trained on him as the witch continues.

"Now you must take the final steps in accepting your new role." Her tentacles whip me around to face the floating orb, which has grown to accommodate a full-size selkie skin suspended within it. Unlike Lawson's, dark spots cover the slate-colored fur in a sporadic pattern. It reminds me of dregs at the bottom of coffee cups. And it is utterly perfect.

"That's ... that's my ..."

"Very good, Your Highness."

The air whooshes past my ears as I am released from the tentacle shackles and my right arm collides with the floor. Pain shoots through every limb, while black spots cloud my vision. Rolling to my back for relief takes more effort than I care to admit.

Lawson's silence in the background is screaming as loud as it can. Craning my neck, I find him glaring at me, hands fisted at his sides. Shame spreads through me as I take in his rage and disappointment.

Whether it's in me as his wife, or how poorly I am obviously handling whatever the hell is going on now, I don't know.

Shame turns to embarrassment as my already shallow breathing almost stops altogether when he looks away. Not wanting to face his disappointment in me any longer than necessary, I slowly scan the room for the witch. I finally track her hundreds of tentacles scaling the wall on the opposite side of the room.

An unnatural warmth begins to spread through my body. And it quickly turns into what I've always imagined it would feel like to be set on fire.

"Queen Eleanor, please confirm you willingly took your new title of wife and ruler."

"Yes ... yes, I did," I choke out through the pain. Aching surges through my fingers and toes as they dig into the stone floor, grappling for a mercy that won't come. My eyes squeeze shut to concentrate on what she's saying. And to make sure my lungs continue working while fire kisses them from somewhere deep inside.

"Do you wish to join the Selkie Kingdom as their Queen?"

"Please ..."

"Ah, ah, Your Highness. Answer the question."

Tears escape my closed eyes, slipping down my cheeks and into my hair, fanned out over the simple stonework. Another jolt of fire rips through me, causing my back to arch off the ground in order to absorb the pain. Unable to form anything coherent, something between a sob and a groan escapes my lips.

"What was that, dearie?"

"Yes!" I scream in between the waves of fire ebbing and flowing through my body.

Off to the side, Gabriel is saying something. Loudly. But my body is shocked into submission when the fire running through it is instantly replaced by shards of ice. A sigh starts to break free but gets caught in my throat. For a brief moment, the cold brings relief to my system. Until the slivers begin to make their way through all of my nail beds. I lie there sobbing on the floor, feeling each nerve deaden, one by one.

"Please," I whisper. My lower lip trembles as more pleading threatens to trickle out. I open my eyes to find her floating directly above me, her face inches from mine.

Cold, clammy hands reach out to touch the sides of my face. Skimming down my cheeks, they stop as they reach the base of my neck. If I didn't know better, I would think the witch was actually showing affection, or maybe even remorse for what she's doing. But I do know better. Through my tears, her bottomless eyes peer into mine.

"Please ... pl—"

My pleas are cut short and are quickly replaced by sharp wailing as she digs her nails into the flesh at the back of my neck, tearing it open. The searing pain almost covers the sound of gems rustling together near my chin.

"Now, now dearie. If you truly want to be the Queen of the Selkies, you must also wear your token. It's how your coat will recognize you, after all," her voice coated in a false pity. I know she is enjoying this.

I let out a whimper as the weight of the pendant touches right above my collarbone.

"And did you know," she continues like she's never talked about a more fascinating subject matter, "the gold of your token comes straight from the gungnir of Odin himself?"

Between two obscenely long, filthy fingernails, she turns my token back and forth. A heaviness fills my chest as she feigns disinterest and drops it back to my neck, shrugging like she just tossed some loose change back to the ground. Not letting my eyes stray, I watch as she moves directly underneath the orb containing my coat. With an unnatural grace, she lifts large bony hands above her head, calling the orb down. Even with its additional area gained by housing my coat, it is still dwarfed by her immense size.

"Let's make sure this fits, shall we?"

I shakily sit up on my elbows to get a better view of my new least favorite person. Pulling my coat from its ethereal container, the Sea Witch holds it up like a cape. And it begins to glow.

If I had any self-preservation left, I would use it to not look shocked at the radiance being exuded by my coat. But all of my survival instincts left this afternoon when I found out Lawson had been serious about this whole predicament. My wide eyes flit from the coat to her and back. When it's apparent I won't be answering her anytime soon, she lets out an annoyed grunt.

"Get up, Queen," she snaps.

With as much energy as I can manage, I scramble to my feet, noticing the ice shards have melted from my fingers and toes. Movement in front of me signals the witch coming closer and I snap my eyes to hers.

"Arms." She holds my coat out like any other winter coat as I lift my arms. "As you may be aware, Your Highness, a selkie can only put on their own coat and only a selkie can put their coat on."

A quick glance at the skin makes me feel like I'm about to wrap myself in a giant, unzipped, hooded sleeping bag. Slipping my arms inside, I step one foot at a time into the tail portion. The inside is warm, but not squishy like I had imagined, almost ... fur-lined? Unwelcome memories of camping with Noah flash through my mind, threatening to break the dam of tears building once more.

Behind me, Lawson and Gabriel are arguing. If I were to listen closely, I'm pretty sure they're trying to tell me what to do. But the cozy sensations brought forth by the coat overtake any instinct to listen to them for direction. For the first time in a long time, I feel *held*. Content. Almost happy, even. The headpiece comes down over my face and all openings instantly seal over. My vision becomes sharper. Better for seeing underwater, if I had to guess. Sinking to the ground slowly, I pull my ebony flippers in front of my face one by one. A small disturbance runs through my body at the extreme comfort I feel being inside. Maybe this is what it's like to be in a straitjacket. As soon as I decide to just stay in here forever, the witch's voice pulls me back to the present.

"Your Highness, time to rejoin the humans." She almost sounds bored. Unsure of how to communicate with her, I cock my head to ask the obvious question. The witch sighs when she finally understands. "Pull your arms toward your core, and then push them out in front of you."

Following her instructions, removing my coat becomes extremely simple. Almost instantly, my coat is laying on the floor beside me as I stand before the witch.

"Welcome back, Your Highness."

"Ellie?"

I turn at the sound of Lawson's voice and find him watching me open-mouthed and wide-eyed. Maybe I did a little better than he thought I would. Hopefully we won't start this marriage by me failing him.

"Lawson," a deep breath comes rushing out from my lungs as I start toward him, "I—"

"Not so fast, Queen Eleanor. There is one more thing."

Halting in my tracks, I carefully turn to face her. My jaw tenses as the Sea Witch looks me up and down, no doubt admiring my soiled wedding dress and muddied hair.

"Are you feeling better? You looked in a bit of pain before?" A wicked glint shines in her eyes. My fists clench at my sides as I take a deep breath before answering.

"Yes," I grind out. And it's the truth—I do feel stronger. "I'm feeling much—"

"Well, that's grand, dearie. Now there's just the matter of your past." I freeze.

"My ... past?"

"Why yes, Your Highness. Our oceanic kingdom can't have you walking around while there are *humans* out there looking for you, can we?" I don't miss the way she talks about humans, like they're a dirty species. *"They", not "we".* A shudder rushes through me as the realization of the abrupt transition hits me.

"What ... what are you suggesting?"

Her dark eyes narrow until the yellow is barely visible. When her sardonic smile disappears, I know I won't like what she is about to say.

"First, Your Highness, I do not suggest anything. Second, I will take care of it. No need to thank me. No one in your human life will remember you now th—"

"What?" I bellow.

"That you have officially joined your new kingdom. You will be erased from their memories. Permanently." The witch thrums her fingers together, watching my reaction. Shaking my head in disbelief, I turn to find Lawson and Gabriel looking at me.

"You knew about this?" I look between the two of them, willing one of them to answer. The only response I get is them looking to one another.

Letting out a frustrated cry, I turn back to the witch. Indifference colors her features, frustrating me further.

"You can't just—"

"I am afraid it's already done, Your Highness."

"No ... How—"

"The moment you sealed your coat, the spell was cast." The wind is knocked out of me and I fall to the floor, tears streaming down my face.

"But ... but Caitlin ... Ana ... Paul ... Graham ..." My face falls to my hands as the sobs erupt from my throat. My shoulders shake in time with my tears as I think of all the people who will never remember I had known them. Large, warm hands gently hold me while I weep into my own.

"Congratulations, Your Highness. Welcome to the Kingdom of the Selkies." I briefly wonder if I imagine the sorrow I hear in the Sea Witch's voice as she extends her regards to my new place in this world.

Those same large hands scoop me up into his chest. Lawson holds me close as I cry for what I've lost and what I've gained, while he carries me out the door and back into the dark.

CHAPTER 15

Lawson

T HE WALK BACK TO OUR SHARED SUITE IS SILENT. ELLIE ROCKS back and forth in my arms while her eyes remain closed from exhaustion. If it wasn't for her irregular breathing, I would think she had fallen asleep. Thinking of her being comfortable enough with me to sleep in my presence without being drunk warms my core. Annoying, but certainly not unpleasant.

Taking in a deep breath to work on my still racing pulse, my wife's normally floral scent is now mixed with salty sweat. My jaw ticks as images of her writhing on the floor in pain float through my memory. The echoes of Ellie's screams are permanently burned into my mind, and I make the conscious effort to not tense beneath her. A glimmer catches my eye and drags my attention down to the woman in my arms. Ellie's new golden pendant reflects the dim lights flickering in the empty corridors, making it look like a tiny sun is hanging from her neck. Oddly, it only looks slightly out of place with her dirty wedding dress.

I look down at my wife in awe as I replay the day's events. I never would have guessed this woman would wake up in my bed, lead me to my lost coat, willingly climb into a boat with me, and marry me all in one day. Not to mention the literal hell the fucking Sea Witch just put her through to accept her coat. There is no way she knows just how amazing she truly is.

Ellie must sense me staring at her, because her eyes flutter open and quickly find mine. A soft pink tints her tan cheeks as I nod down to her and move to open our bedroom door. Seeing where we are, the woman literally jumps out of my arms and freezes. If she doesn't know what to do next, that makes two of us. Wringing her hands together, she turns back to face me when I see that we're not alone.

"Ellie, oh thank Odin." Mary Emma comes running through the bathroom door and embraces my wife. "I was so worried about—" The woman's words come to a crashing halt when she notices me.

I frown, sensing that I seem to have that effect on people.

"King Lawson," she bows before gesturing to a wardrobe on the far side of the room. "Your things were brought over from the other bedroom since this one is bigger."

My eyes track where she pointed and I clear my throat before offering a brief thanks. Kicking Ellie's train off my feet, I make my way to see what there is that's appropriate to wear to bed on your wedding night with a reluctant bride.

The two women whisper amongst themselves, and it suddenly feels as though I am intruding on a private moment. I find some sweats and a plain white T-shirt tucked in the bottom of the wardrobe before turning back to them.

"Er, I can, uh, leave for a bit while you get changed, if you like," I offer to Ellie.

To my surprise, Ellie almost looks insulted. Mary Emma does her best to remain professional, but I can see she would try to take me down if Ellie requested it. Once again, I'm grateful my wife has found a loyal friend. Now I just have to work on getting Mary Emma to redirect her hostility.

"I don't mind if you stay," Ellie whispers. Her blush from earlier returns and I feel a matching one creep up my neck.

"Queen Ellie, why don't we go into the bathroom and get you cleaned up and ready for bed?" Mary Emma suggests. Ellie smiles and nods to her friend before returning her eyes to mine. She regards me curiously as she spies the loungewear in my hands. A small smile pulls at her lips and goes straight to my heart. Mary Emma begins gathering Ellie's train in her arms and starts toward the bathroom.

"I'll, um, just be out here," I mumble clumsily.

The bathroom doors close behind them and I am suddenly alone in Ellie's bedroom. Our bedroom. I make quick work of changing and discard my wedding clothes in a basket set out in the corner. Carefully removing the heavy golden crown, I set it gently inside my wardrobe. It may be simple in decoration and filigree with only small peaks to enhance the circlet's outward appearance, but inside the thick band are the initials of each king that has come before me. A way to tell the coming generations they are not alone. A decoration more important than any gemstone could represent.

Looking around, it dawns on me that I haven't seen these rooms since I was a little boy. And they haven't changed at all since the last time I was here, nearly fifteen years ago. The same plush olive blankets still coat the bed, with a matching canopy attached to the mahogany bed posts. Fluffy down pillows cover the dark headboard. Matching mahogany nightstands still sit on each side of the oversized bed.

The far nightstand is already covered in personal effects from Ellie. Whether that was her or Mary Emma's doing, I'm not sure. Reaching down, I pick up the lightly scented lip balm I've seen Ellie use multiple times since meeting her. I replace the tube and take in the other items littering the table. Another colored lipstick, a battered copy of *Pride & Prejudice*, and a necklace lay strewn about. Sighing, I take the necklace in my hands. Her and Noah's wedding bands hang from the dainty chain, light glinting off the tiny engagement ring stone. Guilt moves through me as I look at the symbol of a real marriage sitting in my hand. Ellie and I may have exchanged rings today, but I will never be the husband she deserves. I do my best to push down the insecurity settling in my gut as I gently lay the rings back down.

On the far wall is the standard writing desk and chair that is housed within each bedroom here. As I take a seat at the desk, the sound of the bathroom door opening surprises me. I promptly jump back up, causing Mary Emma to let out a small musical chuckle. Heat quickly spreads up my neck and across my checks. I run a hand through my hair to distract myself from my discomfort.

Mary Emma walks back into the bedroom with Ellie's all but ruined wedding dress draped over her arms. She gives me a tight smile, a warning lying underneath. The message is clear: hurt her friend and be maimed.

I smile awkwardly in return.

"Goodnight, Queen Ellie," she calls over her shoulder as she heads to the bedroom door. "I'll see you in the morning before training." The chambermaid casts one more semi-threatening glance at me before heading out the door.

What the hell did they talk about in there?

The sound of feet shuffling behind me catches my attention. When I turn around, my heart stops and my mouth immediately goes dry.

My wife walks through the bathroom door in a sleeveless, light pink, floor-length nightgown. It gives the illusion of her tanned skin being even darker than it already is. The silk garment is barely covered with a gauzy robe that sweeps the floor as she walks into the bedroom. Her long, dark hair is pulled on top of her head into a loose ballet bun, with free-hanging strands framing her face and making the dark lashes surrounding her amber eyes appear even darker. Fidgeting draws my eyes downward, in Ellie's hand is her crown, she's clearly unsure of what to do with it.

When I can finally function again, I silently offer my hand. She initially frowns at my gesture. It takes her a moment to understand I mean for her to give me the crown, but she eventually hands it over. Unlike mine, her golden crown is more delicate with its intricate design making up the crown in its entirety. The band itself is made up of thin wisps of gold, forming waves as they crash into one another in a never-ending pattern of oceanic perfection around the queen's head. Even without gems adorning it, it is certainly an exquisite piece of art.

I move toward her nightstand and gently set the crown around her necklace already on the table, a golden ring of protection for what was, what is, and what could be.

"Lawson?" she asks softly. Turning back to face her, her amusement is clear. I raise my brows in question. She lets out a quiet giggle as she takes in my plain gray sweatpants and white T-shirt. "Where on earth did you get sweats?"

I look down at my clothes and shrug.

"Humans love them, so I tried them. I can see the appeal." I cock my head and wait for her reaction.

Ellie smiles, shaking her head. Slowly, she walks toward me, eyes locked on mine. She begins removing her robe and my heart threatens to jump out of my throat. *If what I think is happening is actually happening, I think I'm okay with it.* But Ellie clearing her throat pulls me back to reality.

I blink a couple times to stop my mind from continuing down its current path.

"Do you mind?" she asks, blinking at me in return.

All I can do is stare at the gorgeous woman before me. My mind short circuits when I finally grasp that she's waiting on me to say something. Or move out of the way.

"Of-of course." I nod with a little too much enthusiasm and step out of her way.

Tossing the robe on a nearby chair, Ellie slips into the bed. Our bed.

Quickly, I mumble something about needing to wash my face and practically run into the bathroom. Leaning on the closed door, I let out a deep breath. There is no denying my attraction to her, not that I am even really trying to, anymore. But I need to get a fucking grip and get some priorities in order here. First things, first. Splashing some cold water on my face and reciting my forefather's lineage, I manage to calm down enough to face my wife again. Taking one more deep breath, I open the door to find Ellie reading the book from her nightstand.

The sound of the door opening alerts her. Raising her eyes to meet mine, I give her my best easygoing smile. Like I didn't just about have a mess in the bathroom from the sight of her. Like I am as emotionally detached from this as she is. Like this is strictly business. Royals marry for political reasons all the time, after all.

As I'm trying to figure out what the hell to do next, I remember seeing a stack of old books in my wardrobe. Grabbing one at random, I boldly head toward what will apparently be my side of the bed. When I'm getting under the blanket, I try not to notice how Ellie tenses at my nearness and focus on reading my book.

"Do you keep your ring on all the time?" Her question startles me, and it takes me a moment to understand she doesn't mean my wedding ring. She means my token.

I nod while I contemplate my answer. "Yes. I'm sure you've noticed all selkies wear tokens. Men have rings, women have their necklaces. In typical cases," I don't miss the embarrassed blush creeping across her face as she shifts in her seat, "a selkie baby is born with their token. When a selkie gives birth, the baby is born in their human form and then the skin is birthed. Like an afterbirth, if you will." I wince.

Ellie makes a disgusted face and I can't help but laugh.

"That sounds ... unpleasant," she says. She's clearly trying to be polite, even though she is trying to hide her revulsion. Her comment makes me laugh harder and I see her lips lift into a small smile. Putting down my book, I turn to face my wife fully.

"I'm not saying it's a great experience or anything, please don't misunderstand. But the tokens, we're born with them. So if we try to remove them ... it's very ... painful."

Her dark brows knit together while she considers this new information.

"Will it hurt if I try to remove my necklace?" I'm surprised to hear more curiosity than fear in her voice.

"Honestly, I'm not sure. But I don't think we should test that theory," I say, giving her a knowing look. The grin that spreads across my face is easy, as most of my reactions to this woman are.

Ellie answers with a grin of her own and looks back to her book. I watch her profile as she turns serious. The air between us begins to thicken as she thinks.

"Lawson?"

"Yes, dear?" My answer has the desired effect, breaking the tension and causing her to laugh. When she looks at me, her warm eyes glow as she narrows them.

"If everything … is … successful," her eyes find a spot on the bed in between us, "are we to have children?"

My brain to mouth connection is lost as I consider the possibility of having children with the beautiful woman sitting in bed with me.

"Uh, Lawson?"

"Er, um, well, I—"

"I was just asking. I didn't mean to scare you or any—"

"No, no, no," I shake my head quickly. "You didn't scare me. Just surprised me is all."

"Okay, well—"

"But I think children would be nice," I say hurriedly. "With you, children with you would be nice—"

Ellie puts a hand on my arm, stopping my erratic rambling.

"Please, relax," she says. She rubs my arm and a small smile lights up her face. Without another word, she turns back to her book.

I do my best to pay attention to the novel in my hands, trying to ignore the woman beside me, to whom I am now married, and was just speaking with about having children. By the time we snuff out the candles to go to sleep, I am well aware just how royally fucked I am when it comes to Ellie.

The next couple of days pass in a blur. Meetings with the war council, meetings with noblemen, and meetings with Gabriel on running a civilization. Meetings with citizens as I reacquaint myself with my old life. Meetings with the army and their commanders as I begin figuring out my role as their leader. With Ellie busy learning to use her coat, and about water combat, I don't even see her until the evenings, once we've both returned to our suite. Even meals have been taken during meetings.

In the time before bed, we settle into a comfortable routine of chatting about her training, her favorite books, and how all the meetings go. Ellie asks questions about my childhood, which I typically try to deflect by asking about hers.

Our third night together, I am already situated in bed when she climbs in and abruptly turns to face me. Without turning my body, I eye her from the periphery of my vision.

Shit, I'm awkward. This is just Ellie, for fuck's sake. But there is nothing "just" about Ellie. She is everything.

"Yes?" I manage to ask in the most inelegant fashion.

"What was your home like?"

"You saw my apartment."

"That wasn't your home. You said so yourself." She pauses before continuing. "I mean your memory home. The place where your loved ones carry on." She lets her eyes fall to the comforter. "You don't ask me about Noah or my memories of him." I shrug like the truly awkward creature I am.

"I don't want to upset you," I say softly. Ellie brings her curious gaze to meet mine.

"It won't upset me. He is part of my story and my life. Just like your family and where you grew up is a part of yours."

I understand what she's asking with annoying clarity. No more deflecting, it seems. My eyes find the book I laid down just moments ago.

"I'm not sure where to start," I mumble. Ellie reaches out and gently brushes back some hair that's fallen into my eyes. Instinctively, I close them and lean into her hand as it slides down to my cheek. My wife's floral scent invades my senses, causing my heart to skip a few beats. Opening my eyes, Ellie is already looking back at me, the creases around hers apparent as her encouraging smile warms her whole face. A deep breath escapes my lips as I look away and begin.

"The castle, it is—was—beautiful ..."

"Was?" Her soft voice asks the question I've been afraid to ask myself.

"I don't know what all ... *they've* done to it. So I can't be sure it even still looks the same, anymore." A lump gathers in my throat and I work to push it down. "Many generations of my family lived and ruled there. Because the colors used to build the place were ... cold, our people and our enemies alike began to call it the Ice Castle. And they aren't wrong. Blues, whites, silvers. They cover nearly every surface. Some great ancestor decided it was wise to make much of the ceiling out of faceted glass, further giving it the appearance of ice ... or diamonds." My small chuckle holds no humor. "'Royals are to give off the air of opulence', my father used to say when I asked why the palace looked so stupid. And that's only the half that's above the waterline."

"Above the water?" I turn to see the shock on her face. Apparently, no one had bothered to mention to her that half of our castle was underwater. A smirk slides into place on my lips as I quirk up an eyebrow.

"Yes, Ellie. Half of our castle is underwater. For when we're in our ..." I drift at the end, hoping she will put it together. As usual, she doesn't disappoint me.

"Our coats," she whispers. "Half is under water so we can remain in our coats." I can't hide the proud smile on my face.

"Right. But where the upper and lower halves meet is the Coat Room. Or, at least, that's what my brother and I always called it. Because, intelligence." Ellie laughs at my lame excuse for a joke and the warmth that she always seems to bring begins to bloom once more in my chest. "And while the underwater portion is lovely, I think you'll prefer the upper half."

"Why is that?" Her brows knit together in confusion. I beckon her toward me and cup my hand around my mouth. I would be lying if I said it wasn't to hide my grin.

"Because," I whisper in a conspiratorial volume, "That's where my favorite room lives, the grand library." Her answering grin is infectious, causing my own to stretch even wider. Leaning back onto my pillows, I look toward the dark canopy while my hands blindly find my book. Pulling it back up to my face to find my place, Ellie's voice recaptures my attention.

"Do you ... you think ... I will ever really get to see it?" Sorrow colors her voice, frustrating me. I frown at her question, but don't turn to see her expression.

"Of course you will. The council members are preparing to march on the castle with as little damage as possible ... and that is where you will ... well, you know." I clear my throat to release some of the awkwardness that is starting to gather between us.

"Right. Of course." She nods, knowing what I can't bring myself to say. "Lawson?" Turning to look at her, I find Ellie regarding me with satisfaction. "Thank you for telling me about your home." Without waiting for a response, she turns back to her book.

I had expected to feel anxious telling Ellie about our palace. Instead, something akin to hope begins to bloom in my chest. Maybe, one day, she will think of it as her home too.

CHAPTER 16

Ellie

S WORDS RING OUT LOUDLY AS THEY CLASH TOGETHER. IF I weren't so focused on staying on my feet, I would cover my ears.

"Faster, Your Highness. You cannot let them get the upper hand."

Bryant is taking it slowly with me, and it frustrates me to no end. Watching others sword fight is deceiving. While it appears to be easy and you throw in some fancy footwork, my ego takes blow after blow in these training sessions.

"I know, Bryant." I let out a frustrated sigh. "I still think you should push harder. I need to know what I'm really up against here."

"Your Highness, I—"

"Ellie. My name is Ellie."

"Your Highness, you may be my best friend's wife," he pins me with his gaze as he sets down his sword and wipes sweat from his forehead, "but you are still my queen, and I will address you as such."

Rolling my eyes, I try to reach a compromise.

"Fine. What about 'Queen Ellie?' A little half and half for ya, there."

Bryant chuckles and takes a drink of water, no doubt buying time to consider my offer. Setting the bottle back down, he nods his head.

"Very well, Queen Ellie," he concedes. "And I know you want to go faster, but Lawson's tasked me with making sure you can actually fight before we teach you more about ... well, sirens."

"Which you kill by shoving the sword through their vocal cords and severing their heads, right?"

"Right," he sighs.

"My wife giving you trouble, mate?"

Lawson walks into the outdoor training paddock with an easy grin on his handsome face. I can't help the answering grin that spreads across mine as my husband walks straight to my side and throws an arm over my shoulder. He's clearly not worried about getting sweat all over his khakis and polo.

"She just wants to be ready for the intense stuff, is all." Bryant turns his sword over in his hand, examining it closely. Lawson nods and looks down to meet my eyes. For just a moment, neither of us breathe and I swear I can see the depth of his soul in his questioning eyes.

"Sword," he says, without removing his gaze from mine. Bryant's hesitation is enough for my husband to drag his attention away from me and find his friend.

"Sorry, what?"

"If she wants to know what it will really be like, then so be it."

Bryant stands gaping at him, and Lawson lifts his eyebrow expectantly. Without another moment passing, Bryant tosses Lawson his sword. Concern radiates off Bryant and no one is surprised to hear his next question.

"Are you sure, sir?"

Lawson walks a few paces away and turns back to face me with a smirk.

"Are you sure, Ellie?" he teases.

Unwilling to back down from the challenge, I square up my shoulders and toss my sword from one hand to the other before looking back to Lawson. Narrowing my eyes, I smirk right back as I crouch into the starting position.

"Don't go easy on me, Your Majesty."

"Wouldn't dream of it, baby."

He winks at me before lunging with his sword hand. Raising my hand to meet his, our weapons crash together as I block his attack. Taking a quick inventory of his free hand and feet, I swiftly move to the side and slash my sword downward toward his abdomen. But

Lawson is quicker, intercepting my blow with his own hand. In one swift motion, his sword lifts both mine and his up and over my head. His free hand catches mine, causing me to turn with the motion of our weapons and land with my back to his chest, our clasped hands at my breast, pinning me to him. My breaths heave rapidly in time with his and I notice that Bryant is off to the side, leaning against the fence watching our interaction.

"You'll have to be faster than that, Your Highness." His warm breath hits my ear, sending shivers running down my body.

Using my sweat to my advantage, I twist my hand that's holding his and use the moment of surprise to rip my hand loose. Whirling around to face him, I bring my sword to eye level and slowly move backward.

Lawson's grin is triumphant as he watches me like a predator tracking their prey. In one rapid movement, he peels his shirt up and over his head, tossing it off to the side while sweat glistens in the contours of his chiseled abdomen. My jaw drops as I shamelessly ogle my very attractive new husband. Bryant laughs in the distance while Lawson chuckles to himself right in front of me, because that sneaky little turkey knows exactly what he's doing.

Refusing to let him win like this, an old trick comes to mind. Back in college, whenever Caitlin or I was nervous about a presentation, we would employ the old trick of picturing people in their underwear. Except we didn't picture them in their underwear, we pictured them in those blow-up dinosaur costumes.

Quickly, I conjure up the mental image of Lawson with tiny T-Rex arms as his face shows through the opening for the mouth and I let out a full belly laugh. Confusion washes over his face and I take the opportunity to lunge at him with my sword pointed straight at his throat.

He quickly regains his composure and deflects my sword, but not before I manage to sweep my foot out, taking his legs out from under him. But I over rotate and spin myself to the ground, as well. Beside me, Lawson lets out a laugh and grabs my sword.

"Well, that was ... interesting," he says.

Feeling the annoying shame of defeat, I lie back onto the sandy grass and let out a sigh. The sunlight is suddenly blocked by a large figure looming over me, offering their hand.

"C'mon, Your Highness. Don't need anyone else getting hurt with that fancy footwork of yours."

Taking his hand, Lawson pulls me to my feet. Brushing my palms on my pants, I narrow my eyes at him.

"Yeah, yeah. You just wait. Next time, I'll—"

"Next time, you may just win if you can control your emotions," he says, crossing his arms while his damn shirt continues to lay on the ground. I frown at his response.

"What?"

"He means," Bryant answers, "that you wear your emotions on your face when you fight." Handing Lawson his shirt, he turns back to me. "It's how I beat you every time. I can always anticipate your next move because I can see how angry it makes you when you're at a disadvantage."

Looking at our swords in Bryant's grasp, I feel the disappointment of losing turn into heat trailing up my neck and across my cheeks. Lawson's large, warm hand takes hold of mine and tugs, willing me to look at him.

"Don't worry, El. We'll get you where you need to be." His smile is warm and instantly melts my insides.

"He's right, Your High—"

"Eh, excuse me. But it sounded like you were about to call me something other than what we agreed upon."

Bryant shakes his head and looks to Lawson, who merely shrugs before grinning back at me.

"Like I was saying, Queen Ellie, Lawson is right. We will do everything we can to make sure you are ready to face the Siren Queen."

Lawson shifts awkwardly beside me. Rubbing the back of his neck, he thanks Bryant and leads us out of the training paddock.

Lawson takes over my training for the rest of the day as we move from fighting, to underwater combat in our coats, to general siren knowledge with Gabriel. Watching Lawson in his true selkie form is mesmerizing. His movements are so fluid and graceful, it's almost painful to watch. But he never rushes me and is constantly incredibly patient as I learn the dexterity and boundaries of my coat. Communication in our coats also becomes easier as I spend more time under the water. Lawson radiates pride as things become more natural to me in my selkie form. By the time we get to Gabriel in his office, Lawson is practically beaming, so different from the surly and standoffish man I met only a couple short weeks ago.

Walking hand in hand into Gabriel's warm and cozy office, the thought that wormed its way into my mind on our wedding night takes hold and begins to whisper within my heart. Releasing my hand to hold open the door for me, my eyes meet those of the man I love. His easy smile lights up his face as I grin up at him, walking through the door and taking his hand once more.

As Gabriel greets us, a look of surprise crosses his face. I follow his eyes to where Lawson and my hands meet. Looking back at Gabriel, his eyebrows raise in question, which neither of us answer for him.

"Interesting ..."

I go to pull away, but Lawson tightens his grip, securing me to him. His thumb slowly rubs circles on the back of my hand.

"I just wanted to learn where Ellie is in her history lessons," Lawson offers by way of explanation of his presence. His tone exudes confidence, and Gabriel clears his throat.

"Of course, King Lawson. You are always welcome here. After all, I am sure refreshers are always needed, even for those who have lived amongst us their entire lives."

Lawson's expression hardens as he guides me to the large wingback chairs in front of Gabriel's desk. His hand never leaves mine as we sit, not that I mind. But I am fully aware of Gabriel's mindfulness of us, as well, and I work to not let it make me uncomfortable. Even with Noah, I was never big on physical affection in public, which Caitlin always thought was weird. A wave of sadness washes over me at the thought of my old friend, who's walking around in the world and no longer has any idea who I am.

A squeeze of my fingers pulls me back to the present, where Gabriel is talking about Lawson's lineage and how the sirens have always been on the outside of our realm. A knock at the door causes Gabriel to frown. But ever the polite counselor, he bids them welcome to enter. A young medical soldier named Jensen pokes his head timidly through the doorway.

"Erm, my apologies, High Counselor. I was told the king was— Oh, Your Majesty. Uh, and Queen Ellie. Good afternoon." Jensen makes his way fully into the room and bows so low that I wait for his hat to fall off. Lawson barely turns to acknowledge the newest addition to the room.

"Soldier, what is it?"

"Your Majesty, your attention is required in the Throne Room."

"Is it Esme again?"

Jensen winces and Lawson only sighs in response. My brows knit together in confusion.

"Who's Esme and why do you look like you want to wither away?" I ask my husband. He rubs his free hand down his face.

"She's the annoying daughter of an elderly nobleman who is constantly asking my advice on the most mundane subjects." Turning back to Jensen, he asks, "Isn't there anyone else at all who can assist her?"

A look of sincere apology covers Jensen's face as he shakes his head.

"She refuses to leave until she speaks with you. Only you, sir."

A giggle erupts from my lips and all three men turn to look at me in confusion. Shaking my head, I release Lawson's hand.

"C'mon, Lawson. If you can almost kick my butt at sword fighting, then surely you can handle this woman asking about ... whatever it is she wants."

"You only say that because you've never had to deal with her," he groans. But he grins at me and I only feel the warmth spreading through my chest. With a soft smile, he turns to follow Jensen out the door.

Once the door clicks behind them, I turn back to face Gabriel, only to find he is already watching me.

"What?" I tilt my head to the side, trying not to show my annoyance at being watched like a toddler. "Gabriel?"

"You need to be careful, Ellie."

"What do you mean? With Lawson or the Siren Queen?"

"Well, frankly, both."

My head rears back in surprise at his words. Of course I would be weary of the Siren Queen. That woman wants me dead. But Lawson ... Why would I be careful when it comes to Lawson, the man that Gabriel all but forced me to wed? A man who has been so caring and very aware of this strange transition for me.

"I'm sorry, but I don't—"

"I would imagine you're referring to Lawson, since the Siren Queen's threat is quite evident?"

Nodding my head in response, he stands and moves around his small oak desk to sit in the chair that Lawson previously occupied. Leaning forward in the chair, he takes my hands in his and looks me straight in the eye.

"Ellie," he says solemnly, "Lawson is a particular kind of man. He always has been. If he loves you, he will die for you. But those have been few and far between in his life. I assume you know of his late brother, Lorcan?"

I nod, not allowing my eyes to leave his.

"Well, other than Bryant, Lorcan was about the only person he ever felt that way about. But watching the two of you now ... I believe he may have found someone new to add to that exclusive list. But I beg of you, please do not lead him on." Shock makes my eyes go wide at his statement.

"Gabriel, I would never—"

"I know you wouldn't mean to, dear. But this has all happened so quickly, your circumstances changing, you learning about the prophecy you're to fulfill, your marriage to Lawson." His eyes level my own. "I just don't want to see either you get hurt. Lawson has always felt like a rather strange son to me, and I'll admit I feel a very paternal instinct for you, as well, dear."

The tense feeling in my chest begins to dissipate at his words, and a small smile tugs at my lips. It takes everything in me to not launch myself at this man and envelope him into a tight hug, just like the first time I met him.

"Gabriel, I don't want you to worry about me," I say, looking down at my hands in his. "First, I just want to say that I've never met anyone who felt so instantaneously like family as you did for me. As soon as I saw you on the beach, I knew ... I knew you were *good*." A sniffle pulls my gaze to his face in time to see a small tear run down his cheek.

"Ellie, dear ..."

"Please, let me finish," I insist, smiling at him like a weepy woman of ninety years. "When I met Lawson, he was ... unpleasant, to say the least." Gabriel and I both let out a chuckle at the thought. "But since we've been here, and even before, there's just always been something so different about him. I will admit there was a man I was casually seeing in the town where we were staying." I don't miss the look of astonishment that flashes across his face. "But I've always felt so drawn to Lawson. Even that first night. Like there is some thread that just keeps pulling us together, no matter how many knots we get tangled in." I shake my head, sniffling as I try to will the tears to stay inside. But a frail hand cups my face and pulls up my chin.

"Darling girl, you love him. Don't you?"

Gabriel's soft voice knocks me over the edge and the tears start pouring down my face.

"Yes," I breathe. "I truly do." And no words I have ever spoken have been truer. "But I don't want him to feel obligated to feel that way about me. I want him to be happy, and God, I hope that's with me. But if I can't do what I was brought here to do—"

"Eleanor. Do not think for a moment that Lawson's feelings for you will be conditional."

"But no matter how much I train, I just still feel so unprepared. I don't want to let him down ... And I know what others say about me, how the human girl is no match for what awaits us out there."

Gabriel nods, contemplating this. But when he looks back to me, his eyes show the determination I gave him my first afternoon here.

"There will always be those who doubt, Ellie. It is the burden of any leader to heed those concerns." He leans in toward me and I instinctively mimic his motion as he lowers his voice to a whisper. "But then you take those worries, and you crush them."

Not a hint of humor is in his voice. Of course not. He knows what's at stake here, and he knows that my fears are valid. But he also knows what people say. He's fully aware of what I have to prove, especially if I make it through all of this alive and have to face these people every day for the rest of my life.

"What should I do?" My voice may be hushed, but in this silent office, it can be heard in the farthest recesses. "About Lawson, that is."

"What do you mean?"

"He has enough distractions with everything. And when the time comes, I don't want emotions to get in his way. During the fight." I swallow the lump in my throat as I look to my grandfather-figure. Gabriel looks past me and frowns, like he's trying to solve a complex puzzle. When he finally looks back to me, I can tell he's found his answer.

"I cannot tell you if you should tell him of your feelings right now or not. That is up to you, and only you. I think you know him better than you let on if you are concerned about him becoming enraged in the middle of a war if something were to happen to you. Lawson tends to be rather closed off. But when it comes to those he loves, he will stop at nothing to protect them. And when he can no longer do that, all bets are off."

A chill runs down my spine at the thought of Lawson fighting in a war. For me. For his family. The constricting in my chest about him being in a position to be hurt tells me all I need to know.

"Thank you, Gabriel," I whisper. Getting up to leave, I turn back to him one more time. "I'd appreciate it if you didn't mention this conversation to Lawson." He shakes his head.

"Of course not, dear."

Nodding my acknowledgement, I turn and exit the office.

By the time I make it back to our suite, I've made my decision. Lawson still hasn't returned, which is good. It will give me the time I need to write my letter. While I'm not going to tell him how I feel and complicate things further, I do want to be prepared in case the Siren Queen gets the best of me. Thankfully, Mary Emma is also out of the room. I'd like all the privacy I can get for this.

Opening my wardrobe, I take out my favorite purple and white sweater and pull it over my head. Checking the door once more for any incoming company, I sit down at the desk and begin to write. When the letter is finished, I find an envelope and put it in the bottom desk drawer. Wouldn't want it to be found sooner than necessary.

As I get up from the desk, a glint from my nightstand catches my eye. I pause for just a moment, but I already know what it is. A few quick paces to the stand brings my necklace with mine and Noah's wedding ring set into full view. Fingering the rings, it occurs to me that Lawson has probably held back from developing any real feelings toward me because of these. With that thought, I grab up the set and place them in the drawer with the letter. An apology for any pain it has caused him, and a promise that he is the one who will have my heart for the rest of time.

Glancing at the sun, I decide to go find a sparring partner for one more training session today. I *will* be ready when the time comes. I have to be.

CHAPTER 17

"**W**HAT THE ACTUAL FUCK ARE YOU TALKING ABOUT?" The older General Garren flinches at the venom in my voice. His long mustache sways as he looks over to Bryant for help. Apparently, his advanced age doesn't help with his anxiety of being stuck with me instead of my brother as the new king. Figures. Everyone always liked Lorcan better than me. Fuck, *I* liked Lorcan better than me. But here we fucking are. It doesn't help that I had to listen to Esme ask a bunch of inane questions again today. That lady seriously needs to back off. Bryant takes a breath before coming to the man's aid.

"Some of the scouts have begun seeing things in the nearby waters. Shadows, scales shimmering in the sun. And there have been reports of hearing ... things," Bryant says.

"Hearing things? Like what?" My patience has gotten thinner the past couple of days. Watching Ellie train has made my nerves go into overdrive, knowing what she will have to face. Knowing the depths of my feelings for her. And while she's a natural fighter, it doesn't ease my fears about what could happen to her when the time comes. Watching my family die all those years ago guaranteed I will never feel ease around a siren again, unless it's dead and shredded to pieces.

"Siren songs, Your Majesty," the general says. "They're getting closer. And fast."

"Do you think they've found us?" Gabriel finally speaks up from across the table. The library fire roars behind him, giving him a menacing silhouette as he taps his fingers together, sitting in his wingback chair.

Bryant shifts in his chair, weighing his answer carefully. While he's always been level-headed, I watch as beads of sweat roll down Garren's forehead as he eyes his superior anxiously.

"If they haven't yet, it won't be long now. The queen will need to be ready," Bryant states.

"We can't rush her," I slap the arm of my chair in frustration. "She's only just started training and now you're telling me she has to be ready to—"

"Your Highness, I promise this is not something we're taking lightly."

"Bryant, as my oldest friend, you're saying my wife needs to be ready to kill a siren less than a week after her coronation? After she's accepted her coat?"

"Sir … Lawson," he says softly, "I don't know when the time will come. But all the signs are not showing that time is in our favor. The queen needs to be as ready as she can as quickly as possible. I don't want her to be in a position where she will be unable to defend herself, if need be." I run a hand over my face and try not to let panic take over my body. "Your Highness, we've already ensured the queen is never outside of the castle unless absolutely necessary—much to her protest. And if she is, she is never alone. Again, much to her protest." The man has the gall to give a small chuckle at my wife's brazen complaints.

I meet his gaze across the large table, effectively ending his amusement.

"She will be safe so long as she remains with the guards," he continues soberly, "but we must be prepared for all possible circumstances."

I nod while I contemplate my High General's words.

"What of the scouts who heard the songs in the water?" I ask. The men around the table share glances before General Garren finally speaks up.

"Most have returned to us. But some," he looks down to the table uncomfortably, "some have not been seen since. Only a few. But they were still ours."

"I'd like to meet with their families. Give them my condolences personally," I tell him.

"It will be arranged, sire."

I don't know if this meeting could be going any fucking worse. I rub my temples as I try to keep my anger in check. Suddenly, the library feels much too warm and the fire is too loud in the background. Piece by piece, every single thing about this room slowly makes its way under my skin. As much as I'd like to, exploding all over the men trying to keep tabs on everything is not in my best interest. If Ellie were here, she'd tell me to cut the shit and put my big boy pants on. But at this moment, not even the thought of her snarkiness is bringing a smile to my face.

If sirens are being found in the surrounding waters, there will be little stopping them from entering the village. Our people are in more danger than they can even know. If they find out, panic will run fucking rampant. Rightly so. And every moment we wait to strike, the stronger the sirens grow in my childhood home. As the general continues about the best ways into the siren's lair, my mind continues drifting back to Ellie.

Every day since our arrival, Ellie spends hours training her mind and body to become a killer, so that when the time comes, what needs to be done will be as easy for her as breathing. My sweet, warm Ellie becoming something so cold is difficult to wrap my mind around. This is the woman who is squeamish of eating chicken because she once saw a chicken get run over by a truck and saw the innards all over the road. And now I am asking her to throw away her morals entirely. I should be so fucking ashamed of myself.

A cough from my left catches my attention. Looking up from the maps spread out all over the table, I find everyone's eyes glued to my face. Shit, I must have missed a question.

"Gentlemen, I think the king has had enough strategy council for today," Gabriel announces. "Why don't we break for the afternoon and resume in the morning?"

Gabriel and Bryant nod at one another and stand to leave. The two men exit the library while General Garren stands awkwardly from his chair. As he's gathering the maps, his rotund belly spilling over the table, he stops and looks at me.

"If I may, Your Highness?"

I quirk up my eyebrow, intrigued. *At this point, why the fuck not?*

"I think what you're doing is very brave." My frown must not inspire much confidence because he decides to continue. "Having the woman you love go through with something so dangerous. If she were my wife, I don't know if I could do it. Queen Ellie is so pure. She brings so much life and light to our kingdom. Losing her would be devastating." Garren nods to me and finishes gathering the maps. As he finds the door, I grind my teeth at his words.

As if it's my choice to have Ellie go through with these insane events. As if I signed her up for the task. Rubbing my forehead, the realization dawns on me—that's exactly what I did when I brought her here. Shame and rage flow through me, knowing I brought Ellie here for this. Potentially for her own death. My right hand begins to hurt as my nails bite into the flesh of my fist.

Sighing, I get up from the table and go stand in front of the fireplace. Staring into the flames, I think about all the ways I have failed my wife since the day we met. And apparently, I will fail her until the very end. What I wouldn't give for one normal day with her, like any husband and wife.

Ellie should be back from training by now and, while it usually calms me to see her, I truly don't know what I'll feel after today's meeting. Already feeling defeated, I decide to head back to our suite.

When I walk through the door, I'm greeted by the smell of roses, and I know my wife is already here and clean from today's session. Normally, it would bring a smile. But today, all I can think about is what's lurking in the shallows all around us.

"Lawson? You scared me." Ellie walks through the bathroom door toweling off her long, wet hair.

I shut the door behind me and watch as she eyes me and shifts nervously, finally tossing the newly damp towel over the desk chair.

She's wearing jeans, like all human women seem to love. I'll never understand that, they always look too tight to truly be comfortable. But looking at her now, I understand why men love it when their women wear them. They show off her curves perfectly. The ugly purple and white sweater she's wearing has made frequent appearances over the past week. Almost every single day. Its colors are vibrant and clean, but it looks broken in. Old, but well taken care of. Surely I brought her more shirts to wear than just the one? Mary Emma must wash it every night since Ellie wears it so often. I make a mental note to thank her for accommodating Ellie's obsession with the ugly thing.

When Ellie crosses the room to grab her favorite vanilla lip balm off the nightstand, her tennis shoes squeak. I briefly wonder if she's tracking water through the room from the bathroom, or if she just needs new shoes. She glances timidly at the crown resting on her small table as she replaces the lip balm to its former position.

"Are you alright?" I ask tiredly. In all honesty, the last thing I feel up to doing is talking about anything serious. I watch as she sits on the bed facing the window to tie her shoes.

"Um, just a long day," she says absently. Her hands pause while holding the shoelaces. "Are you okay?"

"Long day," I parrot back, sighing. Stripping off my sweater and shoes, I lay back on my side of the bed in my slacks and undershirt. Her shoulders hold a lot of tension. Taking a chance, I reach across the bed and grasp her shoulder. If possible, her muscles only tighten more. "Ellie?" She sniffs.

Fuck, she's crying.

Doing my best to keep my sigh internal, I get up and go around to her side of the bed so I'm standing in front of her. Her head is tipped down, but I don't miss the silent tears rolling down her cheeks. Crouching down, I tip her chin up to meet my gaze.

"El, what's wrong?" I keep my voice quiet so as not to scare her. Or let my irritation from the day seep into my tone.

"I'm just afraid. That I'm not enough," she sniffs again, "for this. For any of it." She motions around us. "What if I can't do it? What if I screw up and she gets away? What if she manages to kill me before

I can get to her? And then she wins. She wins and these beautiful people who love you so much are ... gone ..." She chokes out a sob and puts her face in her hands, twisting to pull her knees up on the bed.

This time, I don't bother hiding my very large exhale. I do not have time for her to doubt herself, especially not after the council meeting today. Our people, the ones ignorantly carrying on with their lives outside the walls of this castle, don't have time for her to second guess herself. I move to sit beside her on the bed. Resting my elbows on my knees, I let my head hang forward and pick a spot on the rug that needs cleaning.

"Ellie, our entire kingdom is literally in your hands." Rubbing my temples and closing my eyes, I hear her shift beside me. The bed squeaks in protest. "I know you've only been training for a few days. But frankly, we really don't have time for this." I know how this is probably sounding to her, but according to Bryant, we're out of time to fuck around.

Beside me, she sniffs, and I know she's trying to get her crying under control. I realize the only other times I've seen her cry were at our wedding and during her Acceptance Ceremony. And during that horrific phone call in the pub. The thought only makes me angrier, but this time it's at myself.

"Ellie. El. I was just told the sirens are getting closer. They're close to our waters. Do you know what that means?" I chance a look at her. She's staring at a spot on the comforter, but still shakes her head in response. "It means the time for you to fulfill your duty is getting close. Our people out there don't have time for you to be wondering if you're good enough. The danger is getting very real, and there is no time to coddle you anymore."

She scoots back from me, her puffy red eyes wider now. Clearly, this is not the response she expected. I pull my gaze back to the brown rug when I hear her clear her throat.

"I want to be a good queen," she whispers. "One they can be proud of. And if I fail—"

Something in me snaps. Jumping off the bed, I walk purposefully toward the desk and bathroom door with my hands on my hips.

"Ellie, I didn't bring you here to fail," I say through gritted teeth. Turning around to face her, I feel the fury start to move through my body. "I brought you here to fulfill a purpose. One purpose. To save my people from a certain death at the hands of the deadliest creature in the entire fucking ocean. That's all." She leans further away from me and only blinks in response. I know I should stop, but at this point, I'm on a roll. My eyes narrow at her cowardice. "I didn't bring you here to make nice and befriend a civilization. I brought you here for one reason, to put a sword through the Odin-be-damned Siren Queen's vocal cords and shred her to pieces. That woman murdered my entire family in front of me and all of Odin's fat-assed ravens won't let me do a single fucking thing about it. And now, the revenge for my family that I have waited years for is completely up to you, baby."

Spit comes out with each word now and I wipe the evidence away from my chin. Reaching the desk, I grasp the back of the chair for support before I fall over from a coronary issue. After a moment of silence, her tears return as she finally whispers the words I know she's been feeling since she first arrived. I brace myself for the impact of them as the air becomes thicker between us.

"What if I'm not fit to be a queen? What if I'll never be good enough?"

I slap the back of the chair and feel it splinter a bit in my palm. Ignoring the pain in my hand, I focus on the sharp pain in my heart and the even sharper pain in my head. Whipping around to face her, I pin her with my glare and release a sardonic laugh.

"You know what? You may not be good enough. You sure as shit wouldn't have been my first choice. You don't know how to fight. You're not very physically strong. And you're not one of us. You walk around with your little golden pendant that came from Odin's own fucking gungnir itself like it's your Odin-given right to wear my mother's crown. You practice swimming around in a beautifully crafted coat made centuries ago to your exact specifications. But if you don't think you can manage to perform the one fucking task you were brought here to do as the crowned fucking queen of the people I've worked the last half of my life to return to, then maybe you shouldn't be queen."

From across the room, I can see the fire in my eyes reflected back at me through her own. Except in her eyes, the mirror image is coming from the big fat tears rolling down her face. And I am so fucking tired of having to protect her from every bad thing in our world that I don't even have it in me to care.

"I-I'm sorry ... I," she stutters.

"You what? Didn't know how much was riding on this?" My voice is now much louder than I've ever spoken to her. But maybe I'll finally get through.

"Of course I know," she snaps, yelling as she leans forward on her seat. "That's why I'm so worried about what could—"

"Do you not think every person on this Odin-forsaken island is afraid of what will happen if you fail? That we're not all fully aware of your purpose here?" I sneer.

Something in her changes then. I actually watch the change on her face as she puts back up every wall I've worked so hard to bring crashing down since the day I met her. Swallowing, she takes a moment to gather her thoughts. And all I can do is stare at her with contempt.

Her face hardens like she's shut off the valve to her emotions, but her tears don't stop flowing, like they didn't get the memo. All the tension in the air shifts. Suddenly, it feels like she finally has the upper hand. She sniffs once more before looking me in the eye.

"Well, Lawson, I'm sorry to have caused you so much additional stress." She brushes invisible dirt off her pants before squaring her shoulders to me. "If you'll excuse me, I have some training and I'm late." She starts for the door.

I snort and grab at her wrist as she passes by me.

"You don't have another fucking training session tonight—"

She rips her wrist away from me with surprising force and pins me with a tearful glare that could freeze over Hell itself. But her big, fiery tears could thaw even the most frozen of hearts.

"Apparently, I need some further training so I can fulfill my purpose and get out of your hair once and for all." My hand that was just touching her feels like it's on fire. She turns to leave and I panic.

"Ellie, I—"

"Fuck off, Lawson," she calls calmly over her shoulder, as if she had just told me she would see me later.

"Ellie! Ellie, wait. I—"

She slams the bedroom door shut and I hear the slapping of her shoes against the stone floors in the hallway as she takes off. Looking around the empty room, I let out an angry cry now that I'm all alone with the mess I created.

CHAPTER 18

Ellie

H EART RACING, I SLAM THE HEAVY DOOR BEHIND ME EVEN though I can hear Lawson calling to me through it. With no hesitation, I take off running through the echoing halls. Fat tears stream down my face from my red, puffy eyes but I don't even bother to try and hide them. Why should I? Every single person on the island probably heard us yelling and is looking to take cover.

Every guard I pass looks flummoxed at the radiant, sobbing vision that is me. They are all clearly unsure whether to stop me or flee to the far side of the castle and away from my female hormones. I run through dimly lit corridor after corridor. Past the warm library, the ancient chapel, Lawson's cluttered office. My feet don't stop until I come up to the exterior door farthest from our bedroom, mine and my reluctant husband's.

The guard on duty is one I recognize. He is usually stationed near our room, but I can't remember his name thanks to my preoccupied brain. When he sees me, he regards me with surprise as I stand before him with a blotchy tear-stained face and breathing like I'm about to pass out. Then again, maybe I am.

"Your Highness, is everything alright?" he asks, his voice laced with concern. His wide eyes show clear hesitation as to whether or not he actually wants to know the answer.

Trying to respond tells me my voice will be too thick. Clearing my throat, I try again with more success.

"Yes-yes. I would like passage outside, please." The amount of focus it takes to simply stand upright at this moment is absolutely fucking ridiculous.

"But Your Highness, you know the king—"

"Passage outside, now!" I bellow. I know I'll feel bad about that later, but right now there is only anger and sadness coursing through my body. The poor guard falls back into the rigid door, as if my words hit him with actual force. I begin to feel bad sooner than expected, but hold my head high like the queen I'm supposed to be.

"Yes, of-of course, Your Highness. Right-right away," he stutters. He turns and opens the door so fast I'm surprised to see it doesn't literally fly off the hinges.

I'm through the door and outside of the castle walls before he can utter another word. Once I'm immersed in the frigid air and farther away from the constraints of my new title, I slow my pace to a walk. I come to a full-on stop when I find a giant rock that looks perfect to sit and cry on for a while. Hidden enough from the rest of our people that I shouldn't be found, but right off the tree covered path where I won't get lost like the directionally challenged person I am.

Exhaustion sweeps over me. Exhaustion from fighting with Lawson, from running through the castle, and then crying throughout the entire journey. I sink down onto the large flat stone. The cold stone immediately cuts through the material of my jeans, shocking me. Now that the crying seems to have finally slowed, my head begins to pound. I'm no stranger to these kinds of pains. While it's not in and of itself unpleasant, the memories it evokes are. So many times after Noah walked into the ocean, I would spend hours, days, weeks crying. I would fall asleep with tears staining my face, only to wake with a splitting headache. That's what this is. That's why this hurts so much. I feel like I've lost Noah all over again. Because I've lost the man I love all over again. I've lost Lawson.

I love him with all my heart and soul, just as I loved Noah. These feelings are things I didn't even think was possible for me to feel again until only recently. The only difference is that Lawson doesn't know. So, to be completely fair, he has no idea how badly he can hurt me. But Lawson doesn't love me, so I'm sure he will be fine in a little while.

And that stupid fucking letter. I left it in the drawer of the desk in our room. While it's not likely he will find it, it will be mortifying if he does. Just more ammunition for him to use against me. I can see him now, joking with Bryant about how the human girl was stupid enough to actually fall for the guy who is her husband in name and title only. While all the selkie noblewomen throw themselves at him with the hopes he will leave me once the Siren Queen is dead and take them as his new queen. Because I will more than likely be dead, too. Nothing says if I am to make it out of all of this alive. But I know the odds.

The cruelty of Lawson's words play on repeat in my head. My inadequacies. My dreams. My fears. He threw them all in my face. I obviously wouldn't have been his first choice for a wife, since I was only a human until a number of days ago. But to actually hear the one you love say that ... He might as well have ripped out my heart with his bare hands and crushed it. Of course I'm not the strongest fighter on the training field. Until I traveled to this side of the freaking earth, the most exercise I ever did was carry stacks of books around a bookstore. I know I'm not qualified to kill a freaking Siren Queen. But I'm here, and I'm trying to be who my new people need me to be. Even though it's really fucking terrifying and difficult. Even if only half of our people really do see me as their queen. Why did I tell him I wanted to be a queen our people could be proud of? Of course he would laugh at that. He was born into his role. I was born to be a librarian or penmanship enthusiast or something. Since before Day One, Lawson and I have been on two completely separate wavelengths. We have never been compatible. We will never be compatible. And I went and fell for him like a foolish moron.

The hairs on the back of my neck prickle. Then I hear it. Whispering from somewhere behind me makes me hold my breath. I'm not ready to face anyone else yet. Climbing to the ground on the other side of the rock, I crouch until I know I can't be seen. If I didn't look psychotic before, I sure as shit do now.

"Yeah, I heard she was a whore in her human life." A woman's shrill voice breaks through the silence behind me and my new rocky living quarters.

"Really? From how awkward she acts, I don't see how. I just can't believe she nabbed Lawson." Two women. Even better. I roll my eyes so far back I see cerebrospinal fluid. And then it hits me.

Fuck, they're talking about me. When I accept I can't identify the voices, I peek around the rock just enough to see they are two of the young noblewomen who live in town, based on how they're dressed. Their dresses tend to be darker browns rather than the creams and sandy browns of the regular citizens. But I can't think of their names for the life of me.

"I know, right? Ugh. I used to flirt with him all the time when we were young. I'd be lying if I said I didn't hope he'd choose me as his wife. But he picked *her.*" Snob #1 makes the best disgusted sound I've ever heard. It is truly impressive. Even if it is aimed at me.

"Well, he didn't really pick her, Esme," Snob #2 weighs in. "He's stuck with her thanks to the damn royalty clause in the prophecy. Have you tried flirting with him lately?"

"No, I can't really get anywhere near him, at least not for long. *She's* always around—the fake queen—anytime I can get any kind of audience with him," Esme complains.

God, if I have ever sounded that whiny, I would love to be struck down where I sit. It'd actually be a favor. Please and thank you.

"You should try! You never know ... If anything, I bet he's good in bed. Maybe just get some hot sex out of the deal? She's probably really boring in bed. He'd be kissing the ground you walk on. Or anything else you'd like." I can practically hear Snob #2 waggle her eyebrows at Esme.

They both cackle as they finally move out of earshot. Just to be safe, I wait a few more moments before allowing a soft sob to escape from my lips. I desperately wish I could talk to Caitlin. She would kick my ass into shape. Or kick anyone's ass who upset me, like Esme or her bitch buddy. I would give just about anything for one more movie, wine and all-the-crap-we-can-eat night with her. But she doesn't remember me. No one from my life does.

When I go to wipe my nose on my sleeve, which is gross but now officially necessary, I'm reminded I'm wearing the purple and white striped sweater Caitlin made me borrow about six months ago. She had called it her strength sweater. When she wore it, it gave her the strength to do anything by whatever means necessary. She had come to pick me up for dinner one night and it was a bad Noah night. The woman pulled her sweater right off her body then and there and made me put it on, before going to grab something from my closet that she could wear.

Seeing her sweater now only added to the waves of emotions flooding through me. And out comes the ugly crying, not that I was really holding back before. My body begins racking with the sobs. Piece by piece, they break through all of the emotional walls I spent the past year putting up oh so carefully. My knees meet my chest just as my elbows make contact with my jeans.

Burying my head in my hands, I have to make a conscious effort to not move my head too far back and into the very solid rock behind me. A concussion would be less than ideal right about now.

So, if not an accidentally self-inflicted brain injury, then what now? Going back to the castle is not high on my list of desired activities. I would pay a lot of money that I don't currently have to not have to look at Lawson again for the next five hundred years. Or the rest of the day. Whichever comes first, really. And if the little display by Esme and her very best friend was any indication, wandering around the village probably isn't in my best emotional interest, either.

The smell of salt and an oceanic noise catches my attention when I finally remember ... we're on an island. That means the ocean is always close by. Still wanting to put as much space between the castle and myself as I possibly can, I start taking the path leading around the village instead of through it. If I remember correctly, the mouth should pop me out on the northwest side of the island. Far away from anyone at all. Standing up, I brush the dirt off my jeans and start off through the thick greenery.

Cutting around the backside of the village, I can hear their laughter. Their love for one another rings out with every boisterous hoot and sweet giggle. Their sense of community is strong and every step I take, I am reminded of how much I do not belong here.

I want no part of this crown. I want no part of this life. I only wanted Lawson. I always only ever wanted him. But now, every single piece of my life here is a joke. And as much as I love him, I will do well to remember he only ever thought of his people in bringing me here. It's not like he brought me here to be his wife because that's what he wanted out of life. This was all a business transaction. It doesn't matter that he remembered my favorite flowers on our wedding day, or somehow knew my favorite snacks to pack for the insane boat ride here. I had only told him about the flowers that morning, there's no way he could have forgotten by the time we got ready for the ceremony. And he probably just needed a way to shut me up while we were on the boat and figured I could eat my weight in sodium. As much as I would love to believe he did those things out of some kind of quiet love for me, I would only be lying to myself if I did. But what's worse, is that I know I could convince myself of it.

I absentmindedly touch the small gold pendant on my necklace. If I had been thinking, I could have taken my coat out for some practice. Maybe I would have ended up in Fiji, far away from all of this insanity. But then, Lawson wouldn't have trusted me with that, either. It would be one more thing for me to screw up because I shouldn't be the human-girl-turned-Selkie-Queen.

The smell of salt makes me walk faster, knowing I'm so close to the shore. A break in the tree line starts to form in the distance. Nearing the last corner, I hear the one sound that will always make my heart and feet stop. A cold sweat breaks out across my forehead as my breath catches.

"Ellie ..."

I pause only for a moment before breaking into a run, bursting around the last corner of the pathway when I hear it again.

"Ellie ..."

"NOAH!" I scream with abandon. No one from the village or guard will hear me here anyway. Swinging my head back and forth as I look around the beach, nothing but the waves stand out. Cupping my hands around my mouth, I try again. "NOAH!"

With no answer, I venture further out of the tree line. My long, undone hair whips in the winds rolling in off the ocean waves.

"Noah, I know that was you, *mi oso*," I whisper. Realizing I haven't used his nickname since the last time I saw him, I choke down another sob that threatens to bubble out.

Scanning the shoreline as my tennis shoes sink into the sand, I run for the water. The tide is impossibly low today, so I kick my shoes off for better traction. Thankful I thought to put a hair tie on my wrist this morning, I pull my hair into a quick messy bun.

The salt in the wind burns my eyes as the ocean air rolls off the waves. Scanning the immediate water tells me nothing, so I head off to my right. I throw my head in every direction so quickly I'm sure I am going to give myself whiplash.

"Help me, Ellie." It comes from behind me.

Whirling around so hard my bun comes loose, I see him. Lying face down on the beach is Noah. My Noah. I would know that black mess of hair and his cappuccino skin anywhere. He's even wearing the same khaki shorts and faded green T-shirt as the last time I saw him. Only this time, they're soaked through and ripped like something clawed to take his life. Not sure whether to laugh, weep, or dance, I settle on running to him.

Only a few feet away, I drop to my knees as big fat tears of joy stream down my face.

"Noah, it's really you," I manage to choke out, my lower lip quivering. Through my sobs, a laugh escapes my throat. "*Mi oso*, I have so much to tell you. I—"

But just as I extend my hands out to embrace him, he turns his head to face me. And all words left within me disappear. I let out a gasp and stumble backward, landing ass first in the sand.

His face is a deep blue and the skin puffed out, like a sponge that has soaked in too much water. Vascular marbling has started around the edges of his face and slowly makes its way down his neck and through his arms, which are lying motionless by his sides. What's left of his beautiful dark chocolate eyes is covered with gray clouds, and his mouth gapes open, water pouring out. With Noah's black curls wet and stuck to his face, I almost miss the starfish suctioned to his right cheek and eye. Almost.

"Noah," I whisper. Even I can hear the fear in my voice. "*Mi oso...*" My voice and body begin to shake as I take in the sight in front of me. A putrefied hand reaches out to me. I let out a scream, doing the crabwalk to try to get away.

"Ellie, *por favor, mi amor ...*"

Slowly, Noah's body begins to sink inch by inch into the wet sand.

Scrambling to my knees, I can only watch with disbelieving eyes as I lose him one more time. When he is fully covered by sand and I can no longer tell he was even once there, a guttural cry rips from my throat.

"NOAH!" Chunks of sand fly from my hands in every direction as I grab angrily at anything I can. "No! I need more time!" Desperate, hot, angry tears begin streaming down my face. "I need! More! Time!" The scalding tears flow freely now and I don't bother trying to stop the floodgates from throwing themselves open.

My ass hits my heels as I rock back, covering my face with my hands. Only when my sobs begin to wane, and I hear the waves crashing in the background do I feel it, that feeling of being watched. That feeling of being preyed upon.

Slowly, I pull my face out of my hands and use them to tuck my now-loose hair away from my face and behind my ears. Not taking my eyes off the spot where Noah had just been, I begin to listen. For footsteps. For hushed whispers. For anything that tells me I'm not alone. That's when I know. It's behind me.

Cautiously, I lift my head and take a deep breath. Using my hands as leverage, I stand with careful but deliberate movements. My breathing threatens to get away from me and I do my best to keep it in check while I turn over my shoulder. Then my breathing stops completely. Eyes wide and stance frozen, I take in the picture before me.

Standing about ten feet away are three of the most beautiful women I have ever seen. None of them could be shorter than six feet, and each woman has the fairest skin, which almost looks blue with the light reflecting off the holographic blue, purple, pink, and green scales climbing up their legs and ceasing just below their bare navels. Their feet show off the same fair skin, but intricate powder blue webbing extends past their toes to create built-in fins. Labyrinthine cords cover their breasts, which are shielded further by snow-white hair, wavy from the sea salt. But what truly stands out are the eyes, an unnatural bottle green with glowing, golden irises. And they're all focused on me.

Sirens.

"Your Highness," the one standing slightly in front of the others rasps. She pulls her thin lips back, showing teeth filed into dagger-like points. I finally understand she's smiling at me, but her expression holds only malice. The sharp edge of her cheekbones curve upward with the continued tug of her lips.

"Si ... sirens ..." I choke out. My voice sounds foreign to my own ears as I blink incredulously at the sight before me.

The closest siren lets out a laugh, although it's more of what I've always thought it would sound like to rip stuffed animals apart in front of three-year-olds.

"Sisters, the queen knows of what we are," she says. Her eyes never leave me as the other two join in her laughter. She tilts her head, studying me. "I'm surprised the king let you know of us. Bets have been placed he would keep you in the dark and to himself. You're a pretty little thing, after all. He shouldn't waste you."

She takes a step forward and I instinctively take one back. Her grin only spreads wider.

They can smell fear. The first thing Gabriel told me of the species, and it's all I can do to remember to breathe.

"Lillis," one of the sirens behind her speaks. Her high-pitched voice hammers on my nerves like mallets, even with its musical quality. "We mustn't play with the queen's food. Our orders were—"

"I know the orders, Allesandra," Lillis whips her head to bark at the siren.

Allesandra doesn't so much as flinch. Instead, her eyes narrow to thin slits where only her golden irises seep through. From her core, she releases a shrill shriek as she communicates her displeasure to her sister. Lillis echoes the shriek back and claws Allesandra across the face, causing inky black blood to run down her check and stain her light hair.

As the confrontation plays out in front of me, I am actively aware the third siren hasn't let her eyes drift from me even once.

I have to get to Lawson.

Allesandra whimpers behind Lillis as the third sister begins to emit a low growl. Dread begins to fill my core while I watch as her eyes begin to black out, giving her an intense and sinister appearance.

"Zyla," Lillis turns to the third sister, "Come now. We must be hospitable to our honored guest. A queen fit for our queen." Lillis motions to me. All three sirens turn their attention back to me, each pulling on a menacing smile. "Now, Your Majesty, are you ready to die?"

The remaining air in my lungs vanishes as I turn on my heels and head for the tree line. I only make it about four steps before stiletto claws grab onto my sweater and pull, shredding it to pieces as it falls from my body. Another set of claws dig into my arm, yanking me backward and onto my back on the beach. Pain sings through my skull as my vision blurs and I begin to feel the outline of the rocks beneath my body.

Lillis crouches down next to my ear and sighs. Her sudden closeness makes me jump. "Your Majesty, I really did hope you would make this easier on us. If you had, we might have let you say goodbye to your love one last time."

Lawson...

I hear her move away from me and retreat back toward the sea.

"Zyla, you know what to do," she calls over her shoulder.

The most beautiful song surrounds me and a warmth floods over my body. I can't help but close my eyes.

CHAPTER 19

ASOFT KNOCK AT THE DOOR PULLS MY ATTENTION AWAY FROM the bed's dark canopy, where I lay sprawled out underneath, on top of the plush blankets.

"What?" I bark. Hopefully, whoever it is will get the hint to go the fuck away. Unfortunately, I'm not that lucky.

The door to our suite opens and Gabriel steps inside, closing it quietly behind him. I turn my eyes back to the canopy. Neither of us says anything for the longest minute of my life. When I finally have enough patience to ask him to kindly leave, he sighs and sits on the bed, facing away from me.

"What happened, Lawson?" he asks softly.

I refuse to look at him and find his head bowed in shame for me. So I glare harder into the heavy fabric draped above.

"Lawson?" he asks again. Neither demanding nor impatient. Fatherly. Reverently.

Pinching the bridge of my nose, I squeeze my eyes shut and count to ten. Opening my eyes, I let out a deep breath before answering.

"We had an argument," I finally say.

The bed squeaks as he turns to look at me. Bringing my eyes to him, I see the pain that lives there. The same pain Ellie had in her eyes when she ran out of here in tears only an hour ago. The thought of Ellie in pain sears through me, white-hot anger at myself coursing through my veins. Dropping my eyes from his, I turn back to the ceiling.

"I assume you are aware she was running through the castle in tears? She managed to frighten every guard on duty."

"Yes, I'm aware," I grit between my teeth. But I didn't know that. I only know she ran out of here in tears. Now the entire castle staff knows I was an asshole to my wife. *Fuck*.

Sighing, I rub my hands over my face, hoping all this shit will disappear and Ellie will be lying beside me on our bed with a warm smile on her face. But again, I'm not that lucky.

Gabriel sniffs, bringing my attention back to the moment.

"What was the argument about?" Gabriel does his best to sound impartial, but I know he prefers Ellie. I knew it from the moment I brought her here.

Everyone should prefer Ellie. She's the better of the two of us. More thoughtful, more kind, stronger, braver. I rub my temples as I think about how to answer his question.

"She was scared," I say quietly. "She was talking about how she was afraid she's not strong enough and asking what will happen if she fails." I swallow. "Ellie said she wants to be the kind of queen our people deserve and she's afraid of what they'll think of her if she fails." I pause to gauge his reaction.

Gabriel only nods, encouraging me to continue.

"I had just come back from that shitshow of a meeting with you, Bryant, and Garren. Talking about the inevitabilities when the fucking sirens find us, and I just felt so fucking helpless. And then Ellie's saying all these things about what if she fails and I just snapped." Risking a peek at him as I shift to a seated position, I find his full but impassive attention on me. "I told her I didn't bring her here to fail and how everyone was counting on her, so if she didn't think she could be a good queen, then maybe she shouldn't be one." I look down at my hands to distract myself from what I have to share next. "I told her she wouldn't have been my first pick if she had been one of us all along, but how she'll just have to do now." My head drops into my hands and I let out an angry cry. "I didn't even mean it. I was just scared, and her being insecure scared me even more. I said terrible things, things I wished I could take back as soon as they were out of my mouth. But I couldn't stop myself from letting my worries look like anger. Anger at *her*, the one person who makes all of this shit bearable."

Sighing, I pull my head up to look at Gabriel. He continues to listen in silence, unnerving me further. Tears threaten my eyes even though I thought I got everything out after Ellie left.

"I love her, Gabriel. Not because of who she is to our people. Not because she reads more than she talks. Not because she's the most beautiful creature I've ever seen on land or in the water. I love her the way my father loved my mother, wholly and unyielding. I would choose her a thousand times over. I would have married her with or without that fucking royalty clause, which is why I was so mad about it. I wanted it to be her choice to marry me, not because she had to. I want to have a family with her, give her and our kids the world. Ellie is everything to me and I am so desperately in love with her. And I hurt her. I hurt her so fucking badly and I don't know if she'll ever come back. Fuck, fuck, fuck!" I choke out a sob as Gabriel becomes a blur through my scalding tears.

Gabriel shifts on the bed and releases a deep sigh over my strangled weeping. His heavy hand lands on my shoulder closest to him

"Lawson, you both need time to grow accustomed to the other. You were both thrust into a strange situation and you both happened to find someone you love under peculiar circumstances. But now—"

"Wait, what?" I say as I snap my gaze to him. Gabriel frowns.

"You will both need time to learn how to fight fairly with one another—"

"No, go back to the thing you said about loving someone—"

"Because you, especially, have never had an intense relationship like this," he finishes. He gives me a pointed look. "And if I have to repeat the requested piece of information, perhaps you are not ready to hear it. Or read about it."

What the fuck?

"Your wife may have come to visit me after her last training session today. She left me with some very intriguing information."

A dumbfounded look paints my features and he looks over to the desk on the other side of the room before looking back to me. Holding my stare for a moment longer, he gets up and heads to the door.

"Gabriel?" I call after him. But he doesn't even look back at me before closing the door behind him.

Rubbing my eyes, I climb off the bed and go to sit down at the large wooden desk. Since nothing's sitting on top, I start pulling open the drawers. In the bottom drawer is a single envelope addressed to me, and the necklace that haunts my dreams. Looking at the envelope, I realize I've never actually seen Ellie's handwriting until now. It's flowing, large, and romantic. Like someone who loves the romance of letter writing like the iconic literary heroines. Just like Ellie. With shaking hands, I set the necklace on the desktop and pull the letter out of the envelope.

Lawson,

I'll admit I'm not quite sure what to say. But in case something happens to me when I finally face the Siren Queen, I want there to be some record of this. Just in case you ever wonder about this as you tell your children years from now, after I'm gone.

Our entire situation is completely unbelievable and if someone tried to tell me as a child I would become the queen to a mythological society and married to the strangest, sweetest man, I would have thought they were insane. Part of me thinks I'm the one that's insane.

When I met Noah, I was fifteen. He was a sweet boy who became a sweet man, and he was the first boy I ever loved. When I married him, I thought, This is it. This is the rest of my life." And I would have been happy that way. Then he was taken from me and I'll never know why.

But then I came to Scotland to try and connect with him in some way and found something I never thought possible – you. A man who is stubborn, impossible, and surly. But at the same time, you are kind, loving, and brave. You gave me hope when I thought all was lost. You gave me a home and a purpose. You reminded me how to love another person, of how wonderful it could be. I will always treasure what I had with Noah, but he is my past. You, Lawson. You are my future.

When we first learned about the royalty clause, I was angry. I thought it meant I was losing any possibility of a normal future. But when it came time for the ceremony, I realized I was being handed a future with you. No matter what happens when it comes time for me to face the Siren Queen, I will always be grateful for the time I was given with you.

I love you, Lawson. I am not ashamed to be the Selkie Queen, so long as you are my Selkie King. I love you in ways I never thought possible for one person to love another. You are my North Star, my Sun, and my Moon. I love that I've only known you for a small window of time, yet it feels like there was never a time when I couldn't feel your presence in my heart. I love you, Lawson. Not because of the prophecy. Not because of our circumstances. I love you because I feel in my heart that you were meant for me and this was the path we had to take to find each other.

I will love you for the rest of my days. There is something about knowing I cannot love you forever that makes me love you harder while I still can. Hopefully, one day, I will mean as much to you as you do to me. But until then, know that I am always on your side. I love you, Lawson.

With Love Always,
Ellie

Not believing what I'm reading, I read the letter through two more times. I begin to taste salt invading the corners of my mouth and set the letter back down on the desk. Turning the rings over in my hand, I know that she knows how I feel about these. She's given me an apology and a promise with them. Wiping my eyes with the back of my hand, I stand with my hands on my hips and look around the room.

Pieces of Ellie are everywhere. Her clothes drape across our bed. Her shoes are strewn around the floor by her armoire. Her naturally floral smell still lingers in the air from before she ran out not even two hours ago. Then I see it.

On her bedside table sits her crown, like any ordinary thing she uses on a daily basis. Because her status and mindset as our Queen is as natural for her as breathing. She was born for it, even if she didn't know it until very recently. Whereas I fucking grew up knowing I was bound to be King if something happened to Lorcan. But I've been acting like a child damned from our waters by Odin himself.

I need Ellie like I need to breathe, and I need to find her. Now.

Throwing our bedroom door open, I take off down the corridor. I round the third corner when I'm met with three guards whispering to one another and skid to a stop to avoid colliding with them. My sudden presence must startle them because they fly apart like shrapnel.

"Your-Your Majesty," one stutters.

Fuck, I wish Ellie was here. She's the one who always remembers names. The guards fall into line at attention. Staring at them one by one, I take in their nervous expressions. Clearly, they saw Ellie and are concerned I'm about to rip them a new one. They exchange a worried look between them. Crossing my arms, I pinpoint which guard looks the most likely to talk and walk directly to him. His pins tell me he holds no rank.

"Soldier," I say, commanding his attention. He actually winces. My towering over him in height doesn't help the matter.

"Yes-yes? Uh, Your Maj-Majesty?" His stuttering is really starting to piss me off.

"Have you seen my wife?" I'm quickly losing my patience. But if he's seen Ellie and he'll help me get to her quicker, I'll give him a fucking medal myself.

The soldier begins to shrink in on himself while he shakes his head. Another of the men clears their throat to catch my attention.

"She went that way, Your Highness." The man points in the opposite direction of where I've been heading. He doesn't miss my annoyed expression because he decides to elaborate. "I heard she went through the rear exit, sir."

I don't bother saying anything as I turn and take off toward the back of the castle. If word already made it back here that she left the castle, that means she left in a hurry. She even passed the library, which is where I really figured she'd gone. Each guard I pass doesn't hide their surprise as they watch their sorry excuse of a king *run* through the halls after his wife. If I had known I was going to get this much exercise today, I would have hydrated first. Reaching the last few corridors, I begin to slow my movements since my legs are now screaming at me to stop existing completely. But soft voices around the final corner catch my attention and force me to work against my protesting limbs.

"I'm sure she—Lawson?" Gabriel looks up at me, surprised at my sudden appearance. "Are you alright?"

"Not really, no. Now, where's my wife?" I cut straight to the point, doing my best to keep my breathing in check. I've really let myself get lax about exercise since we've been at the Base. Apparently, I'm paying for it now.

"She's not here. She—"

"Others told me she left the castle," I cut Gabriel off, not wasting any time. "If Ellie's outside the walls of this castle, she's supposed to have guards. Who went with her?"

Gabriel and the guard on duty at this exit exchange a look before looking back to me.

"None went with her, sir," the guard replied.

Red begins to impede my vision as my stomach starts to roll. I cross and uncross my arms before putting my hands on my hips. My teeth bite down on my lip, namely so I don't bite someone's fucking head off.

"You're telling me," I work to keep my voice as calm as possible, "that the queen is somewhere out on the island ... with no protection, whatsoever ... completely alone? When there are sirens lurking in the waters?" The guard gulps. "Searching for her and our people? Sirens that want her *dead*?" My anger slips in little by little until I'm shouting.

"I was the only one on duty, Your Majesty, and I couldn't just leave my post—"

"So you left your queen to die?" I hiss back at him.

"No, sir," he shakes his head wildly back and forth. "She was very upset and screamed at me to open the door and—"

"And you let her go," I spit.

His mouth hangs open as he looks to Gabriel for help. Before Gabriel can say anything, a young soldier comes running around the corner.

"Your Majesty," he huffs, "there have been reports of siren songs. Near the north shore."

"There are no villagers near the north shore, Soldier," Gabriel says. I don't move my eyes from the soldier's face, but I can hear the frown in his voice.

"Jensen. Medic Corporal Jensen, sir ... But, uh, things have gotten worse, sir."

"How can things have gotten worse?" I grind out. "They were already at 'worse.'"

"A few of the children, Your Highness," the corporal explains. "They saw the queen walking through the forest," he casts a quick glance at me to see if I'll maim him, "and followed her. They kept to the tree line, but they followed her all the way to the beach. When they could see her again, they hung back because ... she ... she had started screaming. They said ... there was ..." He pauses, shaking his head.

"What did they say?" I press. He swallows.

"They said there was a man. But he looked funny." I frown at him. *A man?* "Apparently, the queen wept when she saw him. But then he disappeared and then—the kids described them as 'tall fish women'—sirens appeared. When the queen tried to escape, one of them sang her to sleep. That's when the kids ran." The floor falls out from under me. Gabriel and the older guard grab for me to help me keep steady.

I stand there staring at the man who just told me my unarmed wife has been found by sirens.

"How long ago?" Gabriel asks urgently.

"Maybe twenty minutes? The kids ran home crying and their mother found a guard, who reported it immediately," Jensen says. Finally, my faculties return and my brain kicks into high gear. I don't even think before I act.

Breaking out of the guard and Gabriel's hold, I run to the door and throw it open. My legs break into a run and follow the path along the outside of the castle. Cold leaves slap my face since I don't bother moving anything out of my way while I run. Behind me, I hear the sounds of heavy breathing and know Gabriel and the two guards have followed me.

Apparently, my life is worth guarding but not Ellie's. My jaw ticks as the thought makes me push faster toward the north shore.

"Lawson!"

I hear Gabriel call out to me from behind, but I don't even slow. If Ellie's in trouble, I have to get to her.

Finally, the echo of waves crashing invades my ears as I round the last corner of the path and break through the tree line. Taking a few steps onto the beach, I survey the sight in front of me while the wind breaks violently against my cheek. The empty beach mocks me as the waves continue reaching the shore with no sign of her.

Gabriel and the guards finally escape the cover of the trees. I briefly wonder if I should worry about Gabriel's heart when something catches my eye. Laying a little ways down the beach upon a pile of sharp rocks near the trees is something dark. Maybe purple? My breathing stops as moments of our argument flash through my mind.

Ellie's sweater was purple.

Taking off in a run toward the item, I stop just short of the jagged rocks. On the rocks is what used to be Ellie's sweater, if it could even really be called that anymore. Crouching down, I scoop up the fabric from the rocks and sand. When I last saw it, the garment was vibrant and clean. This thing is dirty, shredded, and covered with crimson stains. It looks like the life was literally ripped out of it. But this is Ellie's sweater. All the blood drains from my face.

Dropping to my knees, I vomit into the sand as I clutch the sweater to my chest. Hands grip my shaking shoulders and keep me upright until I'm done.

"They have her," I choke out as I continue to shake. "She's hurt and they fucking have her." I thrust the crusted, bloody scraps of fabric to Gabriel, who takes it with care.

Turning, I look to find the others searching the beach and shoreline for her. For Ellie. My wife. Who's been taken by the deadliest creatures in the entire fucking ocean. Not finding anything else, they return to where we sit in the sand and pretend to ignore my vomit and the smell emanating from it. But they don't miss what's in Gabriel's hands. And they both look sick.

"Do you think she's ..." The younger guard is bold, if nothing else. It doesn't stop me from wanting to punch him for asking if my wife is dead. But Gabriel speaks before I can remind him of the pecking order.

"No, they need her alive," Gabriel says softly. "If they've found her, there's only one reason." His eyes scan some invisible document, like he's reading something in his memory.

"Sir?" Corporal Jensen prompts.

"The Queen's Rite," Gabriel whispers, nodding. "She's been taken for the Queen's Rite." His eyes find mine.

"What the hell is that?" My voice comes out in a rasp thanks to my recent display of retching. By the look on his face, I'm not even sure I want to know the answer. He clears his throat before continuing.

"The sirens believe, if their queen consumes another queen in this ancient ceremony, and before that, her closest companions, their queen will be able to unequivocally conquer the people whose queen has been consumed." My stomach rolls as his words begin clicking into place.

"You're telling me the Siren Queen is going to *eat* Ellie?" My voice is hard, even to my own ears. Gabriel doesn't answer. He only nods once.

"But we just found her ..." the young guard whispers. None of us miss the sorrow in his voice. He looks around at each of us. "What do we do now?"

The three men watch me as I stand and take the sweater pieces from Gabriel. Turning it over in my hands, I feel my resolve harden within.

"Now," I say, looking at the young guard, "I go get my wife."

CHAPTER 20

Ellie

NEARBY, A SHRIEK PULLS ME FROM A BLACK AND DREAMLESS sleep. A deep shiver runs through me as I slowly begin to regain consciousness. In addition to the freezing ambient temperature, whatever I'm lying on might as well be a giant block of ice. In fact, I think it is. Slowly, I begin testing my restrained limbs for stiffness, rolling my joints one by one. While definitely sore, nothing seems to be broken. Small blessings, or whatever.

Another shriek cuts through the air, this time much closer. Opening my eyes, I find my three favorite siren sisters entering the room from a small doorway several yards away. When Lillis finds me awake, her lips pull back to make my least favorite face in the world.

"Sisters," she rasps, "our guest of honor has awakened."

Zyla and Allesandra reply with their peculiar version of laughter. With Allesandra remaining near the door, Zyla and Lillis come closer until I can almost feel their icy breath on my freezing body. Lillis crouches down until she's level with my face. I decide on looking her straight in the eye. If she's going to kill me, she's going to look at me while she does it.

"Queen Eleanor, welcome home." Her whisper strikes something deep within me. If she thinks this is home for me, then ...

I look around the room and find that it is completely covered in icy blue hues. Even the windows covering the ceiling are filled with sharp facets, giving them an ice-like quality. Just like Lawson described it. This is the Ice Castle.

I'm in Lawson's childhood home.

The thought of being where he grew up and where all of his memories of his family are held causes my eyes to mist. I quickly try to swallow down my emotions. I can't afford those right now.

But Lillis doesn't miss a beat before she grasps my chin with her nails. She makes me turn to her, her gorgeous but frightening face mere breaths from mine.

"Feel free to cry, Your Highness," saltwater flies from her mouth to my face, "for no one will hear you weep for your fate or your loved ones here."

She violently releases my face and my head involuntarily swings back. Connecting with what I'm positive is an actual block of ice, pain begins to radiate from the contact point. I wince, which only seems to bring her greater satisfaction. I lean my head back slowly and look at the ceiling directly above me, trying to find a point of focus.

Behind her, Zyla makes her impatience with her sister known as a low growl escapes her thin lips. Lillis gnashes her tiny dagger teeth in response.

"We were sent to prepare her, so let's just get to it," Zyla sneers. "And throw out that nasty thing. It reeks of *them*." She points to somewhere near me on the floor. Just out of the corner of my eye, I make out a dark, soaked heap.

They used my coat to get me here. So no one would see me go with them.

It also explains why I am completely dry and their hair still looks damp. That means I can't have been here long. Lawson probably doesn't even realize I'm gone. He may not even care. A pang sings through my chest as his face the last time I saw him floats through my memory. He showed the same anger as when I accepted my coat. At the time, I thought maybe he just didn't want to see me in so much pain. Now I know he really just didn't want me here at all. I frown at the memory. But then something the Sea Witch said during the ceremony comes to mind.

"Only a selkie can put on their coat," I croak. Lillis releases a scratchy laugh.

"That's only true of natural selkies, dear," she says.

"You are an impostor queen," Allesandra calls from the doorway.

"You will never be more than a slightly elevated *human*." The way Zyla calls me a human makes me feel dirty. I struggle for an impartial expression. "Only a plaything for the king, really. Your blood still runs human-red, after all. Not selkie-white."

The sisters laugh in unison, setting my whatever-color blood on edge. I set my jaw to attempt regaining control of my nerves. Around my neck, my pendant pulses at the proximity to my coat. It's extremely uncomfortable, and I abandon my neutral expression as I stretch my neck for relief.

Lillis snatches the necklace and pulls until it releases into her palm. The skin on the back of my neck screams from the pain, but I only squeeze my eyes tightly shut and grit my teeth. I refuse to let them know how much pain they're causing me. Even if they might as well have just ripped out my small intestines.

"Ah, ah. Can't have you trying to escape, now can we?" She wags her finger at me like I'm two years old as she holds my pendant in the other. "The queen wouldn't like that. And it would be such a waste of your dears."

Confusion clouds my expression at her words and a menacing grin spreads across her face. My stomach drops at the sight.

"Oh, Queen Eleanor. It would seem your husband and his advisors left out the best part of your arrival in our icy waters," Lillis says sweetly. "The Queen's Rite is to be held tonight, so our family has been holding the appropriate ceremonies in anticipation of your arrival in our—well, your—home."

"Appropriate ceremonies," I whisper back.

She casually walks down to my feet and takes my right foot in her hands. She runs her hands up and down it like I'm having some kind of perverted massage. My shoes must still be on the beach from when I removed them, but my socks are doing wonders to keep my toes from falling off. Gently, she moves her hands down to my ankle.

"Yes, Queen Eleanor." Without warning, she snaps my ankle outward. A scream rips through my throat as we all hear the ligament rip apart. "Just in case," she says pleasantly. "If you do somehow manage to escape, we might as well make our chase a little more interesting." An ominous smile takes over her features.

Keeping my eyes straight ahead, tears stream down the sides of my face as I try not to whimper. But my lip trembles, giving me away. The sisters cackle in satisfaction. Lillis gently runs a nail over my broken ankle, causing me to pull away from the searing sensation.

"Where was I? Oh, yes. Before the queen can consume your being, you must first be bled. Wouldn't want all that nasty human blood getting in her system." She makes a disgusted sound rivaling that of Esme's only hours earlier. "But before that, the closest companions of the queen to be consumed must be devoured, one each night preceding the sacrificial queen, herself."

I close my eyes to concentrate on what she's saying instead of the searing pain radiating up through my leg. A choking noise escapes from me, but it sounds foreign to my own ears.

"But ... no one ... remembers."

"No one remembers you? Yes ... The tricky little Sea Witch took care of that, didn't she? Fortunately, one of our own had already managed to capture one before you had been wiped from her memories."

Opening my eyes, I find she's moved to stand near her singing sister. They both watch as I start connecting the dots. My eyes go wide as my jaw drops open. But I need to hear them say it. They have to say it. Or else I'll never believe it.

"What was her name?" I whisper with as much force as I can muster. All three simply look at me. "WHAT WAS HER NAME?" It feels good to scream in this frozen home-turned-hell. My breaths come short and rapidly as I wait for their response.

Allesandra taps her chin in fake ponderance.

"What did Ken say she was called?" she asks from her station.

"Ken ..." Ken? Why does that name sound familiar? *Oh, fuck* ...

"Cait ... Caitlin," I choke out. Lillis snaps her fingers in false recognition, smirking. "No, not her." I shake my head as well as I can in disbelief.

"Yes, that's it." Rolling her eyes, Lillis continues, "Zyla had to sing for *hours* before she finally gave up the fight. Tasted a little gamey, if you ask me."

I don't want to believe them. There's no way they could know Caitlin and I were connected.

"I can hear you thinking over there, Your Majesty. Your thoughts are terribly loud." Lillis gives me a knowing look.

"But ... But she had nothing to do with any of this. And no longer anything to do with me," I plead. Fresh, hot tears stream down the sides of my cheeks, betraying me.

"Oh, Queen Ellie. She helped bring you here. She helped facilitate this whole thing. If it weren't for your little friend, you'd still be wasting away on your apartment floor in despair." My eyes snap to Lillis's face.

"What did you just s—"

"Besides, Your Majesty, don't you remember Kenneth? You met him that first night."

"How did you know I—"

"Once he got her away from you and convinced her to write that letter, he—"

"ANSWER ME!" I scream over her. But she doesn't stop the onslaught.

"Used his precious siren song to knock her out long enough to bring her here." That catches my attention and I knit my brows together in confusion.

"But ... he's a ... man ..."

Zyla lets out a snort and looks to her sisters.

"Humans are so stupid," she says to them. Then she turns to look at me. "There are male sirens too, you simpleton." Her tone is condescending, like she's explaining I have to eat to continue living. "And if you still don't believe us, you can just ask Kenneth. He's here in the castle somewhere." She shrugs as she begins to head to the far wall.

My mind goes a mile a minute, trying to remember any indication I received letting me know Caitlin was alive since I read her letter. But I come up empty.

Lillis comes up to the table and leans down next to my face.

I narrow my eyes as I cut them to her sharp features.

"Now, Queen Eleanor, you wanted to know how I knew about your apartment activities?" She gives me a saccharine smile. Tears stream silently down my face as I glare at her. Whether they're from learning about Caitlin, or my throbbing ankle, I'm not even sure anymore. "Well?" She tilts her head slightly, giving her a demented look.

Curtly, I nod.

"Very good," she says. "If you continue to cooperate, I may just let Zyla put you to sleep before we begin to bleed you." She motions to Zyla, who returns to her sister's side with a tray of scalpels and tubes.

My eyes widen involuntarily at the sight before me. The lump in my throat begins to grow, even as I work to swallow it down. Lillis follows my line of sight, a pleased look forming over her predatory features. In the background, Allesandra laughs at my obvious discomfort.

"Our queen has known of you for some time now and has kept a close eye on you. Ever since you were in your twentieth year, I'd say." My eyes find Lillis's as I take in what she's saying. "When you married that half-Latin man, we all thought that was the end of it. There would be no reason for you to visit our waters." She pins me with her narrowed gaze and I don't dare move. "But then he walked into the water. Naturally, we had to seize him. We, of course, knew of his value to you—"

"No," I breathe.

"—And may I just say, he made an excellent side dish to your much more recently deceased friend."

A choked sob makes its way out of my throat while fresh, scalding tears flow harder. Through my blurred vision, I can see Zyla begin setting up the tubing. I pull at the restraints in an attempt to flail. Maybe I could kick one of them, if I'm lucky. But Lillis has other plans as she puts her weapon-like hands on my shoulders to hold me still. She leans back down until her mouth reaches my ear.

"And now," she whispers, "your best friend is dead because of you. Your first love walked away from you and to his own death. The people you rule don't respect you. Your husband doesn't return your misplaced affections. And now, you will die a most painful death, only to be consumed by the rightful queen and fail at your only true purpose in this life." She tsks and gives a soft sigh, shaking her head mockingly. "I ask you this, Queen Eleanor, is it worth it? Is King Lawson worth this?"

I don't have time to answer before I feel the blinding pain as Zyla slices into my limbs, releasing a bloodcurdling scream from my throat.

CHAPTER 21

Lawson

T HE LACK OF SUN THE FARTHER NORTH WE GO CAUSES THE water temperature to drop as we get closer to the Ice Castle. Nerves run wild throughout my body, making it difficult for me to concentrate. This will be the first time I have seen my home in nearly fifteen years and, the last time I was there, my entire family was being slaughtered. Now, the newest member of my family and the start of my future family is there without me, about to be bled out and eaten as part of a ritual.

"Lawson," Bryant calls from in front of me. His dark coat makes him difficult to find in these midnight waters. But when he turns, the reflection in his eyes gives him away. He nods to me, ensuring I haven't lost my fucking mind yet. We're not going fast enough for my liking, but I know precautions must be taken.

I told the group there will be no formalities tonight. First names only, no titles. We don't need to help the sirens know who they've killed and who will still stand against them when Ellie fights their queen to the death.

My heart constricts thinking of my wife and the pain I know she's in. Sensing my panic, Jensen swims level with me, occasionally touching my foreflipper to keep me grounded. I curtly nod in his direction, letting him know I'm good, even if I'm anything but.

Three additional soldiers follow closely behind us, with one more to each side. When General Garren found out about our impromptu expedition, he flipped his shit. Especially when he learned I planned to lead the excursion. Thankfully, Bryant and a few of his loyal subordinates had been in the room with him. Otherwise, my hysterics might not have gotten me as far.

I briefly glance behind me to the soldiers at my flank and a wave of disgust sinks in my core. I don't even know the names of these men. But here they are, brave enough to join me in what is essentially a suicide mission. I would bet everything I own that Ellie knows each of their names. When they heard she was gone, not a single one of them showed any hesitation in helping to get her back. They adore her that much.

"How much farther?" I call to Bryant.

"We're almost there. I recommend we go in through the lower corridor. It's far enough out of the way that I doubt they would have much security there, if any."

"The lower corridor? As in ..."

"The one we used to use to sneak out to the Black Waters? Yes."

"Bryant, we need to get lower to the ocean floor. I'm making out siren scales up ahead," Soldier Cade notifies us.

Without another word, our party of eight stealthily sinks to the ocean floor, our bellies barely missing skimming the bottom. Only moments later, thousands of shimmering holographic scales covered in inky blood lay before us on the dark sands. Dozens of sets of human and tail bones lay scattered amongst them.

"What ... what are these?" Jensen asks.

"It's a siren graveyard," I answer him. "Be careful. Sometimes the living will lay amongst the fallen in despair."

Two of our soldiers move higher in the water to scout, swimming ahead of Bryant.

"Lawson, we're very close now. When I give the signal, swim straight up. We'll be directly underneath the door to the lower corridor. Michael and Samuel are already in position."

"Roger that," I call to my friend. To my right, Jensen brushes my flipper once more.

"Lawson, don't worry. We'll get her. We might not love her the way you do, but we do all love her, too."

I have to nod, swallowing before I can formulate any kind of clear response. But Bryant's voice rings out, catching my attention.

"Now!"

Jensen and I shoot straight up, cutting through the water. That's when I finally see it. After all these years, the Ice Castle looks exactly the same. We both reach Bryant and the others who are already waiting by the door, followed shortly by Soldiers John and Elijah. When we're all present and accounted for, we carefully open the door to the inside.

The long corridor is silent as we swim inside. The icy hues take over our vision, our eyes needing a minute to adjust to the brightness after the murky waters outside. Bryant turns back to face us.

"We'll take the back passageways through the underwater portion of the castle. Once we reach the Atrium, we'll only have moments for all of us to reach the Coat Room before the chances of us getting caught heavily increase."

The men around me nod intently. He starts to return to the front but hesitates before turning back to look each of us in the eye.

"Remember, men. This is not training any longer. These creatures *will* kill you without hesitation. If one starts to sing, screech as loud as you can and then get to her throat. Quickly." His eyes land on me. "Lawson, they know who you are. They've been waiting for your return just as we have. Do not give them a chance to recognize you." I give him a silent agreement before asking the burning question within me. The reason we're here.

"Do you have any idea where Ellie's being kept?"

"According to lore, she will be kept in the Ice Chamber near the library." My face must not convey much confidence, so Bryant continues. "Supposedly, the ... Sacrifice ... is kept on ice until they are to be ... bled. It's to make their blood run more slowly. To ... to make the Sacrifice suffer all the more." He clears his throat, waiting for my response.

I only dare to blink since I'm not sure I can trust myself not to yell out for my wife at this moment. And all that would do is get us killed. Sensing I will give no real answer, Bryant nods and bids us onward.

Quickly, we make our way through several blue-tinted corridors before we finally come upon one standing guard. With her back to us, Soldier Cade sneaks up behind the siren and shoves a flipper claws-first through her throat. He finishes the job by snapping her neck in two with his teeth. She never even had time to scream.

Her body sinks to the floor as we rush past. When we reach the next corner, the sounds of sirens arguing floats through the water straight to us. One of them shrieks their displeasure to the other, causing Jensen to wince at the sound.

"Quiet, sister," one of the sirens screeches. "Or the queen will hear." The other siren is immediately silenced with the comment. "She is not to be disturbed until dawn for the beginning of the Rite with the Selkie Queen."

At the mention of Ellie, every muscle in my body freezes. I pray to Odin they will say more about her so I'll know her condition, but they move on through the hallway to the next stop in their checkpoint. It's not until he begins to draw my blood that I realize Bryant and Jensen are holding me in place as I try to propel myself forward to end the creatures who had just dared to discuss my wife.

"Lawson," Bryant's voice is strong, unyielding. "You must be patient. We will find her." His eyes meet mine with a stern, fatherly look. "But if you go off killing every siren we come across, we will not be able to help her."

I look at each of the men, embarrassment flooding my system. Nodding, I shake the two of them off me.

"How far are we from the Coat Room? We're still in the Lower Castle, right?" one of the younger soldiers asks.

"Not far," I grumble, feeling the need to offer something to the group other than stress. "Only a couple more passageways and then we should reach the Atrium." Bryant nods in agreement.

"Right. That's where the water will begin to recede and the Upper Castle will begin."

"Let's go, then," I grind out, gnashing my teeth together.

Sticking to the dark recessed corners, we move through the next couple of passages without any more siren sightings. As we near the Atrium, the water begins to lighten in color. More lights also begin to appear throughout the corridors. Brighter lighting. Clearer waters. The Atrium is just around the corner.

The blood rushes to my ears as I poke my head above the waterline in my home for the first time in over a decade. Looking around, a small wave of pleasure crashes through me when I see that not much has changed. There may still be a chance to show Ellie my childhood home, after all.

I slip back underneath the water and remain along the wall to avoid detection. While the others have begun swimming ahead, Jensen remains by my side to watch my back. Our eyes meet and I know there's not much longer now. It's not far from the Coat Room to the Ice Chamber. Ellie is almost within my reach.

Dark, black blood floats toward us in the water. Too dark to be any of ours since our blood runs white. They've killed more sirens. Three, given the amount of blood.

"Lawson?" Jensen swims up beside me. "The queen's sweater ... it was covered in blood, as well. But not our blood. It was ... still ... human." I hear the confusion in his voice and feel it mirrored in my expression.

"Odin's bony ass," I whisper, clenching my jaw.

"Sir?"

The fucking Sea Witch. She. Fucking. Knew. I shake my head angrily, doing my best not to draw unwanted siren attention.

"Ellie," I rub my flippers over my face, "sacrifice ..."

"What?"

"When Ellie accepted her coat. The witch said something about never truly belonging somewhere until you're forced to ... sacrifice yourself for your people."

"What does that mean?"

A chorus of siren shrieks halt the conversation and we both shoot forward to catch up with the others. When we reach them, the water is filled with black and white blood mixed together. Two siren corpses slowly sink to the floor, each of them with shredded vocal cords, dancing in the light of the water. Between them, Soldier John's lifeless body bobs toward the ground. Completely covered in scratch marks, his eyes have been clawed from his head and one of his foreflippers is missing.

My mouth opens in shock, causing me to accidentally ingest bloody seawater. I am instantly folded over and vomiting it back into the ocean. Just when I think I'm done, something floats past me in the water. One of Soldier John's severed eyes is level with mine. It has clearly been cut into during the fight, milky liquid floats from the lacerated center and toward the water's surface. Looking away, my body finds what little bile is left in my stomach to send up. Someone comes from beside me and begins patting my back while the retching finally slows.

One of the soldiers, Cade, I think, punches the closest wall and lets out an angry screech. The others hurry him further down the passageway and into the heart of the Atrium.

Beside me, Jensen clears his throat.

"Lawson, we have to move. Now."

Shakily, I nod my head as I look one more time to Soldier John before following Jensen and the others.

When we reach the Atrium's main entrance from the Lower Castle, it's clear the Upper Castle is in a buzz. A dozen sirens talk excitedly about the coming dawn and getting to catch a glimpse of the once-human Selkie Queen. Tucked into an unlit corner, Bryant and I pop our heads barely out of the waterline while the others keep watch and try to help Soldier Cade calm down.

A floor above us, a group of sirens are cackling at something one of them has just said when another chimes in.

"She clearly wasn't born a selkie. She's utterly plain looking."

"I think she's pretty. But so far, she's put up even more of a fight than her friend."

Her friend?

I whip my head to Bryant, but find no answers on his face.

"Maybe it means she will taste better too," the siren continues. A sudden shriek causes Bryant and I to flinch, cowering away from the sound.

"You moron. Only the queen will get to taste her. That's why we have to keep her on ice until then, so she's nice and fresh for Her Majesty. We will only get to use her blood for our skincare later on."

My heart stops as my temperature rises just before I'm yanked underwater.

"Get a grip, mate," Bryant hisses.

"Did you not hear what they just *said*?"

"Yes, I did. But I also heard them confirm Ellie's location. You've got to remain calm if we're going to make it out of here with Ellie still alive." Bryant stares at me hard.

I nod to him tersely and follow him back up to the water's surface. I swear, this woman will be the death of me.

We sink a little lower back into the water as another siren across the way emerges from the surface. Her holographic scales shimmer in the moonlight thanks to the windowed ceilings featured throughout the castle. As she breaks the waterline, her tail begins to split up the middle. The shining scales shift quickly to encase the blue legs that form where her tail was only moments ago. The siren's movement from the ocean water to the floor inside the castle is seamless. She doesn't miss a single beat.

Pressure on my foreflipper breaks my attention away from the siren. Turning back to Bryant, I find he's sunk back below the surface and I slip back down to join him.

"The door to the Coat Room is just across the way, on the opposite wall. If we stay along the wall line, we should be able to make it there with as little attention as possible."

The men listen as Bryant points in the direction where we need to go. Even Soldier Cade seems to be listening intently, and I make a mental note to ask Bryant or Jensen about Cade's relationship with John later.

"Do you think they're using the room for anything?" Jensen asks. Bryant shakes his head confidently.

"I don't know why they would. It's not even the main room that connects the Upper and Lower Castle. Unless they're using it for storage of some kind. But once we're in, we need to store our coats and get out in about thirty seconds in order to avoid detection."

"And from there, the Ice Chamber is only a few doors down the hall."

Soldiers Michael, Elijah, and Samuel turn to look at me in surprise, like they had forgotten I was even here. I have to fight my instincts to scowl at them. But if I am being honest with myself, I know they are not here for me. They're here for Ellie.

"He's right," Bryant agrees, "once we're out of the Coat Room, we'll only be a few paces away from where they're keeping the queen. But that will be when the real trouble begins. They will undoubtedly have multiple guards for her and the room where she's being kept." He looks at me. "Lawson's only goal will be to retrieve the queen. The rest of us will only help him if absolutely necessary because we will be taking care of any sirens that get in our way. Understood?"

A soft chorus of agreement comes from the group as we head out.

With Bryant in the lead and Soldier Samuel watching our backs, we make our way along the sapphire wall toward the door to the Coat Room. Bryant was right, no sirens are even standing guard by the small, unremarkable door. One by one, we all slip into the dark room. When we shut the door, the water begins to recede down the drain located in the middle of the floor. My instincts take over and I head straight to where the first gas lantern hangs.

As the light begins to glow, I see Soldiers Cade, Michael, and Elijah are already out of their coats and are looking for a cobweb-filled cubby to stash them. I don't dare look at whose cubbies are chosen, knowing whoever they are died long ago. Jensen and Soldier Samuel are working their way out of their skins while Bryant moves to turn up the light on another lantern a little farther into the room.

Ten seconds gone. Pulling my arms to my core, I push out of my coat and it drops to the floor. With a light thunk, Bryant's does the same. Without even having to think about it, I pick up my coat and walk it to the cubby with my name engraved above it. A small lump forms in my throat as I look to the next cubby over, where *Lorcan MacCallum* has been painted in a golden script. I can't even bring myself to look at my own name.

Twenty seconds gone. Movement to my right has me turning my head as the others gear up by the exit. Looking down at my own charcoal uniform and weapons, I make sure everything is in place as I rejoin the group.

"Alright men, this is just a small piece of what we have prepared our entire adult lives for," Bryant says to the group. He turns to face me. "Are you ready?"

I nod, ensuring I show no emotion other than strength when I give my response.

"Let's do it."

"Lawson, men, it's a pleasure to serve with you all. Let's go save our Queen."

Thirty seconds gone.

Waiting until there is only silence on the other side of the door, Bryant leads us single file out to the main hallway. Everything is familiar. The hallways are still an icy blue with ornate black sconces lining the walls, emitting a soft glow, giving the illusion of warmth. The floors are still encrusted with white marble that has been buffed to perfection. A faint scent of sea salt and citrus still lingers in the air. So many memories begin fighting their way to the forefront of my mind. I have to actively work to push them back and focus on the mission at hand.

Soldier Michael walks between Bryant and me for another layer of assault protection, but even with all of our combined military training, it's evident we are all sweating profusely from nerves. All swords are drawn, ready for whatever battle awaits us.

Walking quickly, we make our way down the hall. One more turn and we will be at the Ice Chamber's plain, unassuming door. Hugging the wall, Bryant pauses at the corner to listen. Just as expected, there is a siren on guard at the door, pacing back and forth. Only one.

Before Bryant can give the signal to attack, an ear-piercing scream shudders the chamber door. The siren shuffles back toward the door and bangs loudly on the thick wood. My muscles tense. There's only one person that could be.

Jensen slaps his hand to my mouth while Soldiers Cade and Elijah grab onto my arms. Jensen moves to my ear.

"I'm so sorry, Lawson. Bryant's orders if we hear her in pain. He knows you won't be able to think straight." My chest heaves as sweat begins pouring down my temple.

Another cry from Ellie cuts through the thick door and the siren on guard has decided she's had enough.

"Will one of you shut her up?" she hisses.

The sound of the door being thrown open echoes in the hallway, and I can hear Ellie crying clear as fucking day.

"She keeps thrashing."

"Then put her to sleep."

"She was asleep. The blades woke her and she keeps kicking."

"I thought Lillis snapped her ankle?"

"Well, she did. But—"

"Argh! If you want an Odin-damned queen bled out right, you have to do it yourself, Lillis!" The siren on guard goes into the Ice Chamber, slamming the door shut behind her.

Jensen and the others finally let go of me while red colors my vision. Bryant's eyes meet mine and he nods before giving the signal to the rest of the team. Within seconds, we reach the door.

"One," Bryant counts, looking each of us in the eye while I work to not barrel past him. "Two." We each raise our sword for the danger waiting behind the door. "Three!" He throws open the door and we rush the room.

I take a quick survey of the area and see there are only three sirens, all of which are sporting stunned looks on their unnaturally beautiful faces. Bryant and the soldiers waste no time getting to the sirens while Jensen shuts the door to help contain the noise, and hopefully help minimize the number of enemies we have to face. Then I see her.

Ellie is strapped down, lying unconscious on a giant block of ice in nothing more than her jeans, socks and a thin white camisole.

Large tubes are connected to each of her limbs, leading to the floor. At the base of each tube is a pool of red blood with something else beginning to mix itself in. Following the additional lighter substance's path, shock fills my chest as I see it's coming from the tubes.

Blood. White blood. Selkie blood.

She's done it.

My eyes begin to water at the thought of Ellie finally being a part of my kingdom. Of our kingdom. But my pride for my wife will have to wait until we make it out of here alive.

Rushing forward, I rip the first tube and needle from Ellie's arm, effectively waking her as she lets out a bloodcurdling scream, matching the siren shrieks happening behind me. Ellie begins to flail as much as her restraints will let her. I quickly envelope her in a hug and gently pet her hair.

"Shh, shh. Ellie, baby. It's me," I coo.

Sobbing, she finally calms while everyone else rages in battle all around us. And when I pull back, there's only her.

"Lawson?" Her dirty, clawed, tear-stained face breaks my heart. Red, puffy eyes frantically search mine. I choke back my own sob at her current state.

"Yeah, baby, it's me. Lie still while I get these things out, okay?" I beg.

She nods and I set to work removing the rest of the tubing. When I get to the restraints, my hands begin to tremble from the anger coursing through my body. Jensen joins us and unravels the knots in the straps holding her down for me. If I didn't need to get Ellie out of here as quickly as possible, I would murder all of these fucking sirens myself for what they've done to her.

While Jensen finishes up, I look around the rest of the room to find two beheaded sirens with mangled vocal cords and black, bloody holographic scales strewn across the floor. I don't think any of us could tell you which vocal cords went to which siren even if we wanted to. The third siren is backed into a corner with four swords pointed at her throat. But something hanging from her hand catches my eye.

"She has Ellie's token," I bellow.

Bryant turns to me wide-eyed before turning his gaze back to the siren's hand. Regripping his sword, he takes another step toward her.

"Ah, King Lawson. So wonderful to finally meet you." A sinister smile spreads across the siren's face.

"I'm afraid I cannot say the same of you."

"Shame, though I can't say I am all that surprised. The older selkie generations fill the younglings with all kinds of terrible thoughts of our kind. Your wife and I did have a nice chat about you, though."

"Do not speak of her." I instinctively take a step toward Ellie, who is being examined by Jensen.

The siren's grin slowly fades and her eyes narrow, focusing hard on me.

"I must admit," she says, feigning disinterest, "I am rather surprised to find you here. We have watched you with her since she arrived in town, and you always did seem rather—"

"I said, do not—"

"Disinterested in her." The siren tilts her head at me. She crosses her arms and I know she's dangling Ellie's token in front of me.

"What did you say?" I ask, rearing my head back. But I don't get my answer.

Cade lunges forward, putting his sword directly through the siren's throat. Her shrill laughter fills the room until he twists his weapon, effectively severing her vocal cords. The dead siren drops Ellie's token and Bryant races forward to grab it.

"Why the fuck did you just do that?" I roar, seething. I grab Cade with both hands by the shirt and shove him hard up against the wall. A piece of hair falls into my eyes, obstructing my view of the little fucker.

"Because," he spits at me, "she's one of them. She was going to die anyway."

"She was about to give us what could have been valuable information. Don't you care about that?"

"She killed John!"

"No, she didn't—"

"By extension, she did. She's evil, just like the rest of them."

"You don't kill any—"

"Gentlemen," Bryant's authoritative voice cuts through our argument. "Now is not the time. Let's get everyone to safety first, and then we will deal with this." He levels Cade with a stern look.

I let go of Cade's shirt and take a step back, looking at the black blood all over the floor. White blood mixes in spots from injuries Soldiers Elijah and Michael sustained, but other than that, everyone else is still alive.

A small, soft hand touches my arm. Waves of calm radiate through me before I even turn to look at her.

"Lawson?" Her soft voice is void of quivers, helping with my mental state knowing she's okay. Turning to face my wife, I bring my hand up to cup her face and touch her forehead with my own, closing my eyes.

"I thought I'd lost you," I whisper to her.

"You'll have to try harder than that to get rid of me."

A nearby throat clearing pulls us back to the situation at hand. Jensen steps up beside her, helping hold her steady. My brows knit tightly together as I frown in confusion.

"Sir, her ankle. She can't walk on her own," he says.

I look down to find her favoring her right foot. Even through her socks, I can clearly see it's about three times its normal size and resting awkwardly on the ground.

"Fuck, Ellie," I croak as something between rage and dread fill my chest.

"Lawson, we need to leave. Now." I meet Bryant's gaze and see him holding Ellie's token. Next to him, Soldier Elijah holds Ellie's coat in his hands, ready to go.

I nod to Bryant and look back at Ellie, only to find her already looking at me. Without wasting another moment, I scoop Ellie into my arms, relishing the feel of her body against mine.

Bryant and Jensen lead us out the door and down the hall. We quickly slip back into the Coat Room, which is just as we left it. Setting Ellie down, I help Soldier Elijah get her coat ready.

"But my token," she says as she points to Bryant's hand.

"Here, this should work until we can have the Sea Witch, erm, reattach it." He makes quick work of tying the necklace around her wrist. Sure as shit, her coat begins to glow. "Of course, you may not need her help now," Bryant grins at her.

Ellie tilts her head in confusion at him.

She doesn't know about her blood.

"We'll explain later, El. For now, I'll help you swim while you're in your coat. Your ankle will affect your ability." She groans at me in response, eliciting a chuckle from the others in the room.

When her coat is on and she's waiting by the door, I quickly slip my own coat back on. The door to the Atrium is opened and I take my wife's foreflipper as water floods the room.

"Ellie, you good?" I ask hesitantly. My wife nods in response. "Good. Stay with me. We'll get you out of here, baby. I promise."

Bryant and the others slip back into the Atrium, following the wall the same way we came in. Word clearly hasn't made its way through the castle yet about Ellie being gone. Above us, sirens continue shuffling around, talking excitedly. When we reach where Soldier John's remains lie, I take her foreflipper and pull her along as quickly as I can. She may be the strongest woman I've ever met, but that doesn't mean she has to see every bad thing our oceanic world has to offer.

We finally make it back to the lower corridor and through the exterior door to the dark waters outside the castle. When we're all outside and the door is sealed behind us, I guide Ellie to the ocean floor with the rest of the team.

"Lawson?" Ellie's voice cuts through the murky water.

"Yeah, baby?"

"Thank you." Her words stop me and I turn to face her.

"Ellie, you don't have to thank me. I will always come for you. Always." *Because I love you. You mean everything to me.*

Ellie nods, and something in the look she gives me causes my heart to pick up speed at all the possibilities.

CHAPTER 22

Ellie

"**H**OW MUCH FARTHER TO THE BASE?"
I try to keep my voice as light and unburdened as possible. But on the inside, I'm ashamed to admit how thankful I am that the scary siren sisters knocked me out for this obnoxiously long swim. On top of the distance in general, my ankle is killing me. Trying to keep up without showing how much pain I'm in may be quickly coming to an end.

"We're not going to the Base, Your Highness," Soldier Michael calls from behind me.

"What?"

On my right, Lawson somehow manages to look determined, even in his seal form. He hasn't left my side since we made it out of the castle. With my ankle affecting my hind flipper, I'm swimming much more slowly than I would like. And I've seen him swim at full speed. I know going this slowly must be driving him crazy. He looks over our shoulders at Jensen, who's been watching my six.

"How's her flipper responding?"

"The queen is perfectly capable of speaking for herself, sir. She's proven that multiple times." A chorus of snickers surrounds us from the others. Lawson glares back at me.

"I am fully aware of her capabilities, Jensen. I'm asking for a truthful analysis. If I ask her, she will lie and say she is completely fine so I don't worry about her." His gaze shifts to me and, I swear if seals could blush, he does.

He worries about me.

The thought makes my insides do flippy things and my letter comes to mind, still sitting there in the desk drawer in our room.

"She's definitely favoring the right hind flipper. And it is important to note that she has been slowing down over the past few miles." I turn around to glare at him, the little fink. Even propelling forward in the dark water, he visibly shrinks away from me. "I'm sorry, Queen Ellie. But King Lawson scares me more than you do."

Lawson lets out a barking laugh. My glare softens at the sound.

"I suppose I can let you off the hook for helping loosen up my husband, then." Lawson grins over at me. "So anyway, why are we not going to the Base and where are we actually going?"

Bryant stops in the lead, along with the rest of the group. The morning sun casts light down through the blue-black waters, reflecting off his serious eyes as he swims back to me.

"Queen Ellie, we cannot return to the Base for the time being."

"Why not?" He takes a deep breath and my pulse starts to hammer.

"Shortly after you were taken and it was discovered you were gone, a small group of us readied to retrieve you from the sirens." He looks over to Lawson, whose grin has faded and is staring hard at the ocean floor. "When we got ready to leave, several sirens came onto our shores and began wreaking havoc in the village. It was clearly a diversion so that we wouldn't yet notice you were gone. And while our military was able to take down the sirens with swift efficiency, our numbers and resources did take a hit.

"No ..." I breathe, shaking my head.

"We made the executive decision to evacuate the island. The sirens know of our whereabouts. Nothing is stopping them from hurting more of our people now, and we need time to regroup. Lawson told us of your former employer and the extensive housing and land available past the town where you met ... and that she will be out of town for quite a while. It is there that our people have sought out shelter. Other than those of us here, all other survivors are already on the mainland. Hopefully, the human woman will be away long enough that we will not have to ... deal with her ..."

I look around at the other men with us. Each of them have grim looks covering their faces as their eyes remain downcast. When my eyes reach Lawson, I see a look of angered determination in the eyes looking back at me. I nod, looking back to Bryant.

"Isla's land has plenty of privacy and should remain vacant for several weeks."

"That's what I told them," Lawson says softly. "I thought it might be best to go somewhere familiar and safe while we figure out our next steps."

My foreflipper finds his and I hold onto it as best I can without hurting him. The little claws are something I'm still not quite used to.

"It was a great idea." I offer him a soft smile before turning back to Bryant.

"Okay, so to the mainland, then?"

"Yes, Queen Ellie. It's only a few more miles until we reach the shoreline and then we'll head inland toward the moors."

"Well," I narrow my eyes at Bryant, "let's get going then." A squeeze of my flipper makes me look to my husband, who is beaming at me.

By the time we reach the beaches, I am barely holding up my "my ankle is completely fine" act. And Lawson knows it. When the water is shallow enough and we can make out the sky above us, the man is literally just pulling me along beside him.

The foggy beach is completely deserted, and we take advantage of the privacy to strip out of our coats. After I crawl out of mine, Soldier Michael arrives by my side and scoops it up. My face flushes from embarrassment.

"Oh, Michael, you don't have to do that."

"Your Highness, it is an honor to serve you. I am happy to help however I can."

"Oh, um, well. Thank you. I really appreciate it." He gives me a warm smile before heading off to join the others as they begin walking away from the water. Suddenly, warm breath coats my ear.

"You've certainly managed to charm all of them, Queen Ellie." Lawson's breath tickles my ear as he speaks. "Except maybe Bryant, but he's a tough nut to crack." I laugh as I find his arm with my hand to help steady me. He frowns down at me and pauses before drawing me up into his strong arms.

"Lawson, put me down!" I exclaim. He quickly obliges, setting me in front of him. My fists find my hips as he crosses his arms.

"Walk."

"What?"

"You don't want me to carry you, so you must be able to walk just fine on your own. So go ahead." He smirks at me, waiting. I purse my lips and stare at him through narrow eyes. No man has ever carried me and we are sure as shit not about to start now. But a blush starts to creep across my cheeks at the mental image of my big, strong husband carrying me across the misty moors. Straight out of a freaking romance novel. Eager to put a stop to that image, I square my shoulders as I look him in the eye.

"Fine," I huff. Putting one foot in front of the other, I take exactly three steps before I stumble, thanks to my broken ankle. Just as I'm about to fall on my ass, Lawson grabs me mid-fall and holds me upright, facing him. "Fine!" I bellow.

Chuckling, he pulls me back up into his arms and propels us forward. As I rock against his chiseled body, I fold my arms across my chest to match my frown. He only laughs harder when my loose hair whips him in the face, making my lips quirk up involuntarily. But a thought catches me off guard as I reach up to tame my wild mane. I frown up at him.

"Lawson, it's freezing." His head rears back and he frowns back at me.

"You're cold?"

"No, that's just it." I shake my head. "I know the temperature here is literally hovering around freezing and I'm ... not ... cold ..." He smiles down at me sheepishly.

"Well, you're a selkie now. Do you not remember when we rejoined the village? You needed about eight hundred blankets and were confused when I didn't need any?"

"But even when I was training, and then yesterday, on the beach with the sirens," his grip on me tightens at the mention of them, "I had to wear a sweater because—my sweater, where is it?" Panic takes over as I begin patting my husband on the chest, like Caitlin's sweater is hidden somewhere in his shirt.

"The purple one? Uh, well, it's not really wearable anymore." His confusion about my attachment to the sweater is written all over his face. All the color drains from mine.

"What do you mean?"

"The sirens shredded it. And besides, the scraps are all ... bloody." He shrugs. As his eyes search my face for some indication of what's going through my head, I feel it. The tears start to well up and my husband becomes blurry. His eyes widen in alarm and begin darting back and forth, trying to come up with something useful to say. "Uhh, I mean, we can, erm, get you another sweater. Y'know, if you're cold. Which you just said you aren't. But maybe you kind of are?"

My hands cover my face while I try to get my tears under control. If there's anything to be thankful for, it's that the rest of the guys are too far ahead to witness this embarrassing display.

"No, I'm ... not cold," I sniff. More tears. And now I think some snot has gotten involved. This is just the impression I want to make in front of the man I love, who may or may not love me back. Fabulous.

"Is, uh, purple your favorite color ... or something?" My poor husband.

"That ... was Caitlin's ... strength sweater," I explain through snot-infused sniffles. "She gave it ... to me," a deep breath to keep from hyperventilating, "for when I ... needed to be strong." Wiping my nose with the back of my hand, I lean my head on his chest. I don't want to see the pity I know is on his face. His silence is bad enough.

"Ellie," he whispers.

"Please, don't." I sniffle again before closing my eyes and fall asleep to the sway of his steps.

When I wake, the room around me is familiar. I may have only been gone a week, but I don't think I could forget the oddly specific furnishings of Isla's home even if I tried. Light floods the room. Looking around, surprise registers as I find all of my belongings in an open bag on the floor near the bed I am currently occupying. Looking down, I see I'm wearing my favorite flowery pajamas. The old, tattered T-shirt and shorts combo I told myself I wouldn't bring on this trip, but Caitlin took pity on me and packed them anyway. Before I can dwell too long on my friend, I twist a little more and see the nightstand littered with my book, my favorite EOS lip balm, and a golden bangle bracelet I don't recognize. Picking it up, an inscription on the inside catches the light. I frown, realizing it's not in English or Spanish, so I can't read it. If I'm being honest, it reminds me of a bracelet version of the One Ring in the *Lord of the Rings* franchise.

Pulling my lips in, I shift to a sitting position under the too-heavy covers. When I was still only a human, this comforter's weight was perfect for the bitter cold that seeped in through the old glass in the windows. Now, it's almost suffocating. I turn the bracelet over in my hand, looking for any indication that Sauron may be spying on me and is actually working for the Siren Queen.

Movement and hushed voices outside the door tears my attention away from the bangle.

"When will she wake up?" Lawson sounds strained, tired.

"I'm afraid I cannot say, Your Majesty." Jensen's voice comes through the door. I tilt my head to listen. "She sustained some minor head injuries, there are the embalming-like tube entrance wounds to consider. And then, of course, there's her ankle that has to heal correctly. That siren did a number on it."

A growl rips through Lawson and I can easily picture Jensen flinching away.

"So you're telling me there is nothing else we can do? To know if she's okay?"

"Your Majesty, the queen is a strong woman. Her mind and body have been through so much. I'm not a betting man. But if I were, I would bet on her." Jensen pauses.

I can imagine the knowing look he's giving Lawson. It would be the same one I got on my first full day with the selkies. when he gave me a health exam, when I lied and said I had never been pregnant.

"That being said," he continues, "we did use the remaining bottled serum from the Sea Witch on her head wound and her ankle. We will have to wait to see how far that got us."

"Does she need to wear an ankle brace or anything? What about the wounds from the tubes?"

"A brace, for the next several days at least, is not a bad idea, no matter how her ankle looks when she wakes. I will put one on her shortly. King Lawson," he seems to hesitate with whatever he plans to say next, "she will live to fight the Siren Queen, do not doubt that. But you must prepare yourself for any injuries she may sustain in the process."

"Fine," Lawson's voice is hard. Even I wince hearing it, and it wasn't aimed at me. "Can I please just get back to my wife now?"

The doorknob creaks and a wave of panic washes over me. Am I still supposed to be asleep? Should I be touching this bracelet that's obviously not mine? Are these pajamas too ugly to be seen by anyone other than my closest friend? I hastily shove the bracelet under my pillow as the door opens and Lawson and Jensen enter the room.

Lawson skids to a stop just past the doorway when he sees I'm awake, causing Jensen to crash into his broad back.

"Ellie!" Lawson's voice comes out a few decibels louder than necessary, making me wince. Surprising me, he rushes to the bed and proceeds to sit down. Cupping my face with both of his hands, he leans his forehead to mine. "Oh, thank Odin." Pulling his head back, his excited eyes roam my face while his fingers tenderly probe the back of my head.

"Um, Your Majesty. May I?" Jensen appears beside him. A blush covers my handsome husband's face as he moves to sit on the other side of the bed.

Just like my husband, Jensen gently probes the back of my head. Satisfied, he walks down to the end of the bed and lifts the blankets to reveal my ankle. I have to blink a couple times to make sure I'm seeing it right. My ankle only has some minor bruising with a little swelling. My jaw drops and the longer I look at it, the more questions I have.

"It's magic," my husband whispers beside me. I snap my eyes to his.

"What?"

"We've always kept a reserve of serum we extracted from the Sea Witch. Its properties ... they're—"

"Magic?" I finish. He nods his head and watches as Jensen tests the dexterity in my ankle. Each time I wince, Lawson's hand squeezes mine a little tighter.

"We used it a few different places," Jensen pipes in. "Your ankle, obviously. It's remarkable you were able to make it any distance at all." He slips on a tight black ankle brace and secures it in place. "Not very pretty, I'm afraid. But it will help." Moving back up to the head of the bed, he points to my injuries. "Your head and neck, as well. It looked like you had taken a couple of serious hits. If you feel dizziness or any typical concussion symptoms, definitely let me know. But I don't honestly expect you will." Jensen grips my shoulder and smiles warmly at me. "We are so glad you're back safe with us, Your Highness."

"That makes two of us," I laugh. As he picks up my arm closest to him, I realize he left something out. "What did you mean when you mentioned my neck?"

He points to my other wrist as an answer. And I take in a deep breath because I immediately understand. Reaching up my free hand, I lightly touch the base of my neck. My fingers hit the cold gemstones and find my token hanging from the necklace.

"How ..." I breathe. Beside me, Lawson shifts to take my hand from my token.

"I figured you probably didn't want to go see the witch again."

Not that it was, but if my love for this man had ever been in question, it sure as hell isn't anymore. If we were alone, I would tell him every word waiting on the tip of my tongue. I pull my hands from his and throw my arms around his neck, burying my face in his chest.

Lawson chuckles in response and I can feel the rumble in his chest against my cheek as I slide down his torso and back into my sitting position. Keeping my arms hooked around him, I gaze at this man who is beautiful inside and out. Without breaking our stare, he takes care of the only other obstacle in the room.

"Jensen, would you mind if I had a moment alone with my wife?"

"Of course, Your Majesty. Queen Ellie, please let me know if you need me." I move to slide my arms from around Lawson. But he stops me, holding them in place.

The door clicks shut behind him and Lawson finally releases my arms. Kicking off his shoes, he resituates on the bed so that he's comfortably facing me. His eyes flick over my ratty shirt and he blushes when he realizes that I'm watching him.

"Um, Mary Emma changed you. I wanted you to be comfortable and, based on the wear of these, they seemed to be your favorite, so ..."

"Lawson?" He swallows. I offer him a small smile as I cup his heated face with my hand. He leans into it and closes his eyes. A breath releases from deep inside him.

"Yes?"

"I need to tell you something." His eyes flutter open to reveal his crystal-blue eyes. A warmth lives there, and I feel a response deep within my core. He looks at me intently, waiting patiently for me to continue. So I just start. "Lawson, I love you. I—"

"I know."

"You know?" I don't bother to hide the shock in my voice. A smirk spreads on his beautiful face.

"Gabriel, um, led me to your letter. After the fight." Shifting slightly, he pulls the letter from his pants pocket. The letter I wrote only yesterday. "I read it. Obviously." He lets out a nervous laugh. "After a fight where I said absolutely terrible things. None of which

I meant in the least." Putting the letter on the nightstand, he scoops my hands into his. "Ellie, I'm so sorry. And I'll apologize every day for the rest of our lives, if that's what you need. Because I love you, too. So much more than I've ever known was even possible to love another person. You ... you were just supposed to be this human that came along and left once you were done with us. But I've known since our wedding night. I am so in love with you, Eleanor. And I want to stay by your side for as long as we both shall live. If you'll have me, that is."

Tears stream down my face as my husband says the most beautiful words I've ever heard. All the emotions rushing around inside me makes breathing become almost painful. An awkward laugh bubbles out of the back of my throat as he moves his hands to hold my face, using his thumbs to tenderly wipe away my tears. This wonderful man is my husband. I am his wife. And I want him to be my husband in every sense of the word.

"Lawson?"

"Yeah, baby?" Our eyes devour each other, taking in everything we can. Giving this moment a permanent home in our minds.

"Kiss me," I breathe. I don't need to ask twice.

His lips crash into mine, taking everything I offer.

My heart threatens to hammer its way out of my chest, and I feel the desire pooling deep inside. Despite all the love present between us, there is nothing tender about this. This is hungry, raw. Desperate from the weeks of tiptoeing around one another. This is pure need.

My mouth opens in a moan, giving him more access.

His hands begin to move down to my hips as he shifts to cover me, laying me down beneath him with the damn comforter still halfway between us. He traces each curve he comes to along the way, slowly, reverently. When his hands reach the lower edge of my top, they skim the visible sliver of skin, making me shiver in response. He grins against my lips, his closely trimmed beard tickling my chin. Keeping one hand on my hip, he brings the other up and sweeps my hair to one side. Slowly, he begins tracing kisses down my neck to my shoulder and back up again.

Moving the comforter to the side, I reach for his shirt and frantically set to work on the buttons. Finally reaching the last one, I drag his shirt out of his waistband. Leaning back from me, he makes quick work of removing his shirt and throwing it on the floor, his eyes never leaving mine.

My breathing becomes ragged, and I take the opportunity to sit up and discard my own shirt, tossing it to the floor with his. *While I'm at it, screw these shorts.* I shimmy out of my bottom layers and let them join our shirts on the floor.

Lawson lets out a choked, discordant laugh and I hear him undo his belt. I turn to watch him unzip his pants and shift to strip both them and his boxers off as he becomes just as vulnerable in this moment as me.

When my eyes meet his again, a warm blush spreads up my chest, all the way to my cheeks.

His pupils are blown wide, the blue irises barely visible as he rakes his eyes over me, taking me in. Reaching out both hands, his fingers lightly dance down the dip of my waist to the swell of my hips.

"You're so beautiful, Ellie," he breathes.

"Not so bad yourself, Your Majesty." My voice comes out rough, a stark contrast to my fingers that lightly trace his collarbone and chest. I look up at him from underneath my lashes and hold my lower lip between my teeth, all my nerves gone.

Lowering himself back down to me, he kisses me again, his tongue coaxing mine out to dance with his once more.

But this time, something changes.

All the urgency is gone, replaced with the tenderness of the love that now flows freely between us. Now, there is only us.

I bring my hands up to his hair, working them in tight while he presses me deeper into the bed, his body already slick with sweat from the sheer anticipation of us finally being together.

His knee moves to sit between my legs and my hips buck up to meet him. He groans in response, shifting until he's perfectly situated. Releasing a deep breath as he moves to kiss a trail down to my sternum, his hands roam over my body.

My back arches in response, wordlessly begging him for what we both know comes next. Taking in a ragged breath, I sweep a hand under his chin.

His dilated eyes lift to mine, holding a perfect balance of love and lust.

"You're sure?"

"Lawson, my love. I'm yours." I smile down at him and he breathes a sigh of relief.

"Oh, thank Odin." He moves above me, around me, within me, and we finally become one, never to be separated again.

CHAPTER 23

Lawson

I OPEN MY EYES TO A DARK ROOM AND MY BEAUTIFUL WIFE ASLEEP on my chest. Her naturally floral perfume cocoons us, swirling with the telltale scent of the love we've made together. Gently, I move out from under her and pray she doesn't wake. From what I've learned, she is quite the heavy sleeper. I'm proven right as I successfully get up from the bed and hear her give a light snore. A smile pulls at my lips as all the ways my life has changed run through my mind. Even if there is still some kind of hell coming for us, Ellie and I can take it. Together.

After putting my pants and shirt back on, I quietly slip out the door. The hallway is deserted and it causes my footsteps to echo in the long, empty space. It's only a short walk to the house's massive library and it's there that my feet take me now.

Libraries have always been my safe place, even as a child. If my parents ever sent my brother looking for me, he always knew to look there before anywhere else. When the church of Bettyhill took me in that night so many years ago, they asked about my strengths. I initially felt foolish telling him it was books. But when I got to take over the local library, it seemed like a decent way to bide my time while I searched the area for my coat. An added bonus was the apartment on the second floor. No more having to live in the church and accidentally overhear confessionals. If the locals knew what I've heard, they would never be able to look me in the eye again.

The fireplace in the dark library is roaring with life, but the temperature isn't altogether unpleasant. I unbutton my cuffs and roll up my sleeves for a little more comfort as I take a seat in one of the massive wingback chairs in front of the fire. The flames dance together, tall and strong, making it easy to get lost in thought.

A hand touches my shoulder and I about crap my pants.

"Fuck!" I gasp.

The hand withdraws quickly and I turn to see Ellie standing there in sweats from some university I assume she attended. I guess I should ask about that.

"I'm sorry, I thought you heard me come in." Ellie's wide eyes show the shock she tries to cover in her voice.

I rub my hands over my face and into my hair, shaking my head. "Too deep in thought, I guess." Taking her hand, I pull her into my lap and cradle her in my arms.

She looks up at me with a lazy smile.

I can't help myself from kissing her, because now I know that I can anytime I want. And I do want to. All the time. Giving her a moment to breathe, I pull back in time to see a beautiful pink tint paint over her cheeks.

Ellie raises a hand to tuck a stray hair behind my ear, letting her hand slide down the side of my face. When she reaches my trimmed beard, she gives a light scratch that feels incredible. It's safe to say I've never had anyone scratch my beard but me, and I could certainly get used to it. A soft laugh escapes her lips at my apparent enjoyment of the small motion.

Capturing her hand in mine, I press it to my lips before moving it back down to her lap.

"Why are you awake? Are you alright?" Her voice is laced with worry, her brows knitting together. But the question makes me laugh.

"Are you kidding? I got to have sex for the first time, and with my beautiful wife that I've been in love with most of the time that I've known her. And now I'm all cozied up by a fire with her in my lap. I'm definitely better than alright, love."

"For the first time?"

I look down to see confusion written all over her face and I realize my mistake.

Ellie didn't know I was a virgin. Odin's bony ass.

Mortified by my accidental confession, I look around the room for literally anything to distract myself. Or her. Like maybe the house is on fire. Who really knows? I honestly don't know which is hotter, the fireplace in front of us or my face at this moment.

"Lawson, are you telling me that you've really never had sex before, well, any of those times earlier?" She taps on my chest because I'm still looking for something weird to distract her. "Honey?"

My eyes snap to hers. It's the first time she's called me anything other than my name.

One of her hands lands on my chest while the other moves to snake around my neck. Pulling herself up, she plants a soft kiss on my parted lips.

I offer her a timid smile, doing my best to not feel awkward.

"It's okay, y'know? I just figured you had." She shrugs. Her eyes never leave mine and I can feel the sincerity in them.

My hand that's not holding her rubs the back of my neck and I let out a low chuckle. "I guess being a loner in a small town without many prospects, always looking for something that would make anyone else think you were insane, on top of being a ..." I tap my lips a couple times, trying to recall her words, "a 'stupid, arrogant, egotistical asshole' doesn't really make me a hot commodity on the dating scene."

Ellie tips her head back and gives a full belly laugh.

I grin like an idiot. If I can make her laugh like that for the rest of our lives, I won't need anything else.

"I guess it did come out something like that, huh?" Taking my free hand in hers, she plays with my fingers. "But, y'know, I definitely meant it, at the time. You weren't being very nice. Especially if you knew who I was!" She feigns annoyance at me, and I love every moment of it.

I shrug. "I guess I was annoyed."

"At me?"

"No, at all the other men in the pub."

Ellie raises her eyebrow in question.

"That night, the pub was absolutely buzzing with talk of the two beautiful women who had traveled in. I didn't know it was you, yet. Just someone." I look down at our intertwined fingers, thinking of how to say what comes next. "When I first saw you, I knew immediately who you were, like I told you the day we made it to the Base. All the drawings over the years were pretty spot on in likeness. But you looked so sad, content to sit by while your friend handled all the attention. All of those years, I thought I might just be able to talk to you if you were the happy woman depicted for the past several centuries. So when I finally saw you, I panicked. And apparently, I didn't come across very friendly." I smirk at my wife while she listens intently.

"Definitely not," she laughs.

"So anyway, I tried to convince myself I didn't care if you took care of ... other ... needs while you were here. But now I had a problem."

"Other needs?"

"Graham Brightley?"

Her eyes widen at his name when she realizes where I'm going with that. "Graham and I never did anything, just so you know."

I don't want to admit out loud how relieved I am at her statement. So I just nod, hoping she doesn't ask a follow-up question.

"Your problem?"

"What? Oh," putting my thoughts back together, I pick up where I left off, "my problem, right. So, I guess I had, uh, a couple problems, really. First, I still didn't have any idea where my coat was. And if you'll recall from the book I gave you—"

"'A selkie can't return to their home in the sea without their coat,'" she quotes. "I'll admit, I did always wonder why you specifically mentioned selkies. They're—we're—kind of off the beaten path as far as mythological creatures go."

"Right, so I had to make sure you looked them up. Which led to my other problem," I grin at her, "you certainly didn't like me after our introduction and now I had to convince you to help me. So,

I had to start showing up in places I knew you might be. Like the coffee shop."

Ellie frowns, contemplating this.

"How could you have known I would be there? I didn't even know I would be there until nearly two a.m. the night before."

"I was actually still out at the beach then. When I was walking back to my apartment, I saw you. With Graham." Fuck, I sound like a stalker. Her blank expression does nothing to help my self-esteem here, either. "To be clear, I turned around and walked the other way, but Graham saw me when he was driving home and told me about your plans for the next morning. Then I just had to snag you before he got there." I shrug nonchalantly. "I may have paid a few people to hold him up at his booth so I could beat him to the coffee shop."

Ellie's eyebrows shoot up in surprise, but I can't quite tell if it's in a good or bad way.

"When you were drooling over the ice cream case—in nearly literally freezing temperatures, I might add—I figured I had the perfect in to get you to talk to me." I give her a moment to process all the information I just vomited into her lap.

For the next couple of minutes, Ellie just looks at me, blinking occasionally. If I didn't know she loves me, I would seriously be worried for my life right now.

Finally, the tension in my chest inspires me to say something. I shift uncomfortably in the chair, moving her with me.

"Uh, El, could you, y'know, say something?" Relief floods my system as she smiles and slowly shakes her head.

"My mom always did say the way to my heart was through my stomach. Even though that's supposed to be true for men," she laughs.

"So does that mean ice cream will always get me out of trouble in the future?"

She chuckles, hopping off my lap as I waggle my eyebrows. Walking toward the closest bookshelf, she cranes her neck to look at the higher shelves.

Without a single thought, I get up to follow, her pull to me magnetic. Wherever she goes, I will go. When I reach her, I instinctively find her hand with mine. My eyes follow hers as she scans the shelves. She almost seems to be looking for something specific.

Feeling her disappointment, I frown, unsure of what she's looking for. In a place this big, it could be anything. "Are you looking for something in particular?"

"Uh, not really."

"Did I say something wrong?" Maybe I said something to upset her?

She shakes her head, but hesitates so long before answering, I wonder if she will answer at all.

I squeeze her hand for extra encouragement.

"Just thinking about the future is scary, is all." She releases a deep breath, raking a hand through her sloppy ponytail.

So my comment about the future upset her? If possible, I'm now more confused than before.

Ellie begins walking along the length of the library, dragging me along by the hand like a distracted puppy on a leash.

"Anything in particular about the future? Because if it's about kids, well, we've already proven we can do what it takes to make them." My comment pulls a smile to her soft lips.

"I guess it's more about what happens ... after."

"After ..."

"After the queen is slain and we find our new 'normal', if you will."

My jaw tenses as I recall our conversation before, well, everything. The future was the last thing we talked about—fought about. Tension begins to take over my chest at how everything ended. And for how I don't want it to go this time.

"Look, Ellie, all those things I said—"

"I know, you already—"

"No, I apologized, but there's so much more I need to say. Let me? Please?" I beg.

She nods reluctantly.

"First, I want you to know how incredible you truly are." I turn her toward me, taking both of her hands in mine. "You took your position in our kingdom in stride, you married someone you initially didn't even want to tolerate, and started training to kill fucking sirens, literally one of the most dangerous creatures in the sea. And let's not forget what you went through just to get your coat in addition to being stuck in matrimony with my dumb ass." A soft giggle escapes her lips and I can't help but grin. "Eleanor MacCallum, you are the most incredible woman. Everything I said during our fight," I don't miss how her face falls at the mention of our harsh words to one another, "I didn't mean any of it."

"None?" Her voice is laced with sorrow and it spears through my heart.

"Not a single word. I was angry about a terrible meeting with the war council I had just left, that noblewoman Esme has asked for me about three times a day since we returned for the stupidest shit, and—"

Ellie tenses at the mention of the noblewoman. She watches me raise my eyebrows and sighs. "While I've definitely heard others voice their concerns about me and my ... capabilities ... After I made it out of the castle, I overheard Esme talking with one of her friends. I didn't see who the other woman was, or anything, bu—"

"What was said, Ellie?"

"Oh, um, just more not so great things about me."

I bring one of my hands up to pinch the bridge of my nose, closing my eyes. "Ellie, what exactly was said to you?"

"Well, it wasn't said *to* me, to be exact ..."

"Ellie."

"She basically said she figures I must have been a whore during my human life but that she's been trying to cozy up to you because you'll probably get rid of me anyway, and because you're only stuck with me temporarily. Then her friend told her not to give up because, if anything, she could probably get some good sex out of you. Which I can now attest to."

"WHAT?" My vision goes red. Dropping Ellie's hands, I start toward the door. I sure didn't know what she was doing. But Esme's shit ends now.

A small hand grabs my arm and tries to spin me around. There's no way she could physically overpower me, so I help her out by turning in the direction she pulls.

My teeth grind together. I have to work to keep my fists at my sides and not find a wall to put them through. But looking at Ellie and feeling her touch helps my rage start to simmer. Only a little.

"Lawson, please," she pleads, "please, don't make a big deal about this."

"It's not ok."

"I know it's not okay, but we also don't need to make it any wor—"

"There is no way in hell she gets away with saying that shit to her fucking Queen, Ellie."

"Remember, she didn't say it *to* me, just *about* me."

Blinking a couple times, my fists find my hips while I turn Ellie's statement over in my mind before giving up. "What does that mean?"

"Well, when she said it, I overheard her. Because, uh, I was," she wrings her hands together nervously, "uh, sitting down. Where she couldn't see me."

"You were sitting where she couldn't see you?"

"Yes."

"Where?"

"What do you mean?" Ellie tilts her head at me, pinching her brows together.

"Where were you sitting that she couldn't see you when she said ... those things?"

"Oh, behind a rock."

"You were sitting behind a rock," I repeat, still trying to grasp what my wife is telling me.

"Yep."

My fury turns into confused, simmering rage. I try to picture Ellie sitting behind a rock listening to terrible things from an equally terrible woman, but it doesn't compute. "Um, baby, why were you sitting behind a rock to begin with?"

"Uh, because I heard someone coming and I didn't feel like

talking to anyone yet. This was after I yelled at the poor guard at the door to let me out because you had given orders that I wasn't to be let outside unaccompanied."

"For obvious reasons," I point out.

"Yes, well," she looks down to her hands, "I see that now."

Even though I would still love to hand deliver Esme to the sirens, I close the remaining distance between my wife and me. Cupping my hands around her delicate face, I lift it just enough to encourage her to look at me.

Her warm amber eyes search my face for any remaining signs of anger and I hope to Odin she finds none. Because in this moment, nothing else matters other than her.

I press my lips softly to hers. As I move to deepen the kiss and fully wipe away those terrible words from her memory, the sound of the door opening echoes throughout the room.

"Oh!"

Ellie and I turn to see Gabriel standing in the doorway in his brown everyday robes, arms full of books. I let go of Ellie's face and take her hand in its place. I raise an eyebrow to Gabriel and he seems to gather his thoughts while he walks further into the room.

"Ellie, it is so nice to see you up and around. You were in a terrible state when you arrived."

Beside me, Ellie shifts uncomfortably. Why, I'm not sure. I frown down at her.

"Um, yes. Jensen and Lawson told me they used a serum from the Sea Witch?"

"Ah ..."

Ellie flits her eyes up to meet mine, sensing Gabriel's discomfort with the witch. To my annoyance, she releases my hand. But she starts forward and makes her way to Gabriel, enveloping him in a hug. Seeing her with him makes my heart swell with pride. Just another way she has truly embraced our people and culture. From watching them, it's clear she holds a reverence for him. And he clearly adores her like a grandfather would. I make a mental note to ask Ellie about any remaining family members she may have as I watch her offer to carry some of Gabriel's books. A smile spreads across my face as I watch her selflessness at work. Speaking of ...

"Gabriel?"

"Yes, Your Majesty?"

I chuckle, not sure I'll ever get used to him calling me by my new title. "What punishment would you think fitting of someone who has spoken extremely ill of the queen?"

Gabriel's eyebrows shoot up. He looks to Ellie, who has her face hidden beneath one of her hands. But she can't hide the blush creeping up her neck.

"Please, ignore him, Gabriel—"

"Please, do *not* ignore me, Gabriel. I have recently learned of some heinous slander spoken of our Queen and I would like your input on proper procedures."

Gabriel looks between the two of us. A large grin takes over my face as my wife glares at me through her fingers.

"Well," he starts, "I have heard musings of doubt of the queen's abilities to complete her duties foretold within the prophecy ..."

"No, I'm talking about someone attacking her character, not her capabilities."

"Lawson!" If looks could kill, I'm pretty sure I would be toast right about now. But this is about her comfort in our kingdom, and right now, her comfort is at risk. And that's not something I'm willing to take a chance on.

Gabriel rears his head back in horror as I recount what Ellie told me about Esme and whomever her friend may be.

"That one's always been such a terror," he mutters. "And I would imagine her friend would be Joann. Those two have been inseparable since they were born. They're younger than you. And since you never really wanted anything to do with anyone, you never really bothered with them. Or anyone else for that matter." Gabriel laughs to himself and I watch as Ellie smiles at the sound. He turns to Ellie and takes one of her hands in his, patting it with the hand on top. "Don't you worry, dear. I will deal with it."

Ellie looks positively mortified and I stroll over to where they're standing so I can hold my wife. Locking my arms around her waist, I kiss her on the top of her head. "See baby? I told you it would be dealt with. I want you to be as comfortable within your home as possible."

To my relief, she returns the hug and presses her body into mine.

Gabriel whirls around to face us, eyeing us suspiciously. "So, you two," he points between the two of us, "are ... together?" His cautious tone makes me laugh, and I have to hold on tighter to Ellie so I don't accidentally knock her over.

"You do know we're married, right? Or is your age finally getting to you?"

Ellie playfully whacks me on the chest to shame me.

Luckily, Gabriel chuckles. "Oh, yes. I was there. I just meant, you've ... talked? And things are now out in the open?"

"Yep." Ellie pops her "p". "It seems my husband found the letter I wrote detailing my feelings for him."

Gabriel, the devious little devil he pretends not to be, doesn't even pretend to act embarrassed. Instead, he shrugs before grinning at Ellie. "I knew he needed a little push in the right direction, is all."

Ellie, my traitorous wife, grins right back at him.

Using any excuse to get the subject changed to anything other than me, I quickly think up a distraction.

"Did you know this is the room where my coat was hidden?"

Gabriel looks around the room and frowns.

"It's true, right over here," Ellie chimes in. She leads us to the fireplace and shows Gabriel the mechanism of the weathered hourglass. Just like the last time I was in this room, tilting the hourglass opens the hidden door on the opposite side of the fireplace, revealing the hidden room. "I would definitely recommend putting a stool in the doorway, just in case it tries to close on you or something crazy like that," she says.

And just like last time, something deep within me doesn't sit right. But whether it's the hidden room, the library, or this house, I still don't know.

Gabriel walks tentatively into the vault-like room.

Ellie and I watch hand in hand from the doorway.

"I'm going to assume this mess is from your coat, Lawson?" He carefully tries to step around the shards of glass sprinkled all over the floor.

"Yes. My token ... and my coat, just ... reacted ..."

Gabriel nods, lightly tracing the remaining edges of the casing that used to hold my skin. "It's not surprising, really. After so long apart from you, your coat would react violently."

"You've seen something like this before?" Ellie asks.

"No, dear. Just lore from the olden times."

Ellie nods.

I look down at her, in awe of how she takes everything in stride. She is already a brilliant ruler. Give her a little time in the role and she will rule the entire fucking ocean. Squeezing her hand, I lean down so my mouth is level with her ear. Lightly running the tip of my nose along its ridges, I breathe in her intoxicating scent.

"Just because I haven't said it in the past little while, I love you, my darling."

My wife blushes and turns her head to face me. My closeness must surprise her because she startles when her eyes meet mine.

I can't help the grin that comes across my face. After a moment, she regains any lost faculties.

"I love you too, husband," she breathes.

"You know," Gabriel calls from the other side of the cramped vault, "there are still a few hours before everyone else will be awake. We will need both of you in meetings on how to move forward with our plans. Especially given your inside knowledge, dear Ellie. So if there's anything you two need to take care of before then, I would suggest doing so now." He sends a knowing look our way and smiles.

Giggling like school children, my wife and I run to jump back in bed.

CHAPTER 24

Ellie

EVERY SINGLE PERSON IN THIS ROOM LOOKS ABSOLUTELY terrified of Lawson. Maybe not Bryant or Gabriel, but definitely everyone else. One older gentleman literally shakes in his chair whenever Lawson so much as looks in his direction. What was his name? Garren, I think? He looks like he's about to reduce down to a puddle any moment now. I briefly wonder what Isla would think of him. Now that is a woman who doesn't seem easily intimidated.

To everyone else's credit, Lawson looks like he wants to scalp someone. Glowering at whomever is speaking at any given time may be a little much. Especially because they're just trying to help us prepare for ... whatever comes next.

It must be the small amount of space available in this second-floor office that makes it feel so crowded with only eight of us packed in around the dark wooden table. We've pulled chairs from other rooms and they are all touching arms with the chair next to them. Not that I mind. It allows me to hold my husband's hand under the table without calling attention to it. To Lawson's right sits Gabriel, whose hands are also underneath the table where we can't see them. But I highly doubt he's holding Lawson's other hand.

I give Lawson's fingers a squeeze. I'm rewarded with one side of his mouth quirking up into a tiny smirk, but he tries to hide it by biting the insides of his cheeks. Pink slowly creeps up his neck and I can tell it is literal work for him to not turn to me and smile. I grin, rather liking this fun little game I've discovered.

Not wanting to give away his tenderness in front of everyone else, he lightly squeezes my hand back before letting go and moving his palm to my leg.

Suddenly, all I can think about is how grateful I am that no one can see through the table. A blush of my own taints my cheeks. Swallowing, I try to tune back into the conversation.

"Please, be reasonable. After all, we still think it will be best to attack from the boats, Your Majesty," Garren says.

My husband looks at him extremely unimpressed. Did this guy spit in Lawson's cereal or something? Hmm, I wonder if selkies even eat cereal.

"Even though we just successfully aided our Queen in escaping by arriving in the sea?" Lawson counters. "And we saw clear evidence that the sirens are not using the Coat Room, indicated by all the dust and cobwebs."

"What if we did a, sort of, split attack?" All heads in the room turn to look in my direction and I realize my mistake. "Um, that was definitely supposed to be in my head," I say, turning to look at Lawson for support.

The man is quite literally grinning at me. But the grin quickly fades when Bryant starts speaking.

"Queen Ellie, I don't—"

"Shut up and let her talk," Lawson whips his head to pin Bryant with his stare. "So far, there have not been any truly useful ideas proposed this morning. So if the queen wants to share an idea, you will all hear it." He looks blissfully back to me like he hasn't just threatened everyone in this room with some kind of fatal disease if they don't want to listen to me as I rank my favorite Broadway musicals in order. But at least his beautiful smile has returned.

"Okay ... Well, uh, what if we pull the best parts of what's been discussed and mesh them together?"

"'Mesh' them, Your Highness?" Garren gives me an amused look, which is quickly wiped from his face as he looks over at Lawson. What can I say? That man has a potent scowl.

"Now, Garren, don't be a stinker," I say sweetly. Laughter erupts from most of the other men in the room, even my husband, and fills the small office space. Bryant sits quietly in his chair, watching me. But I square my shoulders and look Garren straight in the eye. "But yes, I think we should consider attacking from two points of entry. I didn't have the privilege of watching what way I was brought into the castle. I only awoke in the room where I was tied down and bled."

Every man in the room shifts uncomfortably. Jensen, who sits to my left, leans toward me.

"Queen Ellie, you don't have to—"

I hold up my hand to stop him. "You're going to tell me that I don't have to make others uncomfortable with what happened to me. Well, if me discussing what sirens like to do with their captives is painful for them, then perhaps they shouldn't even be present in this room. What do you think?"

Jensen gapes at me before finally nodding.

Turning back to the others, I continue. "When Lawson and the others led me out of the castle, we went through a clearly unused room you all call the Coat Room. But the problem therein lies that now, reentering the castle that way may not be the surprise it once held for the sirens. You don't think, since they have undoubtedly noticed I was gone and all the bodies we left behind, that they haven't scoured every inch of the castle to figure how we got in? That they haven't noticed the Coat Room has been disturbed?" I turn to look at my husband.

Lawson watches me carefully. His face reminds me of the night we first met, when he looked like he was trying to solve some difficult equation but was missing a key piece of information.

The memory makes me smile.

Lawson's expression softens as mine does, not knowing he's the cause.

A strangled tension fills the air as the others watch our obvious display of affection, which is only fair. The last thing they all knew was that we had to get married simply because it was convenient, not because either of us had any kind of romantic feelings for the other.

"So, you're suggesting we find another route to the inside of the Lower Castle?" Soldier Michael leans forward on the table to get a better view of the maps spread out across it.

"Not exactly ... Was the route we took when we left the same as when you all entered?" I ask.

"Yes."

"And was it just as deserted as when we left?"

"Yes ..."

I nod, considering this. "Then, in that case, I think we should consider using the same, if not a similar, route into the Lower Castle. At the same time, we would have people enter the Upper Castle from the boats. Distract the sirens with the more obvious enemy while also infiltrating from underground. They seem to be very tunnel-vision creatures. They will be so focused on one group that they won't even see the other until it's too late."

Bryant shifts forward in his chair. "And just who would you have march to their deaths so the troops coming in from the Lower Castle would have a better chance at survival, Ellie?"

"Enough." Lawson's face is red as he looks at the High General. "She is your Queen and you will address her as such. Odin's bony ass, Bryant—"

"I'm sorry, Your Majesty, but I can't just sit here while she—"

"You can and you will."

I put a hand on Lawson's bicep to get his attention. "Lawson," I whisper. What I say next will be easier if only one of us has boiling blood. And it needs to be me.

The room is silent as Lawson continues to glare at Bryant while working to bring down his blood pressure. I don't speak until I know which one of us has the more leveled head.

"High General," I make sure my eyes are as steely as my voice, "I have seen your men train. I have had the unfortunate opportunity to see them in battle, even if what I saw was nothing compared to what is coming. And no, I am not naive enough to think we will all make it out. But you have seen to it that we will all have our best chance when the time comes."

Bryant slowly leans back in his chair, his jaw tense.

Beside me, Lawson turns in my direction. There is not one ounce of doubt on his face. He brings our newly intertwined hands to the table, showing everyone our unity.

"Obviously, the strongest fighters will arrive in the boats. But those with the most stealth will come up from underneath their feet. You have taught these men well, Bryant, and how to act as a unit. Do not doubt that. But now we need to use their strengths as individuals. I am sure you will step up to the plate to prepare them for that task, as well." I'm done with this.

Pushing my chair back, I stare at Bryant as I stand and turn to leave the room.

Murmurs fill the air behind me as I head to the door. A chair scrapes the floor and I hear Gabriel calling for order as the door slams shut behind me.

An arm snakes around my waist, whirling me around and straight into an enthusiastic kiss with its very handsome owner. One hand twists up into my hair, holding my head in place while the other presses me into his body. When I pull away, my heart rate is still pounding, but for a very different reason.

"You were brilliant, baby." Lawson grins down at me as he rests his forehead against mine.

"Because I yelled at Bryant?"

He chuckles and I feel the rumble in his chest radiate through my own. "No, not that it hurt anything, though. He needs to be put in his place every now and then." His hands slide on my body to meet in the middle, locking behind me and holding me to him. Crystal-blue eyes find mine, capturing my attention and my heart. "You gave solid advice, and you stood your ground when someone fought you on it. When you brought up something that made everyone else uncomfortable, you defended your words because you weren't bullshitting to make everyone happy, you were telling the reality. And I've never been more proud to call you my wife."

I rock forward on my tiptoes, planting a soft kiss on his lips. We disentangle ourselves and start walking down the hall. Taking Lawson's hand in mine, I guide us in the direction of the front door. A little fresh air would do us both some good.

"Now, just so you know, I do want Jensen to check on your ankle. But if he gives the okay, I want to take over your training. If anyone's going to teach my wife to be a kickass fighter, it's gonna be me."

Rearing my head back, I look over at him and raise my eyebrows in question. "Think I'll try to kill Bryant 'accidentally on purpose' or something?"

Lawson shrugs nonchalantly and grins back at me.

I frown, effectively surprising him.

"What is it? I don't really think you'll kill him, if that's what it is ..."

"No, no ... It's not that. Jensen, he said he used the last of that stuff from the witch, right?"

Lawson eyes me cautiously. "Yes ..."

"Well, what if we—"

He stops and, because we're tethered together, I take one more step before being pulled back to where he still stands in the foyer. "Oh, no, Ellie. I don't want you going near her again unless absolutely necessary."

"If that stuff really could heal my wounds that quickly, then I think it's really important that those fighting for our people's survival have access to it when we have to face the sirens again." I look hard at him, praying he gets that I mean business.

He gives me a pained look, remaining silent for several seconds. Running his free hand through his wavy hair, Lawson lets go of a deep sigh.

"How hard is it to get her to give up the serum stuff, anyway?" I ask.

"About impossible. The stuff we used had been given to us back when my great-grandparents were children."

"... Oh."

"Look, it's a good thought. But we can't even risk going back to the Base right now, let alone to see her."

I nod, feeling dejected. "You really don't think she would help us, do you?"

"I think she is only loyal to herself, and you have to be extremely careful when you ask her for favors. The witch is hundreds of years old and only gave our people your description and dress size after several years of offerings."

My eyes widen in response. "Wait, what?"

Lawson looks around the foyer before landing back on me and smiles. "Feel like some coffee and ice cream?"

When we make it to town, it's like we never left. But in reality, everything has changed. After swinging by Lawson's old apartment above the library for some money, we make our way hand in hand to the coffee shop. The familiar smells from those early days here bring so many emotions rushing forward. My love for Caitlin, the gut-wrenching ache I felt when I thought she left me, shyness and ease with Graham, disdain and confusion about Lawson. And to think there was so much happening that I didn't know.

Walking in public holding hands with Lawson MacCallum earns a girl many confused looks, as I'm finding out. Spending so much time with him—and falling in love with him—has made me forget that the people in this town where he found sanctuary consider him strange, an outsider. But the positive side of that is most people tend to leave him alone and now, by extension, me.

To my surprise, the shop is pretty empty this morning. No one waits in line to order and only a couple of the bistro tables are occupied. I would have figured people would flock to the warm coffee shop on such a bitterly cold day.

"Good afternoon," a young girl behind the counter greets us.

It's not the same young woman who was here that first day, but she has the same spunky attitude. They must be friends.

Her eyes widen at the sight of us, but I'm not sure if it's seeing Lawson, me, or Lawson and me together that surprises her.

I wave at her awkwardly while Lawson just frowns. Very on par for him. I go pick out a table while Lawson places our order. Simply hearing him order the mint chocolate chip ice cream for me makes my mouth water. I practically have to wipe the drool from my chin.

As he walks to our table and lets out a laugh, his warm-honey, wavy hair bounces with his body's movement.

I tilt my head, confused.

"You're looking at the ice cream like a person on some sort of drug. And you're drooling." He points to my chin.

Huh. Guess that wasn't in my head, after all. Wiping my chin, I shrug. "What can I say? You're the one that married a crazy person." I take a big spoonful of the sainted ice cream and shove it in my mouth. A satisfied moan escapes my lips.

Lawson raises a brow in question, looking completely perplexed at my sudden pleasure.

"Don't worry about it," I say, waving my spoon in front of my very full mouth. "But I have to say, never really being cold anymore is quite the star feature of being a selkie. Especially if it means I can eat all the ice cream I want and never have to worry about the temperature again."

"Glad to know being a selkie is such a dream come true for you."

I snort at his deadpan tone and expression before remembering our reason for leaving the property in the first place. "So you were, um, gonna tell me about the offerings?" I say around my mouthful of dessert. Looking at his plate, I see my husband has chosen an extremely oversized brownie for himself. Maybe he'll share.

Picking off a piece of the brownie, he nods his head and considers his response. He pops the piece into his mouth before finally picking up where we had left off.

"Right, so according to legend, when the Sea Witch had the vision of the prophecy, she gave over the general information willingly. But then she said she knew what the Savior looked like and, I guess, the selkies just went nuts because she didn't just offer up the information." He pops another piece of brownie into his mouth while I actively work to not drool over his plate. "So then, the selkies tried all kinds of things to win her favor. Gifts, offerings, that sort of thing. But none of it mattered to her, because she's fucking magic, so why would it?"

I nod my head in acknowledgement, encouraging him to continue. Talkative Lawson is rare, so I make it my mission to capitalize on it when it does happen.

"Well, one day, she told the Selkie King at the time, King Orion, what she required of him that would entice her to give him the information he desired. She wanted a private sanctuary to be located wherever our people would make their safe haven for when the events of the prophecy came about."

"The room where we went for the Acceptance Ritual?"

Lawson nods.

"King Orion didn't have any problem with that, so it was done. The problem was, the witch wouldn't hand over your description until the sanctuary was complete."

"How old is she?"

"Uh, no one really knows, exactly. I would guess at least a thousand years?"

Like the puffer fish I truly desire to be, I blow up my cheeks with air while I think about the fact that the witch could be a thousand years old. I suddenly feel guilty for saying my elderly neighbor, Mrs. Lanahan, was a thousand when I mentioned her at school one day. Little did I know, there were creatures roaming the sea that actually *were* that old. Swallowing the air back down, I look at Lawson so he'll continue.

"Naturally, King Orion pushed for the room to be completed as quickly as possible, but he died before it was finished. His daughter took over the throne and eventually completed the project and even began building the Base itself. When the witch finally gave her your description, she included your dress measurements, as well, but wouldn't tell them why. She just suggested they make you a wedding dress in addition to your coat."

"Wow, I bet that was a gut punch." I laugh at the idea of this poor Selkie Queen hearing she has to have a wedding dress made for a random girl that she may or may not meet.

Lawson laughs, taking a sip of his coffee.

"Why did you want to leave to tell me all of this?"

Looking down at the remaining brownie on his plate, a few moments pass before he says anything. "I guess it's just, what you're talking about wanting to do, with trying to get her to give us more serum ... it's really dangerous. The Sea Witch is an evil creature, serving no master but herself. I don't want you to think she's just there trying to help us. And if some of the people who already are ... concerned about you overheard, it would just give them more ammo against you."

I look over at the ordering counter while I consider this. But it makes sense. Anyone who has already lived in fear for so long wouldn't like what I'm suggesting.

"Ellie, I'm not saying we forget about this idea. But if it's something you're really passionate about, we just need to approach it the right way." Lawson pops another piece of brownie in his mouth. Then, that saint of a man ... selkie ... whatever, slides his plate over to me with a big grin on his handsome face.

I'm pretty sure the look I give him rivals any I've ever given to mall Santas over the years. Sheer adoration with a tiny bit of skepticism.

Lawson's laugh is the most beautiful sound I've ever heard.

"You're remarkably handsome, you know that?"

The man full-on blushes like I asked him to strip naked and dance for me. "Because I gave you the brownie?"

"No ..." My eyes narrow and I really look at him for a moment. And that's when it hits me. "I noticed it that first night. I've seen attractive men before, sure. But you're ... different. You're almost inhumanly attractive."

He leans in close across the table and whispers, "You know, technically, I'm not human. But then, neither are you anymore."

My eyes pop at the thought. Woah, intrigue.

"But I know what you mean. It's a selkie trait. We're ... this way ... to lure prey. Um, if needed." I feel like I probably shouldn't dwell on that thought too long, so I just nod. "Your looks changed some, too. When you accepted your coat. And then a little more in the Ice Castle."

Not really sure how to look at myself at the moment, I hold out my hands to examine them. Are my nails permanently painted? That'd be pretty cool.

Lawson glances at his watch and drains the last of his coffee. "If you're ready, there's something I think you need to see back at the property."

"Well, color me intrigued," I mutter, swallowing the last few drops of caffeinated goodness.

When we arrive back at the property, we head straight for the library. As much as I've bugged him the entire walk back, Lawson has held his ground on what this little surprise is. Perhaps now is a good time for me to tell him I don't like surprises. Walking through the door, I'm greeted by the sight of Gabriel, Bryant, Jensen, and two beautiful noblewomen, who I can only assume are Esme and Joann based on their looks of contrition.

I stop mid-step through the doorway, not really sure if I want to be here or not.

"Queen Ellie, I'm glad you're here. Esme and Joann have something they would like to say to you," Gabriel proclaims proudly.

Nope, I definitely do not want to be here.

Gabriel and Lawson fix the women with pointed looks and the two walk sheepishly toward me, stopping in the center of the room.

"Darling?" Lawson beckons me forward with him, standing much closer to the women than I would like to be. My eyes meet his, catching his waiting amusement.

Taking his proffered hand, I find myself with only a small distance between Esme, Joann, and myself.

"Your Majesty, Joann and I—", the redheaded woman starts.

"Do not address me. Address your Queen." Lawson's voice is hard. It matches the scowl he's giving them.

"Yes ... yes, Your Majesty," Esme says quickly, turning to me with downcast eyes. "Queen Ellie. Your Highness. Joann and I would like to formally apologize for all the things you heard us say that day ... And for everything we have said that you didn't hear." She elbows the other woman standing with her.

"Yes, Your Highness. We are so sorry," Joann chimes in. She nods so enthusiastically I briefly wonder if her head will pop right off.

Lawson releases my hand and throws his arm around my shoulder. Pursing his lips, he turns to look at me. "What do you think, baby? Is that good enough or would you like more? Personally, I wouldn't accept it. But then again, I've heard I'm not as kind as you are." He grins down at me.

The women blush furiously while they wait for my verdict. I grin back up at my husband before turning back to them, deciding to toy with them a bit.

Lawson squeezes me tightly into his side.

"I suppose it will do for the present. But if it should happen again, then we shall see what you mean by 'requiring more.'"

My husband and I share one more glance as the others in the room grin mischievously. Lawson looks back to our current annoyances. "You heard the queen. Now get out."

Esme and Joann hurry out of the library without looking back.

CHAPTER 25

Lawson

I'VE ONLY BEEN APART FROM ELLIE FOR THIRTY SECONDS AND my mood has already turned to shit. The tether attaching my heart to hers pulls more taut with every step I take in the opposite direction, even if she is only with Jensen and Mary Emma working on rehabbing her ankle. Irrational as it may be, I wish I could be the one helping her. But if there is anyone else I would trust with the job, it would be Jensen. He's only younger than me by a couple of years, but I remember him always trying to care for wounded animals he would find. Given his nurturing tendencies and the fact that his father was a medicine man, the career choice certainly isn't a stretch.

And Mary Emma, I swear to Odin that woman would skewer me alive if she thought Ellie was so much as annoyed at me. Even as kids, she never really seemed to care much for me. And it wasn't like she just didn't like me. Like everyone else, she just preferred Lorcan. But either way, I know Ellie's in good hands with that one.

"Your Majesty." A nobleman whose name I can't remember nods as we pass one another in the hall.

I nod back politely, but don't bother removing the frown set on my face. My lips purse while I rack my brain trying to think of that guy's name. Ellie would know it. Maybe I should have her go through flashcards with me. That's what humans do to learn things, right?

Several more people pass by as I make my way through the insanely large estate, but most of them don't bother acknowledging me. Climbing the stairs to the second floor, I hang a right toward the smaller bedrooms and come to the door I set out to find, knocking lightly on it. I wait for a response on the other side, dread spreading through my stomach for the conversation I'm about to have.

A wet-haired Bryant opens the door and eyes me curiously as he works on buttoning his shirt cuffs. Like myself, he has always leaned more toward a formal style of dress. Given our positions now, I guess it's a good thing we prepared when we were younger.

"May I come in?"

He nods shortly. Apparently he's very aware of why I'm here. He shuts the door behind me as I make my way into the dark, tiny bedroom. Even though it's nearly ten in the morning, the curtains are drawn from last night's sleep and the only light seeps in from the en suite, whose door is wide open. Steam seeps from the bathroom and into the bedroom from a recent shower, making it feel at least ten degrees warmer in here than the rest of the estate.

"Mate, how do you even move around in here?" Not that our room is much bigger.

Bryant shrugs disinterestedly and crosses his arms. His dark eyes look almost black in this dimly lit room. Stepping over an opened suitcase, he heads into the bathroom to comb his still dripping hair.

Careful to not kick any of his belongings, I move to the doorway separating the two spaces and lean against the doorframe. Unsure of what to do with my hands, I shove them in my pockets, where I feel some loose cash from the day before and part of a cookie. Ellie must have slipped that in.

"What do you want, Your Majesty?" His tone is clipped and he runs the comb through his short hair with more strength than necessary.

I wince at the rough way he tosses the comb back to the small granite counter. My chest tightens as he moves to get past me back into the bedroom.

"Your Majesty, I'm about to have to leave for another meeting. So if you could make this quick, I would greatly appreciate it."

"Uh, right. You know you don't have to formally address me when it's just the two of us, right? In fact, please don't. It's ... weird."

Bryant grunts in response. Sitting down on a tiny velvet chair near the bed, he starts putting on socks and shoes. "You know, your wife said the same thing."

"About me?"

"No, about herself. I think hearing her title bothers her. She only wanted to be called by her name. But don't worry, I told her I wouldn't address her by anything that would make her uncomfortable."

I feel my eyebrows raise as I lower my chin in question at him.

He doesn't respond immediately and I begin to wonder if he's going to say anything else or simply walk out the door. "Look, was there a reason for your visit or did you just want to stop by and see if my socks were matching today?"

I run my tongue across my teeth, desperate for some kind of movement to help calm me. My fists clench inside my pockets, but other than that, I stand unmoving in front of him. Slowly, I nod my head while staring straight at him. "Fine," I reply, "since you're gonna be a dick about it."

Across all three square feet of the room, Bryant rises to his full height and crosses his arms. His face remains impassive, but I know what is lurking behind that indifferent exterior.

"I don't know what the hell crawled up your ass about Ellie's suggestion, but she—"

"Because you haven't been here!"

My head rears back and I blink a few times before I fully grasp what he says. But he continues before I can open my mouth.

"You haven't been here, Lawson," he says again, shaking his head with disbelief. "When you left—"

"It's not like I had a choice—"

"I know that! But. You. Weren't. Here. For the last fifteen years, I've learned from these men, taught these men. Then you finally come back to us with a woman in tow that you're so far in love with you can't even see straight. And now, your wife is asking me to send these men, who have been like fathers to me, who love her, who are willing to fight for their families ... She thinks we should just let them march to their deaths? I like Ellie, I really do. I think she's good for you. But what she's suggesting ..." Bryant pulls in his lips and runs a hand through his hair, causing mist to spray the air around him.

"You had to know. Taking a military position, what it would mean," I keep my voice low, steady.

"That doesn't mean it's any easier to accept." His tone matches mine. Even in the poor lighting, I watch as the conflict within himself plays out across his face. "And when she said it ... I ... dunno, I just ... snapped." His gaze drops to the floor, bringing his hands to his hips. "You wanna know the worst part?" Bryant brings his eyes up to meet mine, nodding his head. "She's right ... It would absolutely fucking work .... It would work ..."

I bring my hand up to rub the back of my neck, sighing.

Bryant plops back down in the chair so hard that I flinch, waiting for it to break under his weight.

"All those years, I didn't know who was still alive and who had died. Other than my own family," I whisper. "You've had all this time to be with those we love. You knew of the fates of our friends, families, everyone. I didn't have the luxury."

"Lawson, I—"

"My wife and I are very aware of the realities of losing those we care about. But you got the time with these men. I didn't. If anyone is being selfish here, I can promise you it's not Ellie."

Bryant and I stare hard at each other for several seconds before he finally concedes with a deep sigh. "What do you want me to do?"

"I think apologizing to her would be a good start."

He rolls his eyes and I nearly come unglued from the desire to slap him. But since we're no longer kids, I doubt it would go over as well.

"Fine, you're right. Anything else?"

"You will support her plan. If Garren doesn't like it—"

"Ellie could suggest a massive deforestation project and Garren would kiss her feet."

Against my better judgment, I let out a low chuckle. "She definitely has managed to charm him, hasn't she?"

Bryant snorts. "Mate, that woman has charmed the pants off of pretty much everyone in our community. Except for a couple of your personal fans."

Ignoring his last comment, I circle back to the issue at hand. "So you'll support Ellie?"

"I will."

Satisfied, I make my way to the door.

"I mean it, you know."

I pause at the door, my hand on the knob. But something in his voice makes me not want to turn back and face him. I've heard that tone often since I returned. Pity. Pity for my loneliness. Pity for my family's death. Pity for previously being stuck in a marriage they all thought I didn't want. And I don't want to see it from my oldest friend.

"I will support Ellie. She really is good for you. I've never seen you this happy, even ... before ... I'm glad you found her."

"Thanks," I mutter and I exit the room, shutting the door behind me.

Knowing I haven't been gone long enough for Ellie to be done with Jensen, I head to our room for a little peace and quiet. If I can't be with Ellie, I'd rather just be alone. I am almost to our hallway when I hear an annoyingly familiar voice behind me.

"King Lawson," it calls again.

Apparently, my not answering her the first time meant she needed to increase her decibel. The pitter patter of shoes are alarmingly close, and I only make it a few more steps before I feel her tap my shoulder from behind.

"Excuse me, Your Majesty?"

Pursing my lips, I turn slowly over my shoulder and there she is, standing much too close for comfort. I was sure I had gotten rid of her when I made her publicly apologize to Ellie.

"What do you want, Esme?" I don't bother even trying to hide my irritation. To my extreme dismay, she remains undeterred.

Flipping her long red hair over her shoulder, she bats her eyelashes up at me. "I just wanted to check and make sure we were alright after what happened yesterday."

This woman obviously has no shame.

"What makes you think we were fine before yesterday?"

"Because you never seemed at all reluctant to help me before Queen Ellie got her feelings hurt, silly." Her tone is sickeningly sweet and I briefly wonder if I'll vomit just from listening to her talk.

Rolling up my sleeves, I take a step back and put some much-needed distance between us. "Look, I don't know if you've misread some situation or something, but you have got to leave me alone. From now on, if there is some problem, real or imagined, you will receive whatever you require. But not from me. Goodbye."

Esme has the audacity to fucking pout at me and I want nothing more than to rip my own hair out. Quickly turning back toward our room, I hightail it out of this awkward encounter.

Our bedroom door slams shut behind me. Lowering my blood pressure seems like a good next step after getting away from that little cretin, so I drop down on the bed and grab the book on Ellie's nightstand. It's her copy where she's written in the margins and it's fascinating to see part of her stream of consciousness while reading about Elizabeth and Mr. Darcy. I kick off my shoes and get comfortable on our bed as I'm transported to the early 1800s.

A couple of hours go by and I'm still alone in our room with only my wife's favorite fictional couple to keep me company. Knowing Ellie should be back by now, a chill runs down my spine as the last time I didn't know where she was runs through my mind. No way are we fucking with that again.

Hopping off the bed, I pull my shoes back on to go in search of my wife. My first thought is checking the library since a library is her favorite place no matter where she goes. I poke my head inside but come up empty, save for some noblemen perusing the shelves. Frowning, I head back out and down the hall. Just as I'm about to head upstairs to see if Gabriel has seen her anywhere, I hear both of their voices coming from the kitchen.

"But I really think this is something we should consider," Ellie insists.

I know that tone. If Gabriel is just as soft for her as I am, he doesn't stand a chance.

"Have you talked to Lawson about this?"

"Yes. And he did warn me—"

I round the corner just in time to see Ellie stuff a marshmallow in her face. Her eyes widen at my sudden presence, but a huge grin quickly follows.

Like a schoolboy, my heart flutters in response. I walk straight up to my wife and throw my arm around her shoulder as she pops a marshmallow in my waiting mouth.

"What was I warning you about, baby?" I can't help but grin down at her.

She shifts nervously and glances at Gabriel, who is leaning against the counter looking very anxious.

And here I thought I was the only one who could make him look like that. But as I glance between them, I know exactly what they were discussing. "You were talking about visiting the Sea Witch."

Ellie flinches away from me, obviously waiting for me to become upset.

"The queen was just explaining her thoughts on the matter, yes."

Sighing, I remove my arm from around Ellie and take her hand. Her worried eyes find mine, but quickly transform to confusion when she sees the smile resting on my face. "This is really important to you, isn't it?"

"Protecting our people as best we can? You better believe it, Your Majesty." She juts out her chin, but it loses some of its effect as her mouth quirks into a smirk.

I look over at Gabriel. Admiration for my wife is written all over his face, and my chest about bursts as Bryant's comment of Ellie charming everyone comes to mind.

"Gabriel, what do you think about this?"

The old man exhales. "This will not be an easy expedition, my dear. We no longer know what waits for us at the Base, let alone the waters surrounding its island."

"But we left her there? There's no chance she's escaped or anything, right?"

Gabriel stiffens just slightly. A blink and it would have been missed. He looks around the empty kitchen before landing back on us. Leaning toward us, he lowers his voice. "No, that wouldn't be possible ... But if we do this, no one can know we've gone."

I frown at his response, but Ellie beats me to the punch.

"Why couldn't anyone know? Shouldn't we tell someone just in case something happens to us?"

"And who all are you thinking will be going?" I add.

A pained look crosses his face as he looks between the two of us.

Ellie squeezes my hand in anticipation and I'm shocked by her incredible strength. It honestly makes me nervous for when she's pregnant and in labor because she is certainly going to break my hand.

Gabriel sighing pulls my head out of the clouds, where it's imagining my beautiful wife holding our baby.

"Know that nothing about this will be easy and, if you're serious about this, it will be best to get it over with as soon as possible. But given the amount of secrecy that will need to go with this mission, I believe the safest group will be Ellie, you, and myself."

My stomach drops to the floor. If he really feels like this, things must be worse than I feared.

"That's all?" Ellie exclaims. "What about Bryant, or Jensen in case one of us gets hurt?"

Gabriel looks between us and shakes his head.

Ellie peeks up at me, clearly trying to gauge my response to Gabriel's suggestion.

"If you really want to do this, I will support you. And if that's what he's telling us, then so be it." I squeeze her hand back in an attempt to physically show just how much I will support her.

Satisfied with my response, we both turn back to Gabriel. I nod to him, letting him know we've made our decision.

He looks like he's about to expire as he releases a slow breath. "Then we leave in the morning."

CHAPTER 26

Ellie

LAWSON AND I SHUFFLE AROUND EACH OTHER AS WE FILL light packs to be carried within our coats. After some discussion, the three of us agreed coming in through the sea would be the smartest way to get back to the Base. If there were any sirens stalking the waters surrounding the island, we would have an easier time hiding with the cover of the ocean than we would in a boat. And with Jensen's blessing earlier today, my ankle is almost as good as healed, meaning we won't have to worry about it being a hindrance on the journey there or back, so long as I keep wearing the brace for the next few days.

I pull a small first aid kit from my suitcase and toss it into my pack. Better to be prepared than not, especially if none of us will have any extensive medical training. Hearing Lawson close behind me, I turn to watch him put some sealable glass vials inside a padded case before stuffing it into his own pack.

After zipping the pack shut, he rolls his shoulders to relieve some of the tension he's carrying.

Frowning, I walk up behind him and start massaging his shoulders. "Are you okay?"

My hands go still but don't move from him. "Shouldn't I be asking you that? You're the one who looks, um, stressed." I laugh awkwardly to try and lighten the mood.

Lawson moves to face me and takes my hands in his. Curious eyes search my face, for what, I'm not sure.

"Is now when you tell me you want to run away and join the circus?"

He blinks at me a few times, trying to process my question. Maybe he doesn't know what a circus actually is.

"What?"

"You do know what a—"

"I know what a circus is, Ellie."

"Okay, just checking!"

His brows come together over beautiful blue eyes. How I could have ever thought his eyes were cold is beyond me. Releasing one of his hands from mine, he scratches his freshly shaven face.

"Hey, you wanna know what you would be in the circus? You've already got the perfect outfit."

Lawson gives me a pained look, clearly trying to decide if he actually wants to ask.

"You'd be the seal who can balance the ball on its nose! Wait, can you balance a ball on your nose? We should probably clear that up first."

My handsome husband smiles and shakes his head.

I take the opportunity to steal a quick kiss, locking my arms around his neck. But with nearly a foot in between us, it's not as sneaky a maneuver as I intend, and he laughs as I bounce to make sure my arms won't slip.

"I'm just worried, is all. I don't want our people to find any reason to discount our intentions and ..." He brings his hands up to rub up and down my back.

"And you're worried what it'll look like if three of the people in charge are suddenly gone for an undetermined amount of time," I finish for him.

"Right."

Scrunching up my nose, I hesitate before letting my next thought out of my mouth. But Lawson knows me better than that.

"Spit it out, Your Highness."

"What if we told Jensen but swore him to secrecy? And, maybe, didn't tell Gabriel until we were already there ... or only if we absolutely have to?"

Lawson straightens. "But we both heard what Gabriel—"

"Think about it. God forbid something happens to one of us, but if it does, we'll need Jensen's expertise the second we get back." I disentangle myself from him and take a step back, giving him the room I know he'll need to process this.

He crosses his arms and stares hard at a spot on the floor.

Just as I'm about to ask if he's still alive over there, he finally graces me with a response.

"You may be right." His voice is so soft that I'm not sure I even heard him correctly. "It would be the smart thing to do ... The problem is, if we need him to meet us at the beach for medical assistance, we won't be able to contact him. And we don't know how long we'll be gone."

"Well, let's think about this logically. We leave in the morning, about how long will it take for us to get there? Cause it took us a couple hours in the boat that day."

"It will probably take about four hours of swimming. We will have to move more carefully to avoid any possible detection, so it will take longer."

I nod, trying not to show the worry on my face that's quickly sinking in my stomach. "Okay, so double that for the trip there and then the trip back. So that's eight hours we'll be gone, minimum." Lawson grunts his acknowledgment. "So the real question mark is how long we'll be with, er, her."

"Not to mention how long it'll take us to get down to her."

"That's right, it did take forever to get down there. I guess I just chalked it up to nerves from the wedding and for the ritual ... Maybe we should just say a day and a half? Two days at the most? That we'll be gone?"

Lawson nods, considering this. "Do you think Gabriel has already come up with an excuse for our absence?" There's a sadness in his voice that draws my attention to him.

"Uh, maybe? I guess he could always just say we're sick or something." I take his hand, willing him to look at me. Anxious eyes meet mine and I immediately understand why this is so hard for him. "You're afraid ... you're afraid something bad will happen while we're gone, aren't you?"

Lawson shifts awkwardly from foot to foot. He opens his mouth to answer when a knock at the door interrupts him.

"Uh, Queen Ellie?" Bryant's muffled voice comes through the closed door. "If you're in there, could I speak to you for a moment?"

I exchange a look with Lawson and head to open the door while he hides the packs. When it swings open, an oddly casually dressed Bryant stands in the doorway with a sheepish look on his blushing face. And in his hands is a giant chocolate cupcake, complete with fluffy frosting and sprinkles. A smile spreads slowly across my face as I step out of the way enough for him to enter the room.

When Lawson sees the offering, he snickers from his spot by the foot of the bed.

Bryant only shrugs, holding the cupcake out to me.

I don't need to be asked twice. Grinning, I try not to look too eager as I take the cupcake and swipe my tongue across the billowy chocolate icing on top. A moan escapes my frosting-filled mouth. I don't even care that the frosting is probably all over my face, because this is the best damn cupcake I have ever eaten.

"Looks like you've got some competition, mate." Bryant elbows Lawson in the ribs.

Rolling his eyes, Lawson walks over and pulls me into his side.

Carefully selecting a spot in the icing where my tongue didn't just slide through, I get a dollop on my finger and offer it to my husband. As he helps himself to the proffered icing, Bryant contorts his face, showing his disgust.

"Okay, you two are truly nauseating, y'know?"

"Weren't you the one who was saying just this morning how good she is for me?" Lawson raises his eyebrow at his friend.

"You did?"

Bryant gives me a smile that may be small, but great warmth radiates from it.

I grin back at him before taking a bite of the cupcake sponge.

"Ellie, I want to apologize for my behavior yesterday."

"I thought that was what the cupcake was?" I feel Lawson shake beside me from working to contain his laughter.

"Well, with my words, as well. You just ... you struck a chord with your suggested action. But no matter, I shouldn't have spoken to you like that. And I'm sorry."

Stepping out of my husband's hold, I crumple the cupcake wrapper in my hand and walk over to him.

He pulls in his lips, no doubt trying to figure out what the hell I'm doing.

"You called me 'Ellie,'" I say, grinning up at him.

Frowning, his eyes widen in response, like he's just made some colossal mistake.

But before he can say anything ornery, I throw my arms around him, hugging him tight. I feel his entire body stiffen for just a moment before he finally gives in to the hug, even going so far as to awkwardly hug me back. Very awkwardly. The man is an awkward hugger, like he's never been hugged a day in his life.

Come to think of it, with the exception of that weird bro-hug I saw him and Lawson do when we first arrived at the Base, and maybe Mary Emma and myself a couple of times, I don't think I've seen any other selkies hug one another. I make a mental note to ask Lawson about that later as I pull away to put my cupcake wrapper in the trash can. Or Lawson's pocket. I haven't really decided yet.

My beautiful husband leans against the bedpost, arms crossed, watching the interaction. I wouldn't call him a very expressive sort of person, but something akin to tenderness colors his features.

And suddenly, his fears I discovered only moments ago make sense.

Looking between Lawson and his oldest friend, both of whom are watching me and clearly unsure what to do next, I see it. The bond that was forged through the trials brought on by childhood. The kind of love only accomplished watching someone do stupid things and making those decisions right along with them. The loyalty no amount of money can buy. A bond that no number of years apart could ever break. Beautiful, true, non-romantic love for another person.

A single tear slips down my cheek as I quickly swallow the lump of tears that threaten to follow.

To their credit, both men in the room look like they're about to panic because I'm on the verge of tears. Looking at one another, they share a terrified glance.

Lawson makes a mad dash to the bathroom, only to quickly return with a handful of tissues.

"Well, I guess that's my cue." Bryant tries to make a quick escape, but the door shuts on his baggy sweatpants, causing Lawson and me to crack up with laughter. After having to open and reclose the door, he finally escapes.

Once we finally catch our breath, Lawson insists on wiping my face with one of the many tissues in his hand.

"Are you alright, darling?"

I look up at my husband, unable to keep from beaming at him. "I'm just ... just so ... proud of you, is all."

This is clearly not what he expects, but he doesn't ask me to elaborate. Instead, he just blushes furiously, and it only makes me grin at him harder.

"Let's go get some dinner," I say, taking his hand in mine.

Surrounded by so many of our people for a meal feels so natural. The selkies are a proud culture and thrive when they're together. I'm suddenly very grateful Isla already had this insanely long dining table for company she didn't even know she would have.

Lawson certainly still looks a little awkward among them, but if what I've heard is true, he's always lived just on the outside of the main social circle. He and I are alike in that way. But now, he'll have to get used to being the center of attention for the rest of his life.

I suppose I will, too.

"Queen Ellie!" One of the women further down the table calls to me. When I look up from my soup and meet her gaze, she continues, "Will you tell us of your history? Please?"

"Umm," I look to my right, where my husband sits with a warm smile on his face. I shrug awkwardly, a shy smile on mine. "Sure. Where do you, er, want me to start?"

"At the beginning!"

"Why do you wear those clothes with the funny looking pig on them?"

"When you were a child!"

Several people begin throwing out suggestions, making both Lawson and me laugh. Even on my left, Mary Emma gives her own suggestions. But then one question rings out above the rest.

"Did you know you loved King Lawson when you first met him? And how did you two actually meet?"

Biting my lip, I look over at Lawson when someone taps me on the shoulder. Tilting my head back, Gabriel stands between my husband and me with something in his hands held closely to his chest. But the look on his face is one of worry, not the joy shown by the rest of the group.

"Finally! Gabriel, we wondered where you had gotten off to," Bryant says from beside Lawson.

"Yes, please, do forgive my tardiness, everyone." Gabriel looks apologetically down the table.

"Is everything okay?" I ask quietly. If this is about what's to come tomorrow for our little group, I don't want to alert everyone else to the issue.

"Well, Your Highness, I was looking through one of the offices upstairs and found this, um, photograph." He pulls the item from his chest to reveal a stunning golden antique picture frame. "Do you happen to know anyone in this photo?"

I carefully take the picture from him, looking at it closely. It looks like some kind of big family photo.

Lawson leans toward me to look over my shoulder and I feel him stiffen beside me.

Then I see a familiar face. Pointing, I tell Gabriel, "That's Isla. This is her house. What's the big deal?" I hand the frame back to him and look over at Lawson, who looks like he's about to vomit.

Turning to Lawson, Gabriel asks quietly, "Did you know?"

Lawson just shakes his head, his eyes never leaving mine.

"Gabriel, come on. What's the matter?"

With one more look at Lawson, Gabriel crouches down to my ear. "Your Highness, the woman you pointed to. That's the Siren Queen."

ACKNOWLEDGEMENTS

Putting a book out into the world is no small journey. Weeks, months, years later and I have so many people to thank for helping make this first book possible. Because, in all honesty, Ellie and Lawson would still be living in my head if it weren't for these amazing individuals.

To my husband, **Matt Mouser**. Thank you for letting me stew on this weird idea in my head until I was ready to talk about it, only to then have to hear about it every day thereafter. Thank you for all your ideas, feedback, and brainstorming sessions under the pergola. Thank you for your unyielding support throughout this entire process, whether it was hanging out with our pups while I furiously drafted, or listening to all of my hair-brained, unhinged ideas. Thank you. There is no one I'd rather have by my side in this crazy game of life. I love you endlessly.

To my parents, **Bill & Cindy Covington**. From Harry Potter to The Giver to Sherlock Holmes and every other story with which you filled my world, you never failed to show me where books could take me. You never failed to read all the silly stories I wrote, whether it was the anthology of Gippy (sorry, Dad) or one of the many first chapters to stories that will never see the light of day. You always listened to every idea I shared, every weird character name I came up with. Thank you for everything. I love you both.

To my incredible editor, **Katie Ducharme**. Simply put, Ellie and Lawson's story wouldn't be the same without you. From the first time we spoke, I knew these two would be safe in your hands. Not a day goes by that I am not incredibly thankful you believed in them as much as I did. I can't wait to see who else we'll bring to life in the future.

To **Luz Aguirre**, a.k.a. **Rotoscope Design**. I am so thankful Katie introduced us and I'm not exaggerating when I say this book wouldn't be the same without you. First, and foremost, the breathtaking design - you are so talented and have truly brought this book to life! Second, I am so glad to have found your friendship. You are such a beautiful human being inside and out and I am so fortunate to call you my friend.

To my first grade teacher, **Mrs. Evelyn McChristian**. While my parents had already instilled a love of reading in my heart, you were the one who built on that love and made it shine. I still remember being in kindergarten and finding out I would be with you the following year. When I asked if you would help me learn to read my chapter books, you said, "Of course!" without hesitation. I should have known then the special place you would always hold in my heart. Truly, deeply, thank you.

To my fifth grade teacher, **Mrs. Becky DeFreece**. You were the one who built off my thoroughly ingrained love of reading and turned that into a need to tell the stories bouncing around in my ten-year-old brain. You never failed to encourage me, even when I would stand up at your desk and cry because I thought kids couldn't publish books. Then, of course, our next classroom read-aloud was a book published by a group of children. I still remember the pointed look you gave me across the room when you stated the authors. Then at my high school graduation party, you asked if I still planned to write down my stories one day. Thank you for always believing in me.

To my wonderful in-laws, **Bev & Randall Mouser**. Thank you for always supporting me in this crazy dream of mine. Thank you for always supporting my love of books and telling me I can do anything. I love you both dearly.

To my grandparents, **Shirley & Loren Dilbeck**. Thank you for believing that I could actually pull this off, even when I was skeptical. Thank you for always telling me stories to pass the time and encouraging my crazy imagination at every turn. Thank you for being my unyielding cheerleaders. I love you both so much.

To the amazing **Caitlin Ramsey**. To say I wouldn't have made it through college without you would be the biggest understatement in the world. The moment we met in the 3rd Floor Quad kitchen, I knew you'd be around for a long time. Thank you for always supporting me, consoling me, giving me a place to sleep when my roommates were crazy, introducing me to new music, and so many other things. I wouldn't be who I am today without your beautiful friendship.

To my lifelong friend, **Grace Nast**. Thank you for always reading those weird little stories I would write in class and telling me they were good, even when they weren't. Thank you for always encouraging my artsy dreams and for always being willing to pet dogs, talk about books, and eat funky popcorn at restaurants with me.

To the one and only **Tanna Eiland**. We spent many hours over many years talking about this dream and how much we both hoped it would become a reality one day. You were going to sneak my books into the recommended sections of bookstores and libraries whenever you could. Well, it's finally here, and even though you aren't, I know how excited you would be. I love you dearly and I am so thankful you are a part of my story. Until we meet again.

To the wonderful authors who have inspired me, mentored me, encouraged me, and answered my endless questions: **Hannah Whitten, Colleen Oakes, Nicola Tyche, Jennifer Chipman**, and **Carlie Jean**. Thank you for unapologetically sharing your voices. Thank you for putting your stories into the world and showing me that anything is possible.

Last, to all the readers, bloggers, bookstagrammers, and all those who love Ellie and Lawson as much as I do. It's pretty terrifying sending a book out into the world, but your support has been amazing. Thank you for letting me do what I love.

About the Author

MADISON MOUSER writes, watches movies with her husband and pups, and drinks coffee in Northwest Arkansas. When she's not writing, she can be found reading, crafting, cuddling her pups, or trying out a new recipe.

Follow her for updates and cute pictures of dogs:
    @madisonmouserwrites
    www.madisonmouser.com

Photo by Laura Powers